DECADE

The 1950s

DECADE

The 1950s

Science fiction is a developed yet constantly developing area of literary endeavour. It has its roots firmly planted in the nineteenth century, so much so that during the closing years of that century it drew in a number of skilled practitioners. During the opening decade of this century, and on into the teens and twenties, it grew even more, until in the 1930s the first specialist magazines were established. After these stumbling beginnings, new magazines, changed magazines, and changed ideas about what SF could and could not do dominated the forties. The changes were so dramatic that these were called 'the golden years' by many ardent readers. In the fifties new editors with original ideas appeared, and in the sixties the phenomenon of the original anthology came on to the scene. Now, halfway through the seventies, other equally interesting trends can be observed.

The *Decade* anthologies present the eighty-year history of science fiction in the most relevant way—by collecting the stories which have gone to make it up. Each volume, complete in itself, takes from a single decade the tales which are best, not only as history, but as entertainment.

Also in the Decade *series:*

The 1940s

DECADE

The 1950s

Edited by

BRIAN W. ALDISS

and

HARRY HARRISON

ST. MARTIN'S PRESS

NEW YORK

First published in the U.S. by St. Martin's Press 1978
Copyright © 1976 by SF Horizons Ltd.
All rights reserved. For information, write:
St. Martin's Press, Inc., 175 Fifth Ave., New York, N.Y. 10010.
Manufactured in the United States of America
Library of Congress Catalog Card Number: 77-15866

Library of Congress Cataloging in Publication Data
Main entry under title:

Decade, the 1950s.

CONTENTS: Schmitz, J. H.   Grandpa—Maclean, K.
The snowball effect.—Budrys, A.   The edge of
the sea.—Smith, C.   Scanners live in vain. [etc.]
    1. Science fiction, American.   I. Aldiss,
Brian Wilson, 1925-   II. Harrison, Harry.
PZ1.D352   1978   [PS648.S3]   813'.0876   77-15866

Contents

Acknowledgements

'Grandpa,' by James H. Schmitz, Copyright © 1955 by Street & Smith Publications, Inc.; reprinted by permission of Scott Meredith Literary Agency, Inc.

'The Snowball Effect,' by Katherine Maclean, Copyright © 1952 by Galaxy Publishing Corporation; reprinted by permission of the author.

'The Edge of the Sea,' by Algis Budrys, Copyright © 1958 by Mercury Press, Inc.; reprinted by permission of the author.

'Scanners Live in Vain,' by Cordwainer Smith, Copyright © 1948 by Fantasy Publishing Co., Inc.; reprinted by permission of the Estate of Cordwainer Smith.

'The Pedestrian,' by Ray Bradbury, Copyright © 1952 by Fantasy House, Inc.; reprinted by permission of Harold Matson Company, Inc.

'The Last Day,' by Richard Matheson, Copyright © 1953 by Ziff-Davis; reprinted by permission of the author.

'The Holes around Mars,' by Jerome Bixby, Copyright © 1954 by Galaxy Publishing Corporation; reprinted by permission of the author.

'The Star,' by Arthur C. Clarke, Copyright © 1955 by Infinity Publications, Inc.; reprinted by permission of Scott Meredith Literary Agency, Inc.

'Two-handed Engine,' by Henry Kuttner, Copyright © 1955 by Fantasy House, Inc.; reprinted by permission of Harold Matson Agency.

'The Large Ant,' by Howard Fast, Copyright © 1960 by the author; reprinted by permission of John Farquharson Ltd.

'Early Model,' by Robert Sheckley, Copyright © 1956 by Galaxy Publishing Corporation; reprinted by permission of the author.

'Sail On! Sail On!,' by Philip José Farmer, Copyright © 1952 by Startling Stories; reprinted by permission of Scott Meredith Literary Agency, Inc.

Introduction

Each volume in this series of *Decade* science fiction anthologies is a record of the major changes within the field. While it must be said that the fundamental SF concepts do not change, the authors and the editors do stamp each period with a particular and individual imprint.

The thirties marked the growth of the specialized pulp magazines. Hugo Gernsback had launched them in the previous decade, so the forties became the era of consolidation and specialization. It also saw the evolution from author to editor of John W. Campbell, the man who was to shape the course of the forties. This fact is obvious when the *Decade* volume for these years is examined; every story in it is from Campbell's magazine *Astounding*. Nor was this deliberate. The editors of this series have two criteria for selection of any story. Quality first, lasting quality that makes a story stand out in memory thirty years after it was first read. Then temporal relativity, that characteristic of a work of fiction that fixes it firmly in time, nails it solidly into place in one decade or another. The stories in the present volume, the 1950s, were selected in this manner – and only after the contents were determined was it noticed that *Astounding* was not represented at all.

This does not mean that Campbell had stopped editing or that *Astounding* had collapsed. Excellent stories were being published there, and many *Astounding* serials of the decade still enjoy reprint existence in book form. What it does mean is that new editors were editing quite different magazines, inspiring and pushing writers in newer directions, shaping science fiction in a manner totally different from that of the Golden Age forties.

By the early fifties literary science fiction and attention to the softer sciences had arrived. Up until this point the word science in science fiction meant physics or chemistry. Gernsback is said to have believed that if you couldn't patent the idea in an SF story he wouldn't buy it. Campbell was never this didactic, but nevertheless the rockets still flew and there was endless trouble with atomic reactors. Horace Gold changed all that.

Gold was a demon editor, loved and hated at the same time. He was the master of the inspirational and cajoling phone call – a two- or three-hour conversation was not unusual. But many times after stories were bought he would pluck them like chickens, changing endings, rewriting, cutting, making nonsense of sense, leaden weights of soaring prose. Not only that, but he would smile and win your money at his weekly poker game. Despite all this – or perhaps because of it – *Galaxy* had a fire and originality possessed by no other magazine at the time. Perhaps Gold's contribution of greatest value was the attention given to sciences other than the classic two.

Psychology, anthropology, demography, archaeology – they all had their day. In 'The Snowball Effect' Katherine Maclean has the audacity to concern herself with the much-scorned sociology, going so far as to name it by name in her opening sentence. Not that every story had to be based upon a single science. Under the Gold lash Alfred Bester created an entire society of Espers in his serial *The Demolished Man*, later published as a book that is happily still in print.

The magazines reflected the characters of the editors. Campbell had his degree in physics. Gold, shattered by war-time experiences, suffered so greatly from agoraphobia that he could not leave his apartment. Little wonder that psychiatry was so well considered in *Galaxy*.

Anthony Boucher had an equally distinct personality. He was a man of great wit and charm who could tell a good joke and write a fine story. And he was an experienced editor, having been at the helm of *Ellery Queen's Mystery Magazine* for a good number of years, as well as editing with J. Francis McComas what is perhaps the all-time best SF anthology, *Tales of Time and Space*. Not surprisingly *Fantasy & Science Fiction* had all the best traits of its editor. Ray Bradbury's 'The Pedestrian' is typical of this period, as is Henry Kuttner's 'Two-handed Engine'.

While these three magazines still enjoy a happy and continuing existence under new editors, a number of other magazines born in this decade ended even before it did. This was the false dawn of science fiction when it appeared, for a brief time, as though much-scorned SF was finally coming into its own. The Science Fiction Book Club was born, and still thrives mightily on. Hardcover science fiction began to appear from the major publishers while sales of SF paperbacks grew annually. Although these continue today the science fiction magazines are in a steady decline. Yet during the fifties over fifty different SF magazines were published.

There was *Fantastic Universe*, an awe-inspiringly bad title that stood out even among some closely run competition. It was edited by the late Hans Stefan Santesson, the kindest of men, who supported many a writer in times of hardship. Howard Fast's 'The Giant Ant' is from this magazine.

Fantasy Book was an amateur-professional magazine, if such a thing can be said to exist. For the most part it contained badly drawn illustrations and worse stories. Yet it published the first work of Cordwainer Smith, 'Scanners Live in Vain'. This fact alone would have justified its brief existence.

Venture was edited by Robert P. Mills and was the first SF magazine consistently to use adult themes. By today's four-letter-word standards the material may look pretty pale – but it was bold stuff in those shy days. The Budrys story, 'The Edge of the Sea', is from *Venture*.

It was an age of experiment. The old barriers were coming down, pulp taboos were being forgotten, new themes and new manners of writing were being explored. Some of the older writers were flexible enough to bend in these new directions; Kuttner and Pohl are the two represented here. But it was up to the kids to do most of the work. Farmer startled the world by not only writing but publishing a story, 'The Lovers', that was all about *sex*! And none of your normal, homely sex, either, but exobiological miscegenation. This was strong stuff for the troops – who nevertheless enjoyed it. As always the readers were more receptive than the editors who, reluctantly, published something they thought daring only to have it accepted with nods of pleasure.

Robert Sheckley was making a profession of humour in SF.

Before him there were Fredric Brown, Henry Kuttner and precious little else. Sheckley wrote story after story, each with his characteristic wry twist, and eventually developed the immense skills he practises today.

Sheckley, like Maclean, Bixby, Matheson, Budrys – even the editors of this volume – were second-generation writers. With Wells the ancestor of us all, the first generation were the war-horses of the pulps. Two who are still writing today are Jack Williamson and Murray Leinster. Their generation invented the raw material out of which editors and other writers shaped the changes. It may have been crude, but by God it was first, and that says a lot. The garish pulps of the twenties were just as garish in the thirties and were the food and drink of the second generation. We – and this is truth because the editors of this anthology were there – teethed on those proverbial bug-eyed monsters, brass brassières and shredded pulp edges. The SF magazines were read and reread, then recycled through the second-hand-magazine shops in the States, finally bundled as ballast and flogged as Yank mags in Britain. They nurtured a generation of readers who later became the next generation of writers. Some began work in the forties, but the fifties saw the largest numbers being published for the first time.

These cranky kids enjoyed the work of the generation before them – but did not want to keep on repeating it. Therefore the entrance of new plots, new themes, new excitement. James Schmitz wrote 'Grandpa', a story about ecology years before anyone but the specialists had heard the word.

The sphere of science fiction was expanding. It no longer existed in magazines or the fan presses alone. With the coming of the paperback revolution, and the revelation that there were millions of readers everywhere capable of reading about other things than romance and murder, SF found new places to go.

So a notable stream of novels appeared in the fifties which seem now very characteristic of that time. There are the violent heroes of several Heinlein and early André Norton novels, the intellectual heroes of Sprague de Camp's *Lest Darkness Fall* and Robert Crane's briskly fashionable *Hero's Walk*. There are the novels of David Duncan and Charles Eric Maine, very much period pieces, more traditional stories such as Simak's *City*, Asimov's *The Naked Son* and *Caves of Steel*, with robot detectives, and Hal Clement's perennially pleasing *Mission of Gravity*, as well as such signs of new times as Bradbury's *Fahrenheit 451*, and refreshingly maverick early novels by Bester, Philip Dick, and Kurt Vonnegut. This was also the age of Pohl and Kornbluth, whose collaborations include *Wolfbane* and *The Space Merchants*. Nor do we forget such individual achievements as Sturgeon's *More than Human* and Walter Miller's *A Canticle for Leibowitz*.

The British scene, too, blossomed during the decade. In the magazine field, *New Worlds*, *Science Fantasy* and *Nebula* found an eager following. Arthur C. Clarke's *Childhood's End* met with great success, but this was really the day of Wyndham, with *The Day of the Triffids*, *The Kraken Wakes* and *The Chrysalids* being read everywhere. Other native products included Eric Frank Russell's *Three to Conquer* (which William Burroughs praised as 'exceptionally realistic'), John Christopher's *Death of Grass*, Aldiss's *Non-Stop*, and novels by John Brunner, John Boland and the egregious Vargo Statten.

The science fiction pulps began in the twenties and blossomed in the thirties. The forties were Campbell and the *Astounding* years, one man single-handedly inventing modern science fiction and whipping on his willing writers to explore this newly built house. The fifties built on Campbell's foundations, new editors and new writers finding that there were more rooms in this house than anyone had realized before. It was a vital and fascinating time to be alive and writing or reading SF, and that excitement is well reflected in the stories here.

H.H.

James H. Schmitz
Grandpa

A green-winged downy thing as big as a hen fluttered along the hillside to a point directly above Cord's head and hovered there, twenty feet above him. Cord, a fifteen-year-old human being, leaned back against a skipboat parked on the equator of a world that had known human beings for only the past four Earth-years, and eyed the thing speculatively. The thing was, in the free and easy terminology of the Sutang Colonial Team, a swamp bug. Concealed in the downy fur behind the bug's head was a second, smaller, semi-parasitical thing, classed as a bug rider.

The bug itself looked like a new species to Cord. Its parasite might or might not turn out to be another unknown. Cord was a natural research man; his first glimpse of the odd flying team had sent endless curiosities thrilling through him. How did that particular phenomenon tick, and *why*? What fascinating things, once you'd learned about it, could you get it to *do*?

Normally, he was hampered by circumstances in carrying out any such investigation. Junior colonial students like Cord were expected to confine their curiosity to the pattern of research set up by the station to which they were attached. Cord's inclination towards independent experiments had got him into disfavour with his immediate superiors before this.

He sent a casual glance in the direction of the Yoger Bay Colonial Station behind him. No signs of human activity about that low, fortress-like bulk in the hill. Its central lock was still closed. In fifteen minutes, it was scheduled to be opened to let out the Planetary Regent, who was inspecting the Yoger Bay Station and its principal activities today.

Fifteen minutes was time enough to find out something about the new bug, Cord decided.

But he'd have to collect it first.

* * *

He slid out one of the two handguns holstered at his side. This one was his own property: a Vanadian projectile weapon. Cord thumbed it to position for anaesthetic small-game missiles and brought the hovering swamp bug down, drilled neatly and microscopically through the head.

As the bug hit the ground, the rider left its back. A tiny scarlet demon, round and bouncy as a rubber ball, it shot towards Cord in three long hops, mouth wide to sink home inch-long, venom-dripping fangs. Rather breathlessly, Cord triggered the gun again and knocked it out in mid-leap. A new species, all right! Most bug riders were harmless plant-eaters, mere suckers of vegetable juice—

'*Cord!*' A feminine voice.

Cord swore softly. He hadn't heard the central lock click open. She must have come around from the other side of the station.

'Hello, Grayan!' he shouted innocently without looking round. 'Come and see what I've got! New species!'

Grayan Mahoney, a slender, black-haired girl two years older than himself, came trotting down the hillside towards him. She was Sutang's star colonial student, and the station manager, Nirmond, indicated from time to time that she was a fine example for Cord to pattern his own behaviour on. In spite of that, she and Cord were good friends.

'Cord, you idiot,' she scowled as she came up. 'Stop playing the collector! If the Regent came out now, you'd be sunk. Nirmond's been telling her about you!'

'Telling her what?' Cord asked, startled.

'For one thing,' Grayan reported, 'that you don't keep up on your assigned work.'

'Golly!' gulped Cord, dismayed.

'Golly is right! I keep warning you!'

'What'll I do?'

'Start acting as if you had good sense mainly.' Grayan grinned suddenly. 'But if you mess up our tour of the Bay Farms today you'll be off the Team for good!'

She turned to go. 'You might as well put the skipboat back; we're not using it. Nirmond's driving us down to the edge of the bay in a treadcar, and we'll take a raft from there.'

Leaving his newly bagged specimens to revive by themselves and flutter off again, Cord hurriedly flew the skipboat around the station and rolled it back into its stall.

Three rafts lay moored just offshore in the marshy cove at the edge of which Nirmond had stopped the treadcar. They looked somewhat like exceptionally broad-brimmed, well-worn sugar-loaf hats floating out there, green and leathery. Or like lily pads twenty-five feet across, with the upper section of a big, grey-green pineapple growing from the centre of each. Plant animals of some sort. Sutang was too new to have had its phyla sorted out into anything remotely like an orderly classification. The rafts were a local oddity which had been investigated and could be regarded as harmless and moderately useful. Their usefulness lay in the fact that they were employed as a rather slow means of transportation about the shallow, swampy waters of the Yoger Bay. That was as far as the Team's interest in them went at present.

The Regent stood up from the back seat of the car, where she was sitting next to Cord. There were only four in the party; Grayan was up front with Nirmond.

'Are those our vehicles?' The Regent sounded amused.

Nirmond grinned. 'Don't underestimate them, Dane! They could become an important economic factor in this region in time. But, as a matter of fact, these three are smaller than I like to use.' He was peering about the reedy edges of the cove. 'There's a regular monster parked here usually—'

Grayan turned to Cord. 'Maybe Cord knows where Grandpa is hiding.'

It was well meant, but Cord had been hoping nobody would ask him about Grandpa. Now they all looked at him.

'Oh, you want Grandpa?' he said, somewhat flustered. 'Well, I left him . . . I mean I saw him a couple of weeks ago about a mile south from here—'

Nirmond grunted and told the Regent, 'The rafts tend to stay wherever they're left, providing it's shallow and muddy. They use a hair-root system to draw chemicals and microscopic nourishment directly from the bottom of the bay. Well – Grayan, would you like to drive us there?'

Cord settled back unhappily as the treadcar lurched into motion. Nirmond suspected he'd used Grandpa for one of his unauthorized tours of the area, and Nirmond was quite right.

'I understand you're an expert with these rafts, Cord,' Dane said from beside him. 'Grayan told me we couldn't find a better steersman, or pilot, or whatever you call it, for our trip today.'

'I can handle them,' Cord said, perspiring. 'They don't give you any trouble!' He didn't feel he'd made a good impression on the Regent so far. Dane was a young, handsome-looking woman with an easy way of talking and laughing, but she wasn't the head of the Sutang Colonial Team for nothing.

'There's one big advantage our beasties have over a skipboat, too,' Nirmond remarked from the front seat. 'You don't have to worry about a snapper trying to climb on board with you!' He went on to describe the stinging ribbon-tentacles the rafts spread around them under water to discourage creatures that might make a meal off their tender underparts. The snappers and two or three other active and aggressive species of the bay hadn't yet learned it was foolish to attack armed human beings in a boat, but they would skitter hurriedly out of the path of a leisurely perambulating raft.

Cord was happy to be ignored for the moment. The Regent, Nirmond, and Grayan were all Earth people, which was true of most of the member of the Team; and Earth people made him uncomfortable, particularly in groups. Vanadia, his own home world, had barely graduated from the status of Earth colony itself, which might explain the difference.

The treadcar swung around and stopped, and Grayan stood up in the front seat, pointing. 'That's Grandpa, over there!'

Dane also stood up and whistled softly, apparently impressed by Grandpa's fifty-foot spread. Cord looked around in surprise. He was pretty sure this was several hundred yards from the spot where he'd left the big raft two weeks ago; and, as Nirmond said, they didn't usually move about by themselves.

Puzzled, he followed the others down a narrow path to the water, hemmed in by tree-sized reeds. Now and then he got a glimpse of Grandpa's swimming platform, the rim of which just touched the shore. Then the path opened out, and he saw the whole raft lying in sunlit, shallow water; and he stopped short, startled.

Nirmond was about to step up on the platform, ahead of Dane. 'Wait!' Cord shouted. His voice sounded squeaky with alarm. 'Stop!'

He came running forward.

'What's the matter, Cord?' Nirmond's voice was quiet and urgent.

'Don't get on that raft – it's changed!' Cord's voice sounded wobbly, even to himself. 'Maybe it's not even Grandpa—'

He saw he was wrong on the last point before he'd finished the sentence. Scattered along the rim of the raft were discoloured spots left by a variety of heat-guns, one of which had been his own. It was the way you goaded the sluggish and mindless things into motion. Cord pointed at the cone-shaped central projection. 'There – his head! He's sprouting!'

Grandpa's head, as befitted his girth, was almost twelve feet high and equally wide. It was armour-plated like the back of a saurian to keep off plant suckers, but two weeks ago it had been an otherwise featureless knob, like those on all other rafts. Now scores of long, kinky, leafless vines had grown out from all surfaces of the cone, like green wires. Some were drawn up like tightly coiled springs, others trailed limply to the platform and over it. The top of the cone was dotted with angry red buds, rather like pimples, which hadn't been there before either. Grandpa looked unhealthy.

'Well,' Nirmond said, 'so it is. Sprouting!' Grayan made a choked sound. Nirmond glanced at Cord as if puzzled. 'Is that all that was bothering you, Cord?'

'Well, sure!' Cord began excitedly. He had caught the significance of the word 'all'; his hackles were still up, and he was shaking. 'None of them ever—'

Then he stopped. He could tell by their faces that they hadn't got it. Or, rather, that they'd got it all right but simply weren't going to let it change their plans. The rafts were classified as harmless, according to the Regulations. Until proved otherwise, they would continue to be regarded as harmless. You didn't waste time quibbling with the Regulations – even if you were the Planetary Regent. You didn't feel you had the time to waste.

He tried again. 'Look—' he began. What he wanted to tell them was that Grandpa with one unknown factor added wasn't Grandpa any more. He was an unpredictable, oversized life form, to be investigated with cautious thoroughness till you knew what the unknown factor meant. He stared at them helplessly.

Dane turned to Nirmond. 'Perhaps you'd better check,' she said. She didn't add, 'to reassure the boy!' but that was what she meant.

Cord felt himself flushing. But there was nothing he could say or do now except watch Nirmond walk steadily across the platform. Grandpa shivered slightly a few times, but the rafts always did that when someone first stepped on them. The station manager stopped before one of the kinky sprouts, touched it and then gave it a tug. He reached up and poked at the lowest of the bud-like growths. 'Odd-looking things!' he called back. He gave Cord another glance. 'Well, everything seems harmless enough, Cord. Coming aboard, everyone?'

It was like dreaming a dream in which you yelled and yelled at people and couldn't make them hear you! Cord stepped up stiff-legged on the platform behind Dane and Grayan. He knew exactly what would have happened if he'd hesitated even a moment. One of them would have said in a friendly voice, careful not to let it sound contemptuous: 'You don't have to come along if you don't want to, Cord!'

Grayan had unholstered her heat-gun and was ready to start Grandpa moving out into the channels of the Yoger Bay.

Cord hauled out his own heat-gun and said roughly, 'I was to do that!'

'All right, Cord.' She gave him a brief, impersonal smile and stood aside.

They were so infuriatingly polite!

For a while, Cord almost hoped that something awesome and catastrophic would happen promptly to teach the Team people a lesson. But nothing did. As always, Grandpa shook himself vaguely and experimentally when he felt the heat on one edge of the platform and then decided to withdraw from it, all of which was standard procedure. Under the water, out of sight, were the raft's working sections: short, thick leaf-structures shaped like paddles and designed to work as such, along with the slimy nettle-streamers which kept the vegetarians of the Yoger Bay away, and a jungle of hair roots through which Grandpa sucked nourishment from the mud and the sluggish waters of the bay and with which he also anchored himself.

The paddles started churning, the platform quivered, the hair roots were hauled out of the mud; and Grandpa was on his ponderous way.

Cord switched off the heat, reholstered his gun, and stood up. Once in motion, the rafts tended to keep travelling unhurriedly for quite a while. To stop them, you gave them a touch of heat along their leading edge; and they could be turned in any direction by using the gun lightly on the opposite side of the platform. It was simple enough.

Cord didn't look at the others. He was still burning inside. He watched the reed beds move past and open out, giving him glimpses of the misty, yellow and green and blue expanses of the brackish bay ahead. Behind the mist, to the west, were the Yoger Straits, tricky and ugly water when the tides were running; and beyond the Straits lay the open sea, the great Zlanti Deep, which was another world entirely and one of which he hadn't seen much as yet.

Grayan called from beside Dane, 'What's the best route from here into the farms, Cord?'

'The big channel to the right,' he answered. He added somewhat sullenly, 'We're headed for it!'

Grayan came over to him. 'The Regent doesn't want to see all of it,' she said, lowering her voice. 'The algae and plankton beds first. Then as much of the mutated grains as we can show her in about three hours. Steer for the ones that have been doing best, and you'll keep Nirmond happy!'

She gave him a conspiratorial wink. Cord looked after her uncertainly. You couldn't tell from her behaviour that anything was wrong. Maybe—

He had a flare of hope. It was hard not to like the Team people, even when they were being rock-headed about their Regulations. Anyway, the day wasn't over yet. He might still redeem himself in the Regent's opinion.

Cord had a sudden cheerful, if improbable, vision of some bay monster plunging up on the raft with snapping jaws; and of himself alertly blowing out what passed for the monster's brains before anyone else – Nirmond, in particular – was even aware of the threat. The bay monsters shunned Grandpa, of course, but there might be ways of tempting one of them.

So far, Cord realized, he'd been letting his feelings control him. It was time to start thinking!

Grandpa first. So he'd sprouted – green vines and red buds, purpose unknown, but with no change observable in his behaviour-patterns otherwise. He was the biggest raft in this end of the bay, though all of them had been growing steadily in the two years since Cord had first seen one. Sutang's seasons changed slowly; its year was somewhat more than five Earth-years long. The first Team members to land here hadn't yet seen a full year pass.

Grandpa, then, was showing a seasonal change. The other rafts, not quite so far developed, would be reacting similarly a little later. Plant animals – they might be blossoming, preparing to propagate.

'Grayan,' he called, 'how do the rafts get started? When they're small, I mean.'

'Nobody knows yet,' she said. 'We were just talking about it. About half of the coastal marsh-fauna of the continent seems to go through a preliminary larval stage in the sea.' She nodded at the red buds on the raft's cone. 'It *looks* as if Grandpa is going to produce flowers and let the wind or tide take the seeds out through the Straits.'

It made sense. It also knocked out Cord's still half-held hope that the change in Grandpa might turn out to be drastic enough, in some way, to justify his reluctance to get on board. Cord studied Grandpa's armoured head carefully once more – unwilling to give up that hope entirely. There were a series of vertical gummy black slits between the armour plates, which hadn't been in evidence two weeks ago either. It looked as if Grandpa were beginning to come apart at the seams. Which might indicate that the rafts, big as they grew to be, didn't outlive a full seasonal cycle, but came to flower at about this time of Sutang's year, and died. However, it was a safe bet that Grandpa wasn't going to collapse into senile decay before they completed their trip today.

Cord gave up on Grandpa. The other notion returned to him – perhaps he *could* coax an obliging bay monster into action that would show the Regent he was no sissy!

Because the monsters were there all right.

Kneeling at the edge of the platform and peering down into the wine-coloured, clear water of the deep channel they were moving through, Cord could see a fair selection of them at almost any moment.

Some five or six snappers, for one thing. Like big, flattened crayfish, chocolate-brown mostly, with green and red spots on their carapaced backs. In some areas they were so thick you'd wonder what they found to live on, except that they ate almost anything, down to chewing up the mud in which they squatted. However, they preferred their food in large chunks and alive, which was one reason you didn't go swimming in the bay. They would attack a boat on occasion; but the excited manner in which the ones he saw were scuttling off towards the edges of the channel showed they wanted nothing to do with a big moving raft.

Dotted across the bottom were two-foot round holes which looked vacant at the moment. Normally, Cord knew, there would be a head filling each of those holes. The heads consisted mainly of triple sets of jaws, held open patiently like so many traps to grab at anything that came within range of the long wormlike bodies behind the heads. But Grandpa's passage, waving his stingers like transparent pennants through the water, had scared the worms out of sight, too.

Otherwise, mostly schools of small stuff – and then a flash of wicked scarlet, off to the left behind the raft, darting out from the reeds, turning its needle-nose into their wake.

Cord watched it without moving. He knew that creature, though it was rare in the bay and hadn't been classified. Swift, vicious – alert enough to snap swamp bugs out of the air as they fluttered across the surface. And he'd tantalized one with fishing tackle once into leaping up on a moored raft, where it had flung itself about furiously until he was able to shoot it.

'What fantastic creatures!' Dane's voice just behind him.

'Yellowheads,' said Nirmond. 'They've got a high utility rating. Keep down the bugs.'

Cord stood up casually. It was no time for tricks! The reed bed to their right was thick with Yellowheads, a colony of them. Vaguely froggy things, man-sized and better. Of all the creatures he'd discovered in the bay, Cord liked them least. The flabby, sack-like bodies clung with four thin limbs to the upper section of the twenty-foot reeds that lined the channel. They hardly ever moved, but their huge bulging eyes seemed to take in everything that went on about them. Every so often, a downy swamp bug came close enough; and a Yellowhead would open its vertical, enormous, tooth-lined slash of a mouth, extend the whole front of its face like a bellows in a flashing strike; and the bug would be gone. They might be useful, but Cord hated them.

'Ten years from now we should know what the cycle of coastal life is like,' Nirmond said. 'When we set up the Yoger Bay Station there were no Yellowheads here. They came the following year. Still with traces of the oceanic larval form; but the metamorphosis was almost complete. About twelve inches long—'

Dane remarked that the same pattern was duplicated endlessly elsewhere. The Regent was inspecting the Yellowhead colony with field glasses; she put them down now, looked at Cord, and smiled, 'How far to the farms?'

'About twenty minutes.'

'The key', Nirmond said, 'seems to be the Zlanti Basin. It must be almost a soup of life in spring.'

'It is,' nodded Dane, who had been here in Sutang's spring, four Earth-years ago. 'It's beginning to look as if the Basin alone might justify colonization. The question is still' – she gestured towards the Yellowheads - 'how do creatures like that get there?'

They walked off towards the other side of the raft, arguing about ocean currents. Cord might have followed. But something splashed back of them, off to the left and not too far back. He stayed, watching.

After a moment, he saw the big Yellowhead. It had slipped down from its reedy perch, which was what had caused the splash. Almost submerged at the water line, it stared after the raft with huge, pale-green eyes. To Cord, it seemed to look directly at him. In that moment, he knew for the first time why he didn't like Yellowheads. There was something very like intelligence in that look, an alien calculation. In creatures like that, intelligence seemed out of place. What use could they have for it?

A little shiver went over him when it sank completely under the water and he realized it intended to swim after the raft. But it was mostly excitement. He had never seen a Yellowhead come down out of the reeds before. The obliging monster he'd been looking for might be presenting itself in an unexpected way.

Half a minute later, he watched it again, swimming awkwardly far down. It had no immediate intention of boarding, at any rate. Cord saw it come into the area of the raft's trailing stingers. It manœuvred its way between them, with curiously human swimming motions, and went out of sight under the platform.

He stood up, wondering what it meant. The Yellowhead had appeared to know about the stingers; there had been an air of purpose in every move of its approach. He was tempted to tell the others about it, but there was the moment of triumph he could have if it suddenly came slobbering up over the edge of the platform and he nailed it before their eyes.

It was almost time anyway to turn the raft in towards the farms. If nothing happened before then—

He watched. Almost five minutes, but no sign of the Yellowhead. Still wondering, a little uneasy, he gave Grandpa a calculated needling of heat.

After a moment, he repeated it. Then he drew a deep breath and forgot all about the Yellowhead.

'Nirmond!' he called sharply.

The three of them were standing near the centre of the platform, next to the big armoured cone, looking ahead at the farms. They glanced around.

'What's the matter now, Cord?'

Cord couldn't say it for a moment. He was suddenly, terribly scared again. Something *had* gone wrong!

'The raft won't turn!' he told them.

'Give it a real burn this time!' Nirmond said.

Cord glanced up at him. Nirmond, standing a few steps in front of Dane and Grayan as if he wanted to protect them, had begun to look a little strained, and no wonder. Cord already had pressed the gun to three different points on the platform; but Grandpa appeared to have developed a sudden anaesthesia for heat. They kept moving out steadily towards the centre of the bay.

Now Cord held his breath, switched the heat on full, and let Grandpa have it. A six-inch patch on the platform blistered up instantly, turned brown, then black—

Grandpa stopped dead. Just like that.

'That's right! Keep burn—' Nirmond didn't finish his order.

A giant shudder. Cord staggered back towards the water. Then the whole edge of the raft came curling up behind him and went down again smacking the bay with a sound like a cannon shot. He flew forward off his feet, hit the platform face down, and flattened himself against it. It swelled up beneath him. Two more enormous slaps and joltings. Then quiet. He looked round for the others.

He lay within twelve feet of the central cone. Some twenty or thirty of the mysterious new vines the cone had sprouted were stretched stiffly towards him now, like so many thin green fingers. They couldn't quite reach him. The nearest tip was still ten inches from his shoes.

But Grandpa had caught the others, all three of them. They were tumbled together at the foot of the cone, wrapped in a stiff network of green vegetable ropes, and they didn't move.

Cord drew his feet up cautiously, prepared for another earthquake reaction. But nothing happened. Then he discovered that Grandpa was back in motion on his previous course. The heatgun had vanished. Gently, he took out the Vanadian gun.

A voice, thin and pain-filled, spoke to him from one of the three huddled bodies.

'Cord? It didn't get you?' It was the Regent.

'No,' he said, keeping his voice low. He realized suddenly he'd simply assumed they were all dead. Now he felt sick and shaky.

'What are you doing?'

Cord looked at Grandpa's big, armour-plated head with a certain hunger. The cones were hollowed out inside, the station's lab had decided their chief function was to keep enough air trapped under the rafts to float them. But in that central section was also the organ that controlled Grandpa's overall reactions.

He said softly, 'I have a gun and twelve heavy-duty explosive bullets. Two of them will blow that cone apart.'

'No good, Cord!' the pain-racked voice told him. 'If the thing sinks, we'll die anyway. You have anaesthetic charges for that gun of yours?'

He stared at her back. 'Yes.'

'Give Nirmond and the girl a shot each, before you do anything else. Directly into the spine, if you can. But don't come any closer—'

Somehow, Cord couldn't argue with that voice. He stood up carefully. The gun made two soft spitting sounds.

'All right,' he said hoarsely. 'What do I do now?'

Dane was silent a moment. 'I'm sorry, Cord, I can't tell you that. I'll tell you what I can—'

She paused for some seconds again.

'This thing didn't try to kill us, Cord. It could have easily. It's incredibly strong. I saw it break Nirmond's legs. But as soon as we stopped moving, it just held us. They were both unconscious then—

'You've got that to go on. It was trying to pitch you within reach of its vines or tendrils, or whatever they are, too, wasn't it?'

'I think so,' Cord said shakily. That was what had happened, of course; and at any moment Grandpa might try again.

'Now it's feeding us some sort of anaesthetic of its own through those vines. Tiny thorns. A sort of numbness—' Dane's voice trailed off a moment. Then she said clearly, 'Look, Cord – it seems we're food it's storing up! You get that?'

'Yes,' he said.

'Seeding time for the rafts. There are analogues. Live food for its seed probably; not for the raft. One couldn't have counted on that. Cord?'

'Yes, I'm here.'

'I want', said Dane, 'to stay awake as long as I can. But there's really just one other thing – this raft's going somewhere, to some particularly favourable location. And that might be very near shore. You might make it in then; otherwise it's up to you. But keep your head and wait for a chance. No heroics, understand?'

'Sure, I understand,' Cord told her. He realized then that he was talking reassuringly, as if it wasn't the Planetary Regent but someone like Grayan.

'Nirmond's the worst,' Dane said. 'The girl was knocked unconscious at once. If it weren't for my arm – but, if we can get help in five hours or so, everything should be all right. Let me know if anything happens, Cord.'

'I will,' Cord said gently again. Then he sighted his gun carefully at a point between Dane's shoulder-blades, and the anaesthetic chamber made its soft, spitting sound once more. Dane's taut body relaxed slowly, and that was all.

There was no point Cord could see in letting her stay awake; because they weren't going anywhere near shore. The reed beds and the channels were already behind them, and Grandpa hadn't changed direction by the fraction of a degree. He was moving out into the open bay – and he was picking up company!

So far, Cord could count seven big rafts within two miles of them; and on the three that were closest he could make out a sprouting of new green vines. All of them were travelling in a straight direction; and the common point they were all headed for appeared to be the roaring centre of the Yoger Straits, now now some three miles away!

Behind the Straits, the cold Zlanti Deep – the rolling fogs, and the open sea! It might be seeding time for the rafts, but it looked as if they weren't going to distribute their seeds in the bay. . . .

Cord was a fine swimmer. He had a gun and he had a knife; in spite of what Dane had said, he might have stood a chance among the killers of the bay. But it would be a very small chance, at best.

And it wasn't, he thought, as if there weren't still other possibilities. He was going to keep his head.

Except by accident, of course, nobody was going to come looking for them in time to do any good. If anyone did look, it would
be around the Bay Farms. There were a number of rafts moored
there; and it would be assumed they'd used one of them. Now
and then something unexpected happened and somebody simply
vanished; by the time it was figured out just what had happened
on this occasion, it would be much too late.

Neither was anybody likely to notice within the next few hours
that the rafts had started migrating out of the swamps through the
Yoger Straits. There was a small weather-station a little inland,
on the north side of the Straits, which used a helicopter occasionally. It was about as improbable, Cord decided dismally, that
they'd use it in the right spot just now as it would be for a jet
transport to happen to come in low enough to spot them.

The fact that it was up to him, as the Regent had said, sank in a
little more after that!

Simply because he was going to try it sooner or later, he carried
out an experiment next that he knew couldn't work. He opened the
gun's anaesthetic chamber and counted out fifty pellets – rather
hurriedly because he didn't particularly want to think of what he
might be using them for eventually. There were around three hundred charges left in the chamber, then; and in the next few minutes Cord carefully planted a third of them in Grandpa's head.

He stopped after that. A whale might have showed signs of
somnolence under a lesser load. Grandpa paddled on undisturbed.
Perhaps he had become a little numb in spots, but his cells weren't
equipped to distribute the soporific effect of that type of drug.

There wasn't anything else Cord could think of doing before
they reached the Straits. At the rate they were moving, he calculated that would happen in something less than an hour; and
if they did pass through the Straits he was going to risk a swim.
He didn't think Dane would have disapproved, under the circumstances. If the raft simply carried them all out into the foggy
vastness of the Zlanti Deep, there would be no practical chance
of survival left at all.

Meanwhile, Grandpa was definitely picking up speed. And there were other changes going on – minor ones, but still a little awe-inspiring to Cord. The pimply-looking red buds that dotted the upper part of the cone were opening out gradually. From the centre of most of them protruded something like a thin, wet, scarlet worm: a worm that twisted weakly, extended itself by an inch or so, rested, and twisted again, and stretched up a little farther, groping into the air. The vertical black slits between the armour plates looked deeper and wider than they had been even some minutes ago; a dark, thick liquid dripped slowly from several of them.

In other circumstances Cord knew he would have been fascinated by these developments in Grandpa. As it was, they drew his suspicious attention only because he didn't know what they meant.

Then something quite horrible happened suddenly. Grayan started moaning loudly and terribly and twisted almost completely around. Afterwards, Cord knew it hadn't been a second before he stopped her struggles and the sounds together with another anaesthetic pellet; but the vines had tightened their grip on her first, not flexibly but like the digging, bony, green talons of some monstrous bird of prey.

White and sweating, Cord put his gun down slowly while the vines relaxed again. Grayan didn't seem to have suffered any additional harm; and she would certainly have been the first to point out that his murderous rage might have been as intelligently directed against a machine. But for some moments Cord continued to luxuriate furiously in the thought that, at any instant he chose, he could still turn the raft very quickly into a ripped and exploded mess of sinking vegetation.

Instead, and more sensibly, he gave both Dane and Nirmond another shot, to prevent a similar occurrence with them. The contents of two such pellets, he knew, would keep any human being torpid for at least four hours.

Cord withdrew his mind hastily from the direction it was turning into; but it wouldn't stay withdrawn. The thought kept coming up again, until at last he had to recognize it.

Five shots would leave the three of them completely unconscious, whatever else might happen to them, until they either
died from other causes or were given a counteracting agent.

Shocked, he told himself he couldn't do it. It was exactly like
killing them.

But then, quite steadily, he found himself raising the gun once
more, to bring the total charge for each of the three Team people
up to five.

Barely thirty minutes later, he watched a raft as big as the one he
rode go sliding into the foaming white waters of the Straits a
few hundred yards ahead, and dart off abruptly at an angle,
caught by one of the swirling currents. It pitched and spun, made
some headway, and was swept aside again. And then it righted
itself once more. Not like some blindly animated vegetable, Cord
thought, but like a creature that struggled with intelligent purpose to maintain its chosen direction.

At least, they seemed practically unsinkable. . . .

Knife in hand, he flattened himself against the platform as the
Straits roared just ahead. When the platform jolted and tilted up
beneath him, he rammed the knife all the way into it and hung on.
Cold water rushed suddenly over him, and Grandpa shuddered
like a labouring engine. In the middle of it all, Cord had the
horrified notion that the raft might release its unconscious human
prisoners in its struggle with the Straits. But he underestimated
Grandpa in that. Grandpa also hung on.

Abruptly, it was over. They were riding a long swell, and there
were three other rafts not far away. The Straits had swept them
together, but they seemed to have no interest in one another's
company. As Cord stood up shakily and began to strip off his
clothes, they were visibly drawing apart again. The platform of
one of them was half-submerged; it must have lost too much of
the air that held it afloat and, like a small ship, it was foundering.

From this point, it was only a two-mile swim to the shore north
of the Straits, and another mile inland from there to the Straits
Head Station. He didn't know about the current; but the distance

didn't seem too much, and he couldn't bring himself to leave knife and gun behind. The bay creatures loved warmth and mud; they didn't venture beyond the Straits. But Zlanti Deep bred its own killers, though they weren't often observed so close to shore.

Things were beginning to look rather hopeful.

Thin, crying voices drifted overhead, like the voices of curious cats, as Cord knotted his clothes into a tight bundle, shoes inside. He looked up. There were four of them circling there; magnified sea-going swamp bugs, each carrying an unseen rider. Probably harmless scavengers – but the ten-foot wingspread was impressive. Uneasily, Cord remembered the venomously carnivorous rider he'd left lying beside the station.

One of them dipped lazily and came sliding down towards him. It soared overhead and came back, to hover about the raft's cone.

The bug rider that directed the mindless flier hadn't been interested in him at all! Grandpa was baiting it!

Cord stared in fascination. The top of the cone was alive now with a softly wriggling mass of the scarlet, worm-like extrusions that had started sprouting before the raft left the bay. Presumably, they looked enticingly edible to the bug rider.

The flier settled with an airy fluttering and touched the cone. Like a trap springing shut, the green vines flashed up and around it, crumpling the brittle wings, almost vanishing into the long, soft body!

Barely a second later, Grandpa made another catch, this one from the sea itself. Cord had a fleeting glimpse of something like a small, rubbery seal that flung itself out of the water upon the edge of the raft, with a suggestion of desperate haste – and was flipped on instantly against the cone where the vines clamped it down beside the flier's body.

It wasn't the enormous ease with which the unexpected kill was accomplished that left Cord standing there, completely shocked. It was the shattering of his hopes to swim ashore from here. Fifty yards away, the creature from which the rubbery thing had been fleeing showed briefly on the surface, as it turned away from the raft; and that glance was all he needed. The ivory-white body and gaping jaws were similar enough to those of the sharks of Earth to indicate the pursuer's nature. The important difference was that, wherever the White Hunters of the Zlanti Deep went, they went by the thousands.

Stunned by that incredible piece of bad luck, still clutching his bundled clothes, Cord stared towards shore. Knowing what to look for, he could spot the tell-tale rollings of the surface now – the long, ivory gleams that flashed through the swells and vanished again. Shoals of smaller things burst into the air in sprays of glittering desperation, and fell back.

He would have been snapped up like a drowning fly before he'd covered a twentieth of that distance!

Grandpa was beginning to eat.

Each of the dark slits down the sides of the cone was a mouth. So far only one of them was in operating condition, and the raft wasn't able to open that one very wide as yet. The first morsel had been fed into it, however: the bug rider the vines had plucked out of the flier's downy neck fur. It took Grandpa several minutes to work it out of sight, small as it was. But it was a start.

Cord didn't feel quite sane any more. He sat there, clutching his bundle of clothes and only vaguely aware of the fact that he was shivering steadily under the cold spray that touched him now and then, while he followed Grandpa's activities attentively. He decided it would be at least some hours before one of that black set of mouths grew flexible and vigorous enough to dispose of a human being. Under the circumstances, it couldn't make much difference to the other human beings here; but the moment Grandpa reached for the first of them would also be the moment he finally blew the raft to pieces. The White Hunters were cleaner eaters, at any rate; and that was about the extent to which he could still control what was going to happen.

Meanwhile, there was the very faint chance that the weather station's helicopter might spot them.

Meanwhile also, in a weary and horrified fascination, he kept debating the mystery of what could have produced such a nightmarish change in the rafts. He could guess where they were going by now; there were scattered strings of them stretching back to the Straits or roughly parallel to their own course, and the direction was that of the plankton-swarming pool of the Zlanti Basin, a thousand miles to the north. Given time, even mobile lily pads like the rafts had been could make that trip for the benefit of their seedlings. But nothing in their structure explained the sudden change into alert and capable carnivores.

He watched the rubbery little seal-thing being hauled up to a mouth. The vines broke its neck; and the mouth took it in up to the shoulders and then went on working patiently at what was still a trifle too large a bite. Meanwhile, there were more thin cat-cries overhead; and a few minutes later, two more sea-bugs were trapped almost simultaneously and added to the larder. Grandpa dropped the dead sea-thing and fed himself another bug rider. The second rider left its mount with a sudden hop, sank its teeth viciously into one of the vines that caught it again, and was promptly battered to death against the platform.

Cord felt a resurge of unreasoning hatred against Grandpa. Killing a bug was about equal to cutting a branch from a tree; they had almost no life-awareness. But the rider had aroused his partisanship because of its appearance of intelligent action – and it was in fact closer to the human scale in that feature than to the monstrous life form that had, mechanically, but quite successfully, trapped both it and the human beings. Then his thoughts drifted again; and he found himself speculating vaguely on the curious symbiosis in which the nerve systems of two creatures as dissimilar as the bugs and their riders could be linked so closely that they functioned as one organism.

Suddenly an expression of vast and stunned surprise appeared on his face.

Why – now he *knew*!

Cord stood up hurriedly, shaking with excitement, the whole plan complete in his mind. And a dozen long vines snaked instantly in the direction of his sudden motion and groped for him, taut and stretching. They couldn't reach him, but their savagely alert reaction froze Cord briefly where he was. The platform was shuddering under his feet, as if in irritation at his inaccessibility; but it couldn't be tilted up suddenly here to throw him within the grasp of the vines, as it could around the edges.

Still, it was a warning! Cord sidled gingerly around the cone till he had gained the position he wanted, which was on the forward half of the raft. And then he waited. Waited long minutes, quite motionless, until his heart stopped pounding and the irregular angry shivering of the surface of the raft-thing died away, and the last vine tendril had stopped its blind groping. It might help a lot if, for a second or two after he next started moving, Grandpa wasn't too aware of his exact whereabouts!

He looked back once to check how far they had gone by now beyond the Straits Head Station. It couldn't, he decided, be even an hour behind them. Which was close enough, by the most pessimistic count – if everything else worked out all right! He didn't try to think out in detail what that 'everything else' could include, because there were factors that simply couldn't be calculated in advance. And he had an uneasy feeling that speculating too vividly about them might make him almost incapable of carrying out his plan.

At last, moving carefully, Cord took the knife in his left hand but left the gun holstered. He raised the tightly knotted bundle of clothes slowly over his head, balanced in his right hand. With a long, smooth motion he tossed the bundle back across the cone, almost to the opposite edge of the platform.

It hit with a soggy thump. Almost immediately, the whole far edge of the raft buckled and flapped up to toss the strange object to the reaching vines.

Simultaneously, Cord was racing forward. For a moment, his attempt to divert Grandpa's attention seemed completely success-ful – then he was pitched to his knees as the platform came up.

He was within eight feet of the edge. As it slapped down again, he drew himself desperately forward.

An instant later, he was knifing down through cold, clear water, just ahead of the raft, then twisting and coming up again.

The raft was passing over him. Clouds of tiny sea creatures scattered through its dark jungle of feeding roots. Cord jerked back from a broad, wavering streak of glassy greenness, which was a stinger, and felt a burning jolt on his side, which meant he'd been touched lightly by another. He bumped on blindly through the slimy black tangles of hair roots that covered the bottom of the raft; then green half-light passed over him, and he burst up into the central bubble under the cone.

Half-light and foul, hot air. Water slapped around him, dragging him away again – nothing to hang on to here! Then above him, to his right, moulded against the interior curve of the cone as if it had grown there from the start, the frog-like, man-sized shape of the Yellowhead.

The raft rider!

Cord reached up, caught Grandpa's symbiotic partner and guide by a flabby hind-leg, pulled himself half out of the water and struck twice with the knife, fast, while the pale-green eyes were still opening.

He'd thought the Yellowhead might need a second or so to detach itself from its host, as the bug riders usually did, before it tried to defend itself. This one merely turned its head; the mouth slashed down and clamped on Cord's left arm above the elbow. His right hand sank the knife through one staring eye, and the Yellowhead jerked away, pulling the knife from his grasp.

Sliding down, he wrapped both hands around the slimy leg and hauled with all his weight. For a moment more, the Yellowhead hung on. Then the countless neural extensions that connected it now with the raft came free in a succession of sucking, tearing sounds; and Cord and the Yellowhead splashed into the water together.

Black tangle of roots again – and two more electric burns suddenly across his back and legs! Strangling, Cord let go. Below him, for a moment, a body was turning over and over with oddly human motions; then a solid wall of water thrust him up and aside, as something big and white struck the turning body and went on.

Cord broke the surface twelve feet behind the raft. And that would have been that, if Grandpa hadn't already been slowing down.

After two tries, he floundered back up on the platform and lay there gasping and coughing a while. There were no indications that his presence was resented now. A few lax vine-tips twitched uneasily, as if trying to remember previous functions, when he came limping up presently to make sure his three companions were still breathing; but Cord never noticed that.

They were still breathing; and he knew better than to waste

time trying to help them himself. He took Grayan's heat-gun from its holster. Grandpa had come to a full stop.

Cord hadn't had time to become completely sane again, or he might have worried now whether Grandpa, violently sundered from his controlling partner, was still capable of motion on his own. Instead, he determined the approximate direction of the Straits Head Station, selected a corresponding spot on the platform, and gave Grandpa a light tap of heat.

Nothing happened immediately. Cord sighed patiently and stepped up the heat a little.

Grandpa shuddered gently. Cord stood up.

Slowly and hesitatingly at first, then with steadfast – though now again brainless – purpose, Grandpa began paddling back towards the Straits Head Station.

Katherine Maclean
The snowball effect

'All right,' I said, 'what is sociology good for?'

Wilton Caswell, Ph.D., was head of my Sociology Department, and right then he was mad enough to chew nails. On the office wall behind him were three or four framed documents in Latin, but I didn't care at that moment if he papered the walls with his degrees. I had been appointed Dean and President to see to it that the University made money. I had a job to do, and I meant to do it.

He bit off each word with great restraint: 'Sociology is the study of social institutions, Mr Halloway.'

I tried to make him understand my position. 'Look, it's the big-money men who are supposed to be contributing to the support of this college. To them, sociology sounds like socialism – nothing can sound worse than that – and an institution is where they put Aunt Maggy when she began collecting Wheaties in a stamp album. We can't appeal to them that way. Come on now.' I smiled condescendingly, knowing it would irritate him. 'What are you doing that's worth anything?'

He glared at me, his white hair bristling and his nostrils dilated like a war-horse about to whinny. I can say one thing for them – these scientists and professors always keep themselves well under control. He had a book in his hand and I was expecting him to throw it, but he spoke instead:

'This department's analysis of institutional accretion, by the use of open-system mathematics, has been recognized as an outstanding and valuable contribution to—'

The words were impressive, whatever they meant, but this still didn't sound like anything that would pull in money. I interrupted, 'Valuable in what way?'

He sat down on the edge of his desk thoughtfully, apparently recovering from the shock of being asked to produce something

solid for his position, and ran his eyes over the titles of the books
that lined his office walls.

'Well, sociology has been valuable to business in initiating
worker efficiency and group motivation studies, which they now
use in management decisions. And, of course, since the Depres-
sion, Washington has been using sociological studies of employ-
ment, labour, and standards of living as a basis for its general
policies of—'

I stopped him with both hands raised. 'Please, Professor Caswell! That would hardly be a recommendation. Washington, the
New Deal and the present Administration are somewhat touchy
subjects to the men I have to deal with. They consider its value
debatable, if you know what I mean. If they got the idea that
sociology professors are giving advice and guidance— No, we
have to stick to brass tacks and leave Washington out of this.
What, specifically, has the work of this specific department done
that would make it as worthy to receive money as – say, a heart-
disease research fund?'

He began to tap the corner of his book absently on the desk,
watching me. 'Fundamental research doesn't show immediate
effects, Mr Halloway, but its value is recognized.'

I smiled and took out my pipe. 'All right, tell me about it.
Maybe I'll recognize its value.'

Professor Caswell smiled back tightly. He knew his department
was at stake. The other departments were popular with donors
and pulled in gift money by scholarships and fellowships, and
supported their professors and graduate students by research
contracts with the Government and industry. Caswell had to show
a way to make his own department popular – or else.

He laid down his book and ran a hand over his ruffled hair.
'Institutions – organizations, that is' – his voice became more
resonant; like most professors, when he had to explain something
he instinctively slipped into his platform lecture mannerisms, and
began to deliver an essay – 'have certain tendencies built into the
way they happen to have been organized, which cause them to
expand or contract without reference to the needs they were
founded to serve.'

He was becoming flushed with the pleasure of explaining his subject. 'All through the ages, it has been a matter of wonder and dismay to men that a simple organization – such as a church to worship in, or a delegation of weapons to a warrior class merely for defence against an outside enemy – will either grow insensately and extend its control until it is a tyranny over their whole lives, or, like other organizations set up to serve a vital need, will tend to repeatedly dwindle and vanish, and have to be painfully rebuilt.

'The reason can be traced to little quirks in the way they were organized, a matter of positive and negative power feedbacks. Such simple questions as "Is there a way a holder of authority in this organization can use the power available to him to increase his power?" provide the key. But it still could not be handled until the complex questions of interacting motives and long-range accumulations of minor effects could somehow be simplified and formulated. In working on the problem, I found that the mathematics of open system, as introduced to biology by Ludwig von Bertalanffy and George Kreezer, could be used as a base that would enable me to develop a specifically social mathematics, expressing the human factors of intermeshing authority and motives in simple formulas.

'By these formulations, it is possible to determine automatically the amount of growth and period of life of any organization. The U.N.' to choose an unfortunate example, is a shrinker-type organization. Its monetary support is not in the hands of those who personally benefit by its governmental activities, but, instead, in the hands of those who would personally lose by any extension and encroachment of its authority on their own. Yet by the use of formula analysis—'

'That's theory,' I said. 'How about proof?'

'My equations are already being used in the study of limited-size Federal corporations. Washington—'

I held up my palm again. 'Please, not that nasty word again. I mean, where else has it been put into operation? Just a simple demonstration, something to show that it works, that's all.'

He looked away from me thoughtfully, picked up the book and began to tap it on the desk again. It had some unreadable title and his name on it in gold letters. I got the distinct impression again that he was repressing an urge to hit me with it.

He spoke quietly. 'All right. I'll give you a demonstration. Are you willing to wait six months?'

'Certainly, if you can show me something at the end of that time.'

Reminded of time, I glanced at my watch and stood up.

'Could we discuss this over lunch?' he asked.

'I wouldn't mind hearing more, but I'm having lunch with some executors of a millionaire's will. They have to be convinced that by "furtherance of research into human ills" he meant that the money should go to research fellowships for postgraduate biologists at the University, rather than to a medical foundation.'

'I see you have your problems, too,' Caswell said, conceding me nothing. He extended his hand with a chilly smile. 'Well, good afternoon, Mr Halloway. I'm glad we had this talk.'

I shook hands and left him standing there, sure of his place in the progress of science and the respect of his colleagues, yet seething inside because I, the President and Dean, had boorishly demanded that he produce something tangible.

My job isn't easy. For a crumb of favourable publicity and respect in the newspapers and an annual ceremony in a silly costume, I spend the rest of the year going hat in hand, asking politely for money at everyone's door, like a well-dressed panhandler, and trying to manage the University on the dribble I get. As far as I was concerned, a department had to support itself or be cut down to what student tuition pays for, which is a handful of overcrowded courses taught by an assistant lecturer. Caswell had to make it work or get out.

But, the more I thought about it, the more I wanted to hear what he was going to do for a demonstration.

At lunch, three days later, while we were waiting for our order, he opened a small notebook. 'Ever hear of feedback effects?'

'Not enough to have it clear.'

'You know the snowball effect, though.'

'Sure, start a snowball rolling downhill and it grows.'

'Well, now—' He wrote a short line of symbols on a blank page and turned the notebook around for me to inspect it. 'Here's the formula for the snowball process. It's the basic general growth formula – covers everything.'

It was a row of little symbols arranged like an algebra equation. One was a concentric spiral going up, like a cross-section of a snowball rolling in snow. That was a growth sign.

I hadn't expected to understand the equation, but it was almost as clear as a sentence. I was impressed and slightly intimidated by it. He had already explained enough so that I knew that, if he was right, here was the growth of the Catholic Church and the Roman Empire, the conquests of Alexander and the spread of the smoking habit and the change and rigidity of the unwritten law of styles.

'Is it really as simple as that?' I asked.

'You notice', he said, 'that when it becomes too heavy for the cohesion strength of snow it breaks apart. Now, in human terms—'

The chops and mashed potatoes and peas arrived.

'Go on,' I urged.

He was deep in the symbology of human motives and the equations of human behaviour in groups. After running through a few different types of grower- and shrinker-type organizations, we came back to the snowball, and decided to run the test by making something grow.

'You add the motives,' he said, 'and the equation will translate them into organization.'

'How about a good selfish reason for the ins to drag others into the group – some sort of bounty on new members, a cut of their membership fee?' I suggested uncertainly, feeling slightly foolish. 'And maybe a reason why the members would lose if any of them resigned, and some indirect way they could use to force each other to stay in.'

'The first is the chain-letter principle,' he nodded. 'I've got that. The other. . . .' He put the symbols through some mathematical manipulation so that a special grouping appeared in the middle of the equation. 'That's it.'

Since I seemed to have the right idea, I suggested some more, and he added some, and juggled them around in different patterns. We threw out a few that would have made the organization too

complicated, and finally worked out an idyllically simple and
deadly little organization set-up where joining had all the temptation of buying a sweepstakes ticket, going in deeper was as easy
as hanging around a race track, and getting out was like trying to
pull free from a Malayan thumb-trap. We put our heads closer together and talked lower, picking the best place for the demonstration.

'Abington?'

'How about Watashaw? I have some student sociological
surveys of it already. We can pick a suitable group from that.'

'This demonstration has got to be convincing. We'd better pick
a little group that no one in his right mind would expect to grow.'

'There should be a suitable club—'

'Ladies,' said the skinny female chairman of the Watashaw
Sewing Circle. 'Today we have guests.' She signalled for us to rise,
and we stood up, bowing to polite applause and smiles. 'Professor
Caswell, and Professor Smith.' (My alias.) 'They are making a
survey of the methods and duties of the clubs of Watashaw.'

We sat down to another ripple of applause and slightly wider
smiles, and then the meeting of the Watashaw Sewing Circle
began. In five minutes I began to feel sleepy.

There were only about thirty people there, and it was a small
room, not the halls of Congress, but they discussed their business
of collecting and repairing second-hand clothing for charity with
the same endless boring parliamentary formality.

I pointed out to Caswell the member I thought would be the
natural leader, a tall, well-built woman in a green suit, with
conscious gestures and a resonant, penetrating voice, and then
went into a half-doze while Caswell stayed awake beside me and
wrote in his notebook. After a while the resonant voice roused
me to attention for a moment. It was the tall woman holding the
floor over some collective dereliction of the club. She was being
scathing.

I nudged Caswell and murmured, 'Did you fix it so that a
shover has a better chance of getting into office than a non-
shover?'

'I think there's a way they could find for it,' Caswell whispered back, and went to work on his equation again. 'Yes, several ways to bias the elections.'

'Good. Point them out tactfully to the one you select. Not as if she'd use such methods, but just as an example of the reason why only *she* can be trusted with initiating the change. Just mention all the personal advantages an unscrupulous person could have.'

He nodded, keeping a straight and sober face as if we were exchanging admiring remarks about the techniques of clothes repairing, instead of conspiring.

After the meeting, Caswell drew the tall woman in the green suit aside and spoke to her confidentially, showing her the diagram of organization we had drawn up. I saw the responsive glitter in the woman's eyes and knew she was hooked.

We left the diagram of organization and our typed copy of the new by-laws with her and went off soberly, as befitted two social-science experimenters. We didn't start laughing until our car passed the town limits and began the climb for University Heights.

If Caswell's equations meant anything at all, we had given that sewing circle more growth drives than the Roman Empire.

Four months later I had time out from a very busy schedule to wonder how the test was coming along. Passing Caswell's office, I put my head in. He looked up from a student research paper he was correcting.

'Caswell, about that sewing club business – I'm beginning to feel the suspense. Could I get an advance report on how it's coming?'

'I'm not following it. We're supposed to let it run the full six months.'

'But I'm curious. Could I get in touch with that woman – what's her name?'

'Searles. Mrs George Searles.'

'Would that change the results?'

'Not in the slightest. If you want to graph the membership rise, it should be going up in a log curve, probably doubling every so often.'

I grinned. 'If it's not rising, you're fired.'

He grinned back. 'If it's not rising, you won't have to fire me – I'll burn my books and shoot myself.'

I returned to my office and put in a call to Watashaw.

While I was waiting for the phone to be answered, I took a piece of graph paper and ruled it off into six sections, one for each month. After the phone had rung in the distance for a long time, a servant answered with a bored drawl:

'Mrs Searles' residence.'

I picked up a red gummed star and licked it.

'Mrs Searles, please.'

'She's not in just now. Could I take a message?'

I placed the star at the thirty line in the beginning of the first section. Thirty members they'd started with.

'No, thanks. Could you tell me when she'll be back?'

'Not until dinner. She's at the meetin'.'

'The sewing club?' I asked.

'No, *sir*, not that thing. There isn't any sewing club any more, not for a long time. She's at the Civic Welfare meeting.'

Somehow I hadn't expected anything like that.

'Thank you,' I said and hung up, and after a moment noticed I was holding a box of red gummed stars in my hand. I closed it and put it down on top of the graph of membership in the sewing circle. No more members. . . .

Poor Caswell. The bet between us was ironclad. He wouldn't let me back down on it even if I wanted to. He'd probably quit before I put through the first slow move to fire him. His professional pride would be shattered, sunk without a trace. I remembered what he said about shooting himself. It had seemed funny to both of us at the time, but. . . . What a mess that would make for the University.

I had to talk to Mrs Searles. Perhaps there was some outside reason why the club had disbanded. Perhaps it had not just died.

I called back. 'This is Professor Smith,' I said, giving the alias I had used before. 'I called a few minutes ago. When did you say Mrs Searles will return?'

'About six-thirty or seven o'clock.'

Five hours to wait.

And what if Caswell asked me what I had found out in the

meantime.? I didn't want to tell him anything until I had talked it over with that woman Searles first.

'Where is this Civic Welfare meeting?'

She told me.

Five minutes later, I was in my car, heading for Watashaw, driving considerably faster than usual and keeping a careful watch for highway-patrol cars as the speedometer climbed.

The town meeting-hall and theatre was a big place, probably with lots of small rooms for different clubs. I went in through the centre door and found myself in the huge central hall where some sort of rally was being held. A political-type rally – you know, cheers and chants, with bunting already down on the floor, people holding banners, and plenty of enthusiasm and excitement in the air. Someone was making a speech up on the platform. Most of the people there were women.

I wondered how the Civic Welfare League could dare hold its meeting at the same time as a political rally that could pull its members away. The group with Mrs Searles was probably holding a shrunken and almost memberless meeting somewhere in an upper room.

There probably was a side door that would lead upstairs.

While I glanced around, a pretty girl usher put a printed bulletin in my hand, whispering, 'Here's one of the new copies.' As I attempted to hand it back, she retreated. 'Oh, you can keep it. It's the new one. Everyone's supposed to have it. We've just printed up 6000 copies to make sure there'll be enough to last.'

The tall woman on the platform had been making a driving, forceful speech about some plans for rebuilding Watashaw's slum section. It began to penetrate my mind dimly as I glanced down at the bulletin in my hands.

'Civic Welfare League of Watashaw. The United Organization of Church and Secular Charities.' That's what it said. Below began the rules of membership.

I looked up. The speaker, with a clear, determined voice and conscious, forceful gestures, had entered the home stretch of her speech, an appeal to the civic pride of all citizens of Watashaw.

'With a bright and glorious future – potentially without poor and without uncared-for ill – potentially with no ugliness, no vistas which are not beautiful – the best people in the best-planned town in the country – jewel of the United States.'

She paused and then leaned forward intensely, striking her clenched hand on the speaker's stand with each word for emphasis.

'*All we need is more members. Now, get out there and recruit!*'

I finally recognized Mrs Searles, as an answering sudden blast of sound half deafened me. The crowd was chanting at the top of its lungs: 'Recruit! Recruit!'

Mrs Searles stood still at the speaker's table and behind her, seated in a row of chairs, was a group that was probably the board of directors. It was mostly women, and the women began to look vaguely familiar, as if they could be members of the sewing circle.

I put my lips close to the ear of the pretty usher while I turned over the stiff printed bulletin on a hunch. 'How long has the League been organized?' On the back of the bulletin was a constitution.

She was cheering with the crowd, her eyes sparkling. 'I don't know,' she answered between cheers. 'I only joined two days ago. Isn't it wonderful?'

I went into the quiet outer air and got into my car with my skin prickling. Even as I drove away, I could hear them. They were singing some kind of organization song with the tune of 'Marching through Georgia'.

Even at the single glance I had given it, the constitution looked exactly like the one we had given the Watashaw Sewing Circle.

All I told Caswell when I got back was that the sewing circle had changed its name and the membership seemed to be rising.

Next day, after calling Mrs Searles, I placed some red stars on my graph for the first three months. They made a nice curve, rising steeply as it reached the fourth month. They had picked up their first increase in membership simply by amalgamating with all the other types of charity organizations in Watashaw, changing the club name with each fusion, but keeping the same constitution – the constitution with the bright promise of advantages as long as there were always new members being brought in.

By the fifth month, the League had added a mutual baby-sitting service and had induced the local school board to add a nursery school to the town service, so as to free more women for League activity. But charity must have been completely organized by then, and expansion had to be in other directions.

Some real-estate agents evidently had been drawn into the whirlpool early, along with their ideas. The slum improvement plans began to blossom and take on a tinge of real-estate planning later in the month.

The first day of the sixth month, a big two-page spread appeared in the local paper of a mass meeting which had approved a full-fledged scheme for slum clearance of Watashaw's shack-town section, plus plans for rehousing, civic building, and re-zoning. And good prospects for attracting some new industries to the town, industries which had already been contacted and seemed interested by the privileges offered.

And, with all this, an arrangement for securing and distributing to the club members *alone* most of the profit that would come to the town in the form of a rise in the price of building sites and a boom in the building industry. The profit-distributing arrangement was the same one that had been built into the organization plan for the distribution of the small profits of membership fees and honorary promotions. It was becoming an openly profitable business. Membership was rising more rapidly now.

By the second week of the sixth month, news appeared in the local paper that the club had filed an application to incorporate itself as the Watashaw Mutual Trade and Civic Development Corporation, and all the local real-estate promoters had finished joining *en masse*. The Mutual Trade part sounded to me as if the Chamber of Commerce was on the point of being pulled in with them, ideas, ambitions and all.

I chuckled while reading the next page of the paper, on which a local politician was reported as having addressed the club with long flowery oration on their enterprise, charity and civic spirit. He had been made an honorary member. If he allowed himself to be made a *full member* with its contractual obligations and its lures, if the politicians went into this, too. . . .

I laughed, filing the newspaper with the other documents on the Watashaw test. These proofs would fascinate any businessman with the sense to see where his bread was buttered. A businessman is constantly dealing with organizations, including his own, and finding them either inert, cantankerous, or both. Caswell's formula could be a handle to grasp them with. Gratitude alone would bring money into the University in car-load lots.

The end of the sixth month came. The test was over and the end reports were spectacular. Caswell's formulas were proven to the hilt. After reading the last newspaper reports, I called him up.

'Perfect, Wilt, *perfect*! I can use this Watashaw thing to get you so many fellowships and scholarships and grants for your department that you'll think it's snowing money!'

He answered somewhat uninterestedly, 'I've been busy working with students on their research papers and marking tests – not following the Watashaw business at all, I'm afraid. You say the demonstration went well and you're satisfied?'

He was definitely putting on a chill. We were friends now, but obviously he was still peeved whenever he was reminded that I had doubted that his theory could work. And he was using its success to rub my nose in the realization that I had been wrong. A man with a string of degrees after his name is just as human as anyone else. I had needled him pretty hard that first time.

'I'm satisfied,' I acknowledged. 'I was wrong. The formulas work beautifully. Come over and see my file of documents on it if you want a boost for your ego. Now let's see the formula for stopping it.'

He sounded cheerful again. 'I didn't complicate that organization with negatives. I wanted it to *grow*. It falls apart naturally when it stops growing for more than two months. It's like the great stock boom before an economic crash. Everyone in it is prosperous as long as the prices must keep going up and new buyers come into the market, but they all know what would happen if it stopped growing. You remember, we built in as one of the incentives that the members know they are going to lose if membership stops growing. Why, if I tried to stop it now, they'd cut my throat.'

I remembered the drive and frenzy of the crowd in the one early meeting I had seen. They probably would.

'No,' he continued. 'We'll just let it play out to the end of its tether and die of old age.'

'When will that be?'

'It can't grow past the female population of the town. There are only so many women in Watashaw, and some of them don't like sewing.'

The graph on the desk before me began to look sinister. Surely Caswell must have made some provision for—

'You underestimate their ingenuity,' I said into the phone. 'Since they wanted to expand, they didn't stick to sewing. They went from general charity to social welfare schemes to something that's pretty close to an incorporated government. The name is now the Watashaw Mutual Trade and Civic Development Corporation, and they're filing an application to change it to Civic Property Pool and Social Dividend, membership contractual, open to all. That social dividend sounds like a Technocrat climbed on the band wagon, eh?'

While I spoke, I carefully added another red star to the curve above the thousand-member level, checking with the newspaper that still lay open on my desk. The curve was definitely some sort of log curve now, growing more rapidly with each increase.

'Leaving out practical limitations for a moment, where does the formula say it will stop?' I asked.

'When you run out of people to join it. But, after all, there are only so many people in Watashaw. It's a pretty small town.'

'They've opened a branch office in New York,' I said carefully into the phone, a few weeks later.

With my pencil, very carefully, I extended the membership curve from where it was then.

After the next doubling, the curve went almost straight up and off the page.

Allowing for a lag of contagion from one nation to another, depending on how much their citizens intermingled, I'd give the rest of the world about twelve years.

There was a long silence while Caswell probably drew the same graph in his own mind. Then he laughed weakly. 'Well, you asked me for a demonstration.'

That was as good an answer as any. We got together and had lunch in a bar, if you can call it lunch. The movement we started will expand by hook or by crook, by seduction or by bribery or by propaganda or by conquest, but it will expand. And maybe a total world government will be a fine thing – until it hits the end of its rope in twelve years or so.

What happens then, I don't know.

But I don't want anyone to pin that on me. From now on, if anyone asks me, I've never heard of Watashaw.

Algis Budrys
The edge of the sea

The Overseas Highway, two narrow white lanes on yellowed concrete piers, lay close to the shallow water, passed over the key, and went on.

All afternoon the sea had been rising. Long, greasy-faced green swells came in from the Atlantic Ocean and broke on the rocks with a sudden upsurge of surf. At midday, the water had been far down among the coral heads. Now it was in the tumbled limestone blocks and concrete prisms that had been dumped there to build up the key. In a little while it would be washing its spume over the highway itself, and it might well go farther, with the increasing wind.

It was dark with twilight, and darker with clouds thick as oil smoke covering the sun over the Gulf of Mexico. The Gulf was stirring, too, and bayous were flooding in Louisiana. But it was over the Atlantic that the hurricane was spinning. It was the broad, deep, deadly ocean that the tide and wind were pushing down through the gloom on to the side of the key where Dan Henry was struggling grimly, his massive back and shoulders naked and running with spray.

His eyes were red-rimmed with salt and his hide was slashed shallowly in a dozen places where he had lost his balance on the stones and fallen. He had been lurching through the surf all afternoon, working to save what he had seen, leaden and encrusted, rolling ponderously at the edge of the water. His shirt, the seat covers from his car – the fan-belt, too – and what few scraps of rope and wire had been in the trunk, all had gone for him to twist into an incredible rag of a hawser.

The men who built the Overseas Highway on the old railroad right-of-way had built up the little key, but it was still no more than a hundred feet in diameter. If the thing trapped on the rocks had chosen any other islet to wash against, there would have been a reasonable chance of saving it. But there was no one living here, and nothing to use for tools or anchors. The thing was rolling and grinding against the rocks, too heavy to float but too bulky to resist the push of storm-driven water. There were bright silver gouges on its metal flanks, and in a little while it would break up or break free, and be lost either way. The rope – the stubborn, futile rope passed around the two struts at its nose and wrapped around the great concrete block it was now butting at with brute persistence – was as much use as though Dan Henry had been a spider and tried to hold this thing in a hurriedly created web. But he had had to try, and he was trying now in another way. He jammed the soles of his feet against one concrete block and pushed his shoulders against another. With his belly ridged and his thighs bulging, his face contorted and his hands clenched, he was trying to push another massive piece of stone into place behind the plunging metal thing, though his blood might erupt from his veins and the muscles tear open his flesh.

The thing was as thick through as a hogshead, and as long as two men. There was a thick-lipped, scarred opening a foot across at one end, where the body rounded sharply in a hemispherical compound curve. There were three stumpy fins rooted in the curve, their tips not extending beyond the bulge of the body, and two struts at the blunt nose like horns on a snail but bent forward so that the entire thing might have been fired out of a monstrous cannon or launched from the tubes of some unimaginable submarine. There were no visible openings, no boltheads, no seams. The entire thing might have been cast of a piece – might have been solid, except for the tube in the stern – and though barnacles clung to it and moss stained it, though the rocks gouged it and other blows had left their older scars on its pitted surface, still the thing was not visibly damaged.

Dan Henry strained at the rock, and sand grated minutely at its base. But the world turned red behind his eyes, and his muscles writhed into knots, and his breath burned his chest with the fury of fire. The sea broke against him and ran into his nose and mouth. The wind moaned, and the water hissed through the rocks, crashing as it came and gurgling as it drew back. The thing groaned and grated with each sluggish move. The day grew steadily darker.

Dan Henry had stopped his car on the key at noon, pulling off the highway on to the one narrow space of shoulder. He had opened the glove compartment and taken out the waxed container of milk and the now stale sandwich he had bought in Hallandale, above Miami, at ten that morning. He lit a cigarette and unwrapped the sandwich, and began to eat. The milk had turned warm in the glove compartment and acquired an unpleasant taste, but Dan Henry had never cared how his food tasted. He paid no attention to it as he chewed the sandwich and drank the milk between drags on the cigarette. He had bought the food when he stopped for gas, and when he finished it he planned to go on immediately, driving until he reached Key West.

There was nothing specific waiting for him there. Nothing in his life had ever been waiting for him anywhere. But, everywhere he went, he went as directly and as efficiently as possible because that was his nature. He was a powerful, reasonably intelligent, ugly man who drew his strength from a knowledge that nothing could quite overcome him. He asked no more of the world. He was thirty years old, and had been a construction foreman, a police officer, an M.P. sergeant in Germany and a long-haul trailer-truck driver. In addition to these things he had been born into a derrick rigger's family in Oklahoma and raised in his father's nomadic, self-sufficient tradition.

When he first saw the dull colour of metal down among the rocks, he got out of the car to see what it was. He was already thinking in terms of its possible usefulness when he reached the thing. Once near it, the idea of salvage rights came naturally.

Looking at it, he felt immediately that it had to be a military instrument of some kind. The Navy, he knew, was constantly firing rockets from Cape Canaveral, up in central Florida. But the longer he looked at the thing the longer he doubted that possibility. The thing was too massive, too obviously built to take the kind of vicious punishment it was receiving at the hands of the sea, to be the light, expendable shell that was a missile prototype or a high-altitude test-rocket. There were tons of metal in it, and the barnacles were thick on it. He wondered how long it had been surging along the bottom, urged and tumbled by the great hidden forces of the ocean, drifting this way and that until this morning the first high tide had heaved it up here to lie caught and scraping on the rocks, steaming as it dried under the early sun.

He did not know what it was, he decided finally. Rocket, torpedo, shell, bomb, or something else, whatever it was, it was valuable and important. The Navy or the Army or Air Force would need it or want it for something.

There was nothing on it to mark it as anyone's property. If anything had ever been written or engraved on that hull, it was gone now. He began to think of how he might establish his rights until he could reach a Navy installation of some kind. The only reason he had for going to Key West was that he had a friend in the sponge-diving business down there. The friend did not know he was coming, so there was no reason not to delay for as long as this business might take him.

He had begun with nothing more than that to urge him on but, as the afternoon grew, the sea and the thing between them had trapped him.

The thing lay awash with half its length over the usual high-water mark, and even when he found it, at low tide, the water curled among the rocks above it. He had thought about that, too, but he had not thought that a hurricane might have taken an un-expected turn during the night, while he drove his old car without a radio to tell him so. Only when the clouds turned grey and the water swirled around his knees like a pack of hounds did he stop for a moment and look out to sea.

He had been clearing the smaller rocks away from around the thing and piling them in an open-ended square enclosing its forward sections, and had been scraping a clean patch in the barnacles with a tyre iron. It had been his intention to make it obvious someone was working on the thing, so he could then leave it and report it with a clear claim. The few cars going by on the highway had not stopped or slowed down – there was no place to stop, with his car on the bit of shoulder, and no real reason to slow down – and after a while the cars had stopped coming entirely.

It was that, telling him the storm had probably caused the

highway to be blocked off at either end, together with the look of the sea, that made him go up to the car and try to make a hawser. And by then he could not have left the thing. It was too obvious that a man had begun a job of work here. If he left it now, it would be too plain that someone had let himself be backed down.

If he had gotten in his car and driven away, he would not have been Dan Henry.

The water was almost completely over the thing now. He himself was working with the waves breaking over his head, trying to dislodge him. More important, the thing was rocking and slipping out of its trap.

The next nearest key was a third of a mile away, bigger than this one, but still uninhabited. The nearest inhabited place was Greyhound Key, where the rest stop was for the buses, and that was out of sight. It would be battened down, and probably evacuated. Dan Henry was all alone, with the highway empty above him and the sea upon him.

He set his back once more, and pushed against the concrete block again. If he could wedge the thing, even a storm tide might not be able to take it away from him. He could untangle his home-made rope and put the fan-belt back on his car. Then he could drive away to some place until the storm died down.

The blood roared in Dan Henry's ears, and the encrusted concrete block opened the hide over his shoulders. A coughing grunt burst out of his mouth. The block teetered – not much, but it gave a little way. Dan Henry locked his knees and braced his back with his palms, pushing his elbows against the block, and when the next wave threw its pressure into the balance he pushed once more. The block slipped suddenly away from him, and he was thrown aside by the wave, flung into the wet rocks above. But the thing was wedged. It could roll and rear as much as it wanted to, but it could not flounder back into the sea. Dan Henry lay over a rock, and wiped the back of his hand across his bloody mouth in satisfaction.

It was over. He could get out of here now, and hole up somewhere. After the storm, he would come back and make sure it was still here. Then he would make his claim, either at one of the little

Navy stations along the chain of keys, or at the big base at Boca Chica. And that would be that, except for the cheque in the mail. The bruises and breaks in his skin would heal over, and become nothing more than scars.

He took his rope off the thing and took it apart far enough to pick out the fan-belt. He let the rest of it wash away, shredded. As he got out of the surging water at last, he scowled slightly because he wondered if the car's spark plugs weren't wet.

It was dark now. Not quite pitch-black, for the hurricane sky to the west was banded by a last strip of sulphur-coloured light at the horizon, but dark enough so that his car was only a looming shape as he climbed up to it. Then, suddenly, the wet finish and the rusty chrome of the front bumper were sparkling with the reflections of faraway lamps. He turned to look southward down the highway, and saw a car coming. As it came nearer, its headlights let him see the clouds of spray that billowed across the road, and the leaping white heads of breakers piling up on the piers and rebounding to the level of the highway. The storm was building up even more quickly than he'd thought. He wondered what kind of damned fool was crazy enough to drive the stretches where the highway crossed open water between keys, and had his answer when a spotlight abruptly reached out and fingered him and his car. Either the state or the county police were out looking to make sure no one was trapped away from shelter.

The police car pulled up, wet and hissing, half-blocking the highway, and the driver immediately switched on his red roof-beacon, through force of habit or training, though there was no oncoming traffic to warn. The four rotating arms of red light tracked monotonously over the road, the key, and the water. By their light, Dan Henry realized for the first time that it was raining furiously. The spotlight was switched off, and the headlights pointed away, up the highway. It was the red beacon that lit the scene and isolated the two men inside its colour.

The officer did not get out of the car. He waited for Dan Henry to come around to his side, and only then cranked his window down halfway.

'Trouble with the car?' he asked, hidden behind the reflection on the glass. Then he must have thought better of it, seeing Dan

Henry's broken skin. He threw the door open quickly, and slid out with his hand on the bone-gripped butt of his plated revolver. He was thick-bodied, with a burly man's voice and brusqueness, and he kept his eyes narrowed. 'What's the story here, Mac?'

Dan Henry shook his head. 'No trouble. I was down on the rocks. Waves threw me around some.'

The officer's uniform pants and leather jacket were already sodden. Water ran down his face and he wiped it out of his eyes. 'What were you doin' down there? No brains?' He watched carefully, his hand firm on his gun.

Dan Henry had been a policeman himself. He was not surprised at the officer's attitude. A policeman was paid to be irritated by anything that didn't have a simple answer.

'I've got something down there I was salvaging,' he said reasonably. 'Storm caught me at it and knocked me around some before I got finished.' Telling about it made him realize he was tired out. He hoped this business with the policeman would be over in a hurry, so that he could fix his car and get into its shelter. The wind was chilly, and the constant impact of water on his skin was beginning to make him numb.

The officer risked a glance down at the thrashing surf before he brought his eyes back to Dan Henry. 'I don't see nothin'. What kind of a thing was it? What're you carryin' that belt around for?'

'It's metal,' Dan Henry said. 'Big. Never seen anything just like it before. I was using the belt to hold it.'

The officer scowled. 'What's holdin' it now? What d'you mean, big? How big? And how come I can't see it?'

'I pushed a rock behind it,' Dan Henry said patiently. 'It's damn near as big as a car. And it's under water, now.'

'Buddy, that don't begin to sound like a likely story.' The policeman pulled his gun out of the holster and held it down alongside his thigh. 'What kind of a lookin' thing is it?'

'Kind of like a rocket, I guess.'

'Now, why the hell didn't you say so!' the policeman growled, relaxing just a little. 'That makes sense. It'll be one of those Navy jobs. They've got 'em droppin' in the ocean like flies. But you ain't goin' to get anything out of it, Buddy. That's government property. You're supposed to turn it in. It's your duty.'

'I don't think so.'

'What d'you mean, you don't think so?' The policeman's gun arm was tense again.

'It doesn't look like a Navy rocket. Doesn't look like anybody's rocket that I know of. I said it was *kind* of like a rocket. Don't know what it is, for sure.' Now Dan Henry was growing angry himself. He didn't like the way things were going. He kept his attention carefully on the gun.

'Know all about rockets, do you?'

'I read the papers. This thing isn't just a piece. It isn't the bottom stage or the top stage. It's one thing, and it never was part of anything bigger. And it's been in the water maybe a couple of years without getting broken up. You show me the Navy rocket that's like that.'

The policeman looked at him. 'Maybe you're right,' he said slowly. 'Tell you what – suppose you just step over here and put my spotlight on it. Reach through the window.' He stepped back casually.

Dan Henry reached around and switched the spot on. He swept it down across the water, a little startled to see how far up the breakers had come. Under the light, the water was a venomous green, full of foam, rain-splotched and furiously alive. A gust of wind rocked the car sharply, and the light with it. The pale beam shot over the sea before it fell back, reaching beyond the swinging cross of red from the roof beacon, and out there the waves disappeared in a mist of rain.

He found the thing, finally, after having to hunt for it. For an instant he thought it had been swept away after all, and felt a stab of anger. But it was still there, heaving under the waves, with only the dim, broad mottling of its back near enough to the surface to be seen at all, that and a constant stirring in the water, rolling it like an animal. 'There it is.' He was surprised how relieved he felt. 'See it?'

'Yeah. Yeah, I seen enough of it,' the officer said. 'You got somethin' down there, all right.' There was a sudden hardness in his voice that had been waiting all along for him to make the decision that would bring it completely out. 'I got my gun on you, buddy. Just step back from that car easy. Anybody foolin' around out here in a hurricane must want somethin' awful bad. If that somethin's a Navy rocket, I guess I know what kind of a son of a bitch that would be.'

'Jesus Christ,' Dan Henry whispered to himself. He was angry with the kind of rage that is almost a pleasure. And not because the cop thought he was a Commie, either, Dan Henry suddenly realized, but because he persisted in not understanding about the rocket. Or whatever it was.

He turned around with a jump. The fan-belt in his hand whipped out with all the strength in his arm and all the snap in his wrist, and snatched the cop's gun out of his hand. It skittered across the wet concrete of the highway, and Dan Henry pounced after it. He scooped it up and crouched with the muzzle pointed dead at the cop's belly.

'Back off,' he said. 'Back off. You're not takin' that thing away from me. I sweated blood to hang on to it, and you're not goin' to come along and throw me in jail to get it away.'

The cop retreated, his hands up without his being told, and waited for his chance. Dan Henry backed him up the highway until the cop was past the cars, and opened the door of his own car. He threw the gun inside, together with the belt. He slammed the door and said, 'You can get that back later. Or you can try and take it away from me now, barehanded.' He was shaking with the tension in his bunched shoulders, and his arms were open wide. He was crouched, his chest deep as his lungs hunted for more and more oxygen to wash the rush of blood his heart was driving through his veins. The red flood of beacon on the police car swept over him in regular flashes.

'I'll wait,' the cop said.

'Now,' Dan Henry said, 'I want to use your radio. I want you to call in and report this. Only I want you to report it to the Navy before you call your headquarters.'

The cop looked at him with a puzzled scowl. 'You on the level?' he asked, and Dan Henry could see him wondering if he hadn't made a mistake, somewhere, in his thinking about what was going on here. But Dan Henry had no more time for him. The wind was a steady pressure that made him brace his left leg hard against it.

The water flying across the highway was coming in solid chunks, instead of spray, and the two cars were rocking on their springs. The rain was streaming over them, leaving the officer's jacket a baggy, clinging mess. The sea was smashing violently into the highway piers, thundering to the wind's howl, and even here on solid ground the shock of the impacts was coming up through Dan Henry's bones.

His throat was raw. Bit by bit, he and the officer had had to raise their voices until they had been shouting at each other without realizing it. 'Get in the car and do it!' he yelled, and the officer came forward as he backed away to give him room.

The policeman got into his car, with Dan Henry standing watchfully a little behind the open door-frame, and switched on his radio. 'Tell them where we are,' Dan Henry said. 'Tell them my name – Daniel Morris Henry – tell them what I said about it's not being one of their rockets – and tell them I'm claiming salvage rights. Then you tell them the rest any way you see it.'

The officer turned the dials away from their usual settings. After a minute, he picked his microphone out of the dashboard hanger and began calling Boca Chica in a stubborn voice. At intervals, he said, 'Over,' and threw the Receive switch. They heard the peculiar, grating crackle of radiotelephone static, trapped in the speaker. And only that.

'Look, buddy,' the policeman said at last, 'we're not goin' to get any answer. Not if we ain't got one by now. Boca Chica radio may be knocked out. Or maybe my transmitter's shorted, with all this wet. Could be anything.' He jerked his head toward the water. 'How much longer you want us to stay out here?' Probably because he had seen many hurricanes, he was beginning to grow nervous.

'Try it again,' Dan Henry said. He watched the officer closely, and couldn't see him doing anything wrong. Dan Henry didn't know the Boca Chica frequency; that was where the trouble might be. But he'd used a police radio often enough so that any other trick wouldn't have gotten by him.

The officer called Boca Chica for another five minutes. Then he stopped again. 'No dice. Look, buddy, you've had it. Maybe you're just a guy looking for some salvage money, like you say you are. Maybe not. But there's goin' to be waves coming across this road in a little while. Why don't we get out of here and straighten things out when this blows over?'

Dan Henry set his jaw. 'Get the vibrator out of that radio. Do it.' Now he had no choice. If he went with the cop, that was that. They'd throw him in some jail for resisting arrest and assaulting an officer, and keep him there until they were good and ready to let him out. By then, whatever happened to the thing down here, somebody would have figured out some way to get that Navy cheque instead of him. The only thing to do was to cripple the cop's radio and send him down the highway until he reached a phone. There was no guarantee that the radio wouldn't work on the police frequency.

Maybe the cop would call the Navy right after he called his headquarters. Or maybe, even if he didn't, some higher brass at the headquarters would report to the Navy. Either way – if you believed it was a Navy rocket or if you didn't – it was government business. Then, maybe, the Navy would get here before the cops did. Or soon enough afterward so he'd still be here to talk to them. Once he got taken away from here, that chance was gone.

On that decision, he was ready to cling to a hundred-foot key in the middle of an Atlantic hurricane. 'Let's have that vibrator. Right now.'

The officer looked at him, and reached under the dash. He fumbled in the narrow space where the radio hung, and pulled the sealed aluminium cylinder out of its socket. But he was getting ready to grab for Dan Henry if he could reach him quickly enough.

'Okay,' Dan Henry said, 'drop it on the road and clear out of here. You can get it back along with your gun. And just in case you have some brains in your head, when you get to a phone, call the Na—'

The policeman had dropped the vibrator, and the wind had rolled it under Dan Henry's Chevrolet. Dan Henry had been in the act of letting the police car door close, when a thread of brilliant violet fire punched up from the water, through the red light, up through the rain, up through the black clouds, and out to the stars beyond.

'There's something *in* that thing!' the officer blurted.

Dan Henry threw the door shut. 'Get out of here, man!'

Down in the drowned rocks, an arc hissed between the two struts in the thing's nose. The water leaped and bubbled around it but, for all the breakers could do, the blaze of light still illuminated the thing and the rocks it ground against, turning the sea transparent; and from the crown of the arc the thin violet column pointed without wavering, without dispersing, straight as a line drawn from hell to heaven.

The police car's tyres smoked and spun on the pavement. 'I'll get help,' the officer shouted over the squeal and the roar of his engine. Then he had traction and the car shot away, headlights slashing, glimmering in the rain and the spray, lurching from side to side under the wind's hammer, roof beacon turning at its unvarying pace, the siren's howl lost in the boom of the water. And Dan Henry was left in the violet-lanced darkness.

Without the windbreak of the police car in front of him, he was pushed violently backward until his own car's fender stopped him. Water struck his eyes, and the night blurred. He bent forward and rubbed his face until the ache of the salt was dulled to a steady throbbing, and then he staggered across the highway to the guard rail on the Atlantic side. The tops of the incoming waves washed over his shoes, just as the surf at noon had lapped at him, twelve feet below.

The rain and the spray streamed over him. He cupped one hand over his nose, to breathe, and hung on the rail.

There was nothing more to see. The pillar of light still shot up from the arc, and the bulk of the thing loomed, gross and black, down there in the water. It was feet below the surface now, cushioned from the smash of the waves, and it stirred with a regular motion like a whale shark in a tank.

The radio, he thought. It had felt the radio in the police car. Nothing else had happened to bring it to life at that particular moment. It had waited a little – perhaps analysing what it had encountered, perhaps then noticing the flash of the car's roof beacon for the first time. And for the first time since the day, years ago, when it entered the sea it had found a reason for sending out a signal.

To where? Not to him, or the policeman. The light was not pointed toward the highway. It went up, straight up, going out of sight through the clouds as his eyes tried to follow it before the lash of water forced his head down again.

There was no one inside the thing, Dan Henry thought. There couldn't be. He had scraped on the side with regular, purposeful strokes, clearing an exactly square patch, and gained no response. And the thing had lain in the ocean a long time, sealed up, dragging its hide over the bottom as the currents pushed and pulled it, rolling, twisting, seamless, with only those two horns with which to feel the world about it.

He could be wrong, of course. Something could be alive in there, still breathing in some fantastic way from a self-contained air supply, eating tiny amounts of stored food, getting rid of its wastes somehow. But he didn't see how. It didn't seem logical that anything would trap itself like that, not knowing if it was ever going to escape.

He could be wrong about it all. It might not have been reacting to anything that happened on the highway. It might be ignoring everything outside itself, and following some purpose that had nothing to do with this world or its people. But whether it was that, or whether he was at least partly right, Dan Henry wondered what was sending things to drop down on the Earth and make signals to the stars.

The water came higher. It came up the key too quickly to split and go around it, and spilled over the highway to plunge into the rocks on the Gulf side. It broke halfway up the side of his car. He remembered the policeman's vibrator. That would be far to the west of him now, skipping at a thrown stone's velocity over waves whose tops were being cut off by the wind. Dan Henry's mouth twisted in a numb grimace. Now he'd have to buy one. They probably wouldn't let him get away that cheaply. They could make that stick for a robbery charge. And destroying public property. While, on the other hand, if he was swept off this key they wouldn't even have to pay for his burial. He laughed drunkenly.

A wave broke over him. He had made a sling for himself by knotting the legs of his dungarees around one of the guard-rail uprights, and when the wave was past he lolled naked with the bunched tops of the dungarees cutting into his chest under his arms. The wind worked at him now, with a kind of fury, and then the next wave came. It was warm, but the wind evaporating it as soon as he was exposed again made his skin crawl and his teeth chatter. He reached behind him with a wooden arm and felt the knot in the dungaree legs to make sure it was holding. The pressure had tightened it into a small hard lump.

That was good, at any rate. That and the blessed practicality of the engineers who built the highway. When they laid the roadway where the hurricane-smashed railroad had been, they had cut the rusted rails up with torches, set the stumps deep in the concrete, and welded the guard-rails together out of T-shaped steel designed to hold a locomotive's weight.

Dan Henry grinned to himself. The rail would hold. The dungarees would hold, or the trademark was a liar. Only about Dan Henry was there any doubt. Dan Henry – hard, sure Dan Henry, with his chest being cut in half, with his torn skin being torn again as the waves beat him against the highway, with his head going silly because he was being pounded into raw meat.

Dear God, he thought, am I doing this for *money*? No, he thought, as a wave filled his nostrils, no, not any more. When that thing turned its light on and I didn't jump in the car with that cop, that's when we found out I wasn't doing it for the money. For what? God knows.

He floundered half over on his side, arched his neck, and looked at the violet arrow through the clouds. Signal, you bastard! Go ahead and signal! Do anything. As long as I know you're still there. If you can stay put, so can I.

Well, what *was* he doing this for? Dan Henry fought with the sling that held him, trying to take some of the pressure off his chest. God knew, but it was up to Dan Henry to find out for himself.

It wasn't money. All right – that was decided. What was left – vanity? Big Dan Henry – big, strong, Dan Henry . . . take more than a hurricane to stop big, strong, wonderful Dan Henry – was that the way his thoughts were running?

He croaked a laugh. Big, strong Dan Henry was lying here

limp as a calico doll, naked as a baby, praying his pants wouldn't rip. The storm had washed the pride out of him as surely as it had his first interest in the salvage money.

All right, *what*, then! He growled and cursed at his own stupidity. Here he was, and he didn't even know why. Here he was, being bludgeoned to death, being drowned, being torn apart by the wind. He was stuck out here now, and nobody could save him.

A wave roared over the highway and struck his car a blow that sent a hubcap careening off into the darkness. The car tilted on to the Gulf-side guard-rail. The rail bellied outward, and the car hung halfway over the rocks on the other side. Successive waves smashed into it, exploding in spray, and the guard-rail groaned in the lull after each strike. Dan Henry watched it dully in the violet light, with the water sluicing down over his head and shoulders for a moment before the wind found it and tore it away in horizontal strings of droplets.

The car's door panels had already been pushed in, and the windows were cracked. Now the exposed floor-boards were being hammered. The muffler was wrenched out.

With the next smash of solid water, the horizontal rail broke its weld at one end and the car heeled forward to the right, impaling its radiator on an upright. It hung there, gradually tearing the radiator out of its brackets, spilling rusty water for one instant before a wave washed it clean, scraping its front axle down the sharp edge of the roadway, breaking loose pieces of the concrete and raising its left rear wheel higher and higher. The radiator came free with a snap like a breaking tooth, and the car dropped suddenly, its front end caught by the edge of the left wheel, kept from falling only by the straining uprights still jammed against it farther back on the right side. The hood flew back suddenly and was gone with a twang in one gust of wind.

Am I going to have to buy that cop a new gun, too? Dan Henry thought, and in that moment the wind began to die. The water hesitated. Three waves rolled across the road slowly, much higher than when the wind was flattening them, but almost gentle. The rain slackened. And then the eye of the storm had moved over him, and he had calm.

* * *

He pushed himself to his feet at last, after he sagged out of the hold the dungarees had on his chest. He leaned against the guard-rail and stared woodenly at the ocean and the thing.

The beam went up out of sight, a clean, marvellously precise line. But down at the surface the sea was finally hiding the thing, and making a new noise that had none of a storm-sea's clean power. It filled his ears and unnerved him.

With the wind and the pressure gone, the waves were leaping upward, clashing against each other, rebounding, colliding again, peaking sharply. Dan Henry could hear the highway over the water booming faintly as the waves slammed up against its under-side. But he could actually see very little. It had grown darker, and what he saw were mostly the tops of the exploding waves, glimmering pale violet.

The thing was buried deep, where it lay at the foot of the key, and the arc that had diffused most of the light was visible only as a fitful glow that shifted and danced. The violet beam seemed to spring into life of itself at the plunging surface, and it kept most of its light compressed within itself.

Dan Henry swayed on the guard-rail. It was stifling hot. The mugginess filled his lungs and choked him. He lolled his head back. The clouds were patchy overhead, and the stars shone through in places.

There was a high-pitched chime, and a circle of ice-blue flame came hurtling down the beam. It came out of the sky and shot into the water, and when it touched the glimmer of the arc there was another chime, this time from the thing, and this time the water quivered. The violet beam flickered once, and a red halo spat up with a crackle, travelling slowly. When it was a hundred feet over Dan Henry's head it split in two, leaving one thin ring moving at the old rate, and a larger one that suddenly doubled its speed until it split again, doubled its speed and split again, accelerated again, and so blazed upward along the violet beam's axis, leaving a spaced trail of slowly moving lesser rings behind it. They hung in the air, a ladder to the stars. Then they died out slowly, and before they had stopped glowing the violet beam was switched off.

The sky was empty, and the thing lay quiescent in the water

once more. Dan Henry blinked at the flashes swimming across his eyes. It was pitch dark. He could barely see the white of swirling water as it dashed itself into the rocks at his feet.

Far up the highway, coming towards him, were two headlights with a swinging red beacon just above them.

The police car was plastered with wet leaves and broken palm fronds. The policeman slammed it to a halt beside him, and flung the door open. He stopped long enough to turn his head and say, 'Jesus Christ! He's still here! He ain't gone!' to someone in the front seat with him, and then he jumped out. 'What happened?' he asked Dan Henry. 'What was that business with the lights?'

Dan Henry looked at him. 'You made it,' he mumbled.

'Yeah, I made it. Got to this Navy skywatch station. Phone was out, so I couldn't call in to headquarters. Found this Navy professor up there. Brought him down with me when the eye came over. He figures we got maybe twenty minutes more before the other side of the hurricane comes around.'

The other man had slid out of the car. He was a thin, bony-faced man with rimless glasses. He was dressed in a badly fitted tropical suit that was pleated with dampness. He looked at Dan Henry's purpled chest, and asked, 'Are you all right?'

'Sure.'

The man twitched an eyebrow. 'I'm assigned to the satellite-tracking station north of here. What is this thing?'

Dan Henry nodded toward it. 'Down there. It got an answer to its signal, acknowledged and switched off. That's what I think, anyhow.'

'You do, eh? Well, you could be right. In any case, we don't have much time. I'll notify the naval district commandant's office as soon as the telephones are working again, but I want a quick look at it now, in case we lose it.'

'We're not going to lose it,' Dan Henry growled.

The professor looked at him sharply. 'What makes you sure?'

'I wedged it,' Dan Henry said with a tight note in his voice. 'I almost ruined myself and I almost drowned, but I wedged it. I took a gun away from a cop to keep it from getting left here without anybody to watch it. And I stayed here and got almost drowned, and almost cut in half, and almost beat to death against this highway here, and *we're not going to lose it now.*'

'I . . . see,' the professor said. He turned to the policeman. 'If you happen to have some sedatives in your first-aid kit, they might be useful now,' he murmured.

'Might have something. I'll look,' the policeman said.

'And put your spotlight on the thing, please,' the professor added, peering over the guard-rail. 'Though I don't suppose we'll see much.'

The yellow beam of the spotlight slid over the top of the water. If it penetrated at all, it still did not reach any part of the thing. The policeman hunted for it, sweeping back and forth until Dan Henry made an impatient sound, went over to him, and pointed it straight. 'Now, leave it there. That's where it is.'

'Yeah? I don't see anythin' but water.'

'That's where it is,' Dan Henry said. 'Haven't been here all this time for nothin'.' He went back to the railing, but there was still nothing to see.

'You're sure that's where it is?' the professor asked.

'Yes. It's about ten feet down.'

'All right,' the professor sighed. 'Tell me as much as you can about its activities.'

'I think it's a sounding rocket,' Dan Henry said. 'I think somebody from some place sent that thing down here a while ago to find out things. I don't know what those things are. I don't know who that somebody is. But I'm pretty sure he lost it somehow, and didn't know where it was until it signalled him just now. I don't know why it worked out that way. I don't know why the rocket couldn't get its signal through before this, or why it didn't go home.'

'You think it's of extraterrestrial origin, then?'

Dan Henry looked at the professor. 'You don't think so?'

'If I did, I would be on my way to district headquarters at this moment, hurricane or no hurricane,' the professor said testily.

'You don't believe it?' Dan Henry persisted.

The professor grew uneasy. 'No.'

'Wouldn't you *like* to believe it?'

The professor looked quickly out to sea.

'Here,' the policeman said, handing Dan Henry a flat brown

half-pint bottle. 'Sedative.' He winked.

Dan Henry knocked the bottle out of the cop's hand. It broke on the pavement.

'Look up!' the professor whispered.

They turned their heads. Something huge, flat, and multi-winged was shadowed faintly on the stars.

'Oh, Lord,' the officer said.

There was a burst of chiming from the thing down in the water, and violet pulses of light came up through the water and burst on the underside of the thing up in the sky.

Answering darts of tawny gold came raining down. The thing in the water stirred, and they could see the rocks move. 'Tractor rays,' the professor said in a husky voice. 'Theoretically impossible.'

'What's it going to do?' the policeman asked.

'Pick it up,' the professor answered. 'And take it back to wherever it comes from.'

Dan Henry began to curse.

The thing in the sky slipped down, and they could feel the air throb. After a moment, the sound came to them – a distant, rumbling purr, and a high metallic shrieking.

The thing in the water heaved itself upward. It struggled against the rocks.

'We'd better get back,' the professor said.

The distant sound grew stronger and beat upon their ears. The professor and the policeman retreated to the car.

But Dan Henry did not. He straightened his back and gathered his muscles. As the tawny fire came down, he leaped over the guard-rail into the water.

He swam with grim fury, thrown and sucked by the water, sputtering for breath, his feet pounding. Even so, he would not have reached the thing. But the water humped in the grip of the force that clutched at the thing, and the waves collapsed. Dan Henry's arms bit through the water with desperate precision, and just before the thing broke free, he was upon it.

'No, sir,' he grunted, closing his hand on one of the struts. 'Not without me. We've been through too much together.' He grinned coldly at the hovering ship as they rose to meet it.

Cordwainer Smith
Scanners live in vain

Martel was angry. He did not even adjust his blood away from anger. He stamped across the room by judgement, not by sight. When he saw the table hit the floor, and could tell by the expression on Luci's face that the table must have made a loud crash, he looked down to see if his leg was broken. It was not. Scanner to the core, he had to scan himself. The action was reflex and automatic. The inventory included his legs, abdomen, chestbox of instruments, hands, arms, face and back with the mirror. Only then did Martel go back to being angry. He talked with his voice, even though he knew that his wife hated its blare and preferred to have him write.

'I tell you, I must cranch, I have to cranch. It's my worry, isn't it?'

When Luci answered, he saw only a part of her words as he read her lips: 'Darling . . . you're my husband . . . right to love you . . . dangerous . . . do it . . . dangerous . . . wait. . . .'

He faced her, but put sound in his voice, letting the blare hurt her again: 'I tell you, I'm going to cranch.'

Catching her expression, he became rueful and a little tender: 'Can't you understand what it means to me? To get out of this horrible prison in my own head? To be a man again – hearing your voice, smelling smoke? To *feel* again – to feel my feet on the ground, to feel the air move against my face? Don't you know what it means?'

Her wide-eyed worrisome concern thrust him back into pure annoyance. He read only a few words as her lips moved: ' . . . love you . . . your own good . . . don't you think I want you to be human? . . . your own good . . . too much . . . he said . . . they said. . . .'

When he roared at her, he realized that his voice must be particularly bad. He knew that the sound hurt her no less than did the words: 'Do you think I wanted you to marry a Scanner? Didn't I tell you we're almost as low as the habermans? We're dead, I tell you. We've got to be dead to do our work. How can anybody go to the Up-and-Out? Can you dream what raw Space is? I warned you. But you married me. All right, you married a man. Please, darling, let me be a man. Let me hear your voice, let me feel the warmth of being alive, of being human. Let me!'

He saw by her look of stricken assent that he had won the argument. He did not use his voice again. Instead, he pulled his tablet up from where it hung against his chest. He wrote on it, using the pointed fingernail of his right forefinger – the talking nail of a Scanner – in quick cleancut script: *Pls, drlng, whrs crnching wire?*

She pulled the long gold-sheathed wire out of the pocket of her apron. She let its field sphere fall to the carpeted floor. Swiftly, dutifully, with the deft obedience of a Scanner's wife, she wound the cranching wire around his head, spirally around his neck and chest. She avoided the instruments set in his chest. She even avoided the radiating scars around the instruments, the stigmata of men who had gone Up and into the Out. Mechanically he lifted a foot as she slipped the wire between his feet. She drew the wire taut. She snapped the small plug into the high-burden control next to his heart-reader. She helped him to sit down, arranging his hands for him, pushing his head back into the cup at the top of the chair. She turned then full-face toward him, so that he could read her lips easily. Her expression was composed.

She knelt, scooped up the sphere at the other end of the wire, stood erect calmly, her back to him. He scanned her, and saw nothing in her posture but grief which would have escaped the eye of anyone but a Scanner. She spoke: he could see her chest-muscles moving. She realized that she was not facing him, and turned so that he could see her lips.

'Ready at last?'

He smiled a *yes*.

She turned her back to him again. (Luci could never bear to watch him go under the wire.) She tossed the wire-sphere into the air. It caught in the force-field and hung there. Suddenly it glowed. That was all. All – except for the sudden red stinking roar of coming back to his senses. Coming back, across the wild threshold of pain.

When he awakened, under the wire, he did not feel as though he had just cranched. Even though it was the second cranching within the week, he felt fit. He lay in the chair. His ears drank in the sound of air touching things in the room. He heard Luci breathing in the next room, where she was hanging up the wire to cool. He smelt the thousand and one smells that are in anybody's room: the crisp freshness of the germ-burner, the sour-sweet tang of the humidifier, the odour of the dinner they had just eaten, the smells of clothes, furniture, of people themselves. All these were pure delight. He sang a phrase or two of his favourite song:

'*Here's to the haberman, Up-and-Out!*
Up – oh! – and Out – oh! – Up-and-Out!...'

He heard Luci chuckle in the next room. He gloated over the sounds of her dress as she swished to the doorway.

She gave him her crooked little smile. 'You sound all right. Are you all right, really?'

Even with this luxury of senses, he scanned. He took the flash-quick inventory which constituted his professional skill. His eyes swept in the news of the instruments. Nothing showed off scale, beyond the nerve compression hanging in the edge of *Danger*. But he could not worry about the nerve-box. That always came through cranching. You couldn't get under the wire without having it show on the nerve-box. Some day the box would go to *Overload* and drop back down to *Dead*. That was the way a haberman ended. But you couldn't have everything. People who went to the Up-and-Out had to pay the price for Space.

Anyhow, he should worry! He was a Scanner. A good one, and he knew it. If he couldn't scan himself, who could? This cranching wasn't too dangerous. Dangerous, but not too dangerous.

Luci put out her hand and ruffled his hair as if she had been reading his thoughts, instead of just following them: 'But you know you shouldn't have! You shouldn't!'

'But I did!' He grinned at her.

Her gaiety still forced, she said: 'Come on, darling, let's have a good time. I have almost everything there is in the icebox – all your favourite tastes. And I have two new records just full of smells. I tried them out myself, and even I liked them. And you know me—'

'Which?'

'Which what, you old darling?'

He slipped his hand over her shoulders as he limped out of the room. He could never go back to feeling the floor beneath his feet, feeling the air against his face, without being bewildered and clumsy. As if cranching was real, and being a haberman was a bad dream. But he *was* a haberman, and a Scanner. 'You know what I meant, Luci . . . the smells, which you have. Which one did you like, on the record?'

'Well-l-l,' said she, judiciously, 'There were some lamb chops that were the strangest things—'

He interrupted: 'What are lambtchots?'

'Wait till you smell them. Then guess. I'll tell you this much. It's a smell hundreds and hundreds of years old. They found about it in the old books.'

'Is a lambtchot a Beast?'

'I won't tell you. You've got to wait,' she laughed, as she helped him sit down and spread his tasting-dishes before him. He wanted to go back over the dinner first, sampling all the pretty things he had eaten, and savouring them this time with his now-living lips and tongue.

When Luci had found the music wire and had thrown its sphere up into the force-field he reminded her of the new smells. She took out the long glass records and set the first one into a transmitter.

'Now sniff!'

A queer, frightening, exciting smell came over the room. It seemed like nothing in this world, nor like anything from the Up-and-Out. Yet it was familiar. His mouth watered. His pulse beat a little faster; he scanned his heartbox. (Faster, sure enough.) But that smell, what was it? In mock perplexity, he grabbed her hands, looked into her eyes and growled:

'Tell me, darling! Tell me, or I'll eat you up!'

'That's just right!'

'What?'

'You're right. It should make you want to eat me. It's meat.'

'Meat. Who?'

'Not a person,' said she, knowledgeably, 'a Beast. A Beast which people used to eat. A lamb was a small sheep – you've seen sheep out in the wild, haven't you? – and a chop is part of its middle – here!' She pointed at her chest.

Martel did not hear her. All his boxes had swung over toward *Alarm*, some to *Danger*. He fought against the roar of his own mind, forcing his body into excess excitement. How easy it was to be a Scanner when you really stood outside your own body, haberman-fashion, and looked back into it with your eyes alone. Then you could manage the body, rule it coldly even in the enduring agony of Space. But to realize that you *were* a body, that this thing was ruling you, that the mind could kick the flesh and send it roaring off into panic! That was bad.

He tried to remember the days before he had gone into the haberman device, before he had been cut apart for the Up-and-Out. Had he always been subject to the rush of his emotions from his mind to his body, from his body back to his mind, confounding him so that he couldn't scan? But he hadn't been a Scanner then.

He knew what had hit him. Amid the roar of his own pulse, he knew. In the nightmare of the Up-and-Out, that smell had forced its way through to him, while their ship burned off Venus and the habermans fought the collapsing metal with their bare hands. He had scanned then: all were in *Danger*. Chestboxes went up to *Overload* and dropped to *Dead* all around him as he had moved from man to man, shoving the drifting corpses out of his way as he fought to scan each man in turn, to clamp vices on unnoticed broken legs, to snap the sleeping-valve on men whose instruments showed they were hopelessly near *Overload*. With men trying to work and cursing him for a Scanner while he, professional zeal aroused, fought to do his job and keep them alive in the Great Pain of Space, he had smelled that smell. It had fought its way along his rebuilt nerves, past the haberman cuts, past all the safeguards of physical and mental discipline. In the wildest hour of tragedy, he had smelled aloud. He remembered it was like a bad cranching, connected with the fury and nightmare all around him. He had even stopped his work to scan himself, fearful that the First Effect might come, breaking past all haberman cuts and ruining him with the Pain of Space. But he had come through. His own instruments stayed and stayed at *Danger*, without nearing *Overload*. He had done his job, and won a commendation for it. He had even forgotten the burning ship.

All except the smell.

And here the smell was all over again – the smell of meat-with-fire. . . .

Luci looked at him with wifely concern. She obviously thought he had cranched too much, and was about to haberman back. She tried to be cheerful: 'You'd better rest, honey.'

He whispered to her: 'Cut – off – that – smell.'

She did not question his word. She cut the transmitter. She even crossed the room and stepped up the room controls until a small breeze flitted across the floor and drove the smells up to the ceiling.

He rose, tired and stiff. (His instruments were normal, except that heart was fast and nerves still hanging on the edge of *Danger*.) He spoke sadly:

'Forgive me, Luci. I suppose I shouldn't have cranched. Not so soon again. But, darling, I have to get out from being a haberman. How can I ever be near you? How can I be a man – not hearing my own voice, not even feeling my own life as it goes through my veins? I love you, darling. Can't I ever be near you?'

Her pride was disciplined and automatic: 'But you're a Scanner!'

'I know I'm a Scanner. But so what?'

She went over the words, like a tale told a thousand times to reassure herself: 'You are the bravest of the brave, the most skilful of the skilled. All Mankind owes most honour to the Scanner, who unites the Earths of mankind. Scanners are the protectors of the habermans. They are the judges in the Up-and-Out. They make men live in the place where men need desperately to die. They are the most honoured of mankind, and even the Chiefs of the Instrumentality are delighted to pay them homage!'

With obstinate sorrow he demurred: 'Luci, we've heard that

all before. But does it pay us back—'

' "Scanners work for more than pay. They are the strong guards of mankind." Don't you remember that?'

'But our lives, Luci. What can you get out of being the wife of a Scanner? Why did you marry me? I'm human only when I cranch. The rest of the time – you know what I am. A machine. A man turned into a machine. A man who has been killed and kept alive for duty. Don't you realize what I miss?'

'Of course, darling, of course—'

He went on: 'Don't you think I remember my childhood? Don't you think I remember what it is to be a man and not a haberman? To walk and feel my feet on the ground? To feel a decent clean pain instead of watching my body every minute to see if I'm alive? How will I know if I'm dead? Did you ever think of that, Luci? How will I know if I'm dead?'

She ignored the unreasonableness of his outburst. Pacifyingly, she said: 'Sit down, darling. Let me make you some kind of a drink. You're overwrought.'

Automatically, he scanned. 'No, I'm not! Listen to me. How do you think it feels to be in the Up-and-Out with the crew tied-for-space all around you? How do you think it feels to watch them sleep? How do you think I like scanning, scanning, scanning month after month, when I can feel the Pain of Space beating against every part of my body, trying to get past my haberman blocks? How do you think I like to wake the men when I have to, and have them hate me for it? Have you ever seen habermans fight – strong men fighting, and neither knowing pain, fighting until one touches *Overload*? Do you think about that, Luci?' Triumphantly he added: 'Can you blame me if I cranch, and come back to being a man, just two days a month?'

'I'm not blaming you, darling. Let's enjoy your cranch. Sit down now, and have a drink.'

He was sitting down, resting his face in his hands, while she fixed the drink, using natural fruits out of bottles in addition to the secure alkaloids. He watched her restlessly and pitied her for marrying a Scanner; and then, though it was unjust, resented having to pity her.

Just as she turned to hand him the drink, they both jumped a little as the phone rang. It should not have rung. They had turned it off. It rang again, obviously on the emergency circuit. Stepping ahead of Luci, Martel strode over to the phone and looked into it. Vomact was looking at him.

The custom of Scanners entitled him to be brusque, even with a Senior Scanner, on certain given occasions. This was one.

Before Vomact could speak, Martel spoke two words into the plate, not caring whether the old man could read lips or not:

'Cranching. Busy.'

He cut the switch and went back to Luci.

The phone rang again.

Luci said, gently, 'I can find out what it is, darling. Here, take your drink and sit down.'

'Leave it alone,' said her husband. 'No one has a right to call when I'm cranching. He knows that. He ought to know that.'

The phone rang again. In a fury, Martel rose and went to the plate. He cut it back on. Vomact was on the screen. Before Martel could speak, Vomact held up his talking nail in line with his heartbox. Martel reverted to discipline:

'Scanner Martel present and waiting, sir.'

The lips moved solemnly: 'Top emergency.'

'Sir, I am under the wire.'

'Top emergency.'

'Sir, don't you understand?' Martel mouthed his words, so he could be sure that Vomact followed. 'I . . . am . . . under . . . the . . . wire. Unfit . . . for . . . space!'

Vomact repeated: 'Top emergency. Report to Central Tie-in.'

'But, sir, no emergency like this—'

'Right, Martel. No emergency like this, ever before. Report to Tie-in.' With a faint glint of kindliness, Vomact added: 'No need to de-cranch. Report as you are.'

This time it was Martel whose phone was cut out. The screen went grey.

He turned to Luci. The temper had gone out of his voice. She came to him. She kissed him, and rumpled his hair. All she could say was, 'I'm sorry.'

She kissed him again, knowing his disappointment. 'Take good care of yourself, darling. I'll wait.'

He scanned, and slipped into his transparent aircoat. At the window he paused, and waved. She called, 'Good luck!' As the air flowed past him he said to himself, 'This is the first time I've felt flight in – eleven years. Lord, but it's easy to fly if you can feel yourself live!'

Central Tie-in glowed white and austere far ahead. Martel peered. He saw no glare of incoming ships from the Up-and-Out, no shuddering flare of Space-fire out of control. Everything was quiet, as it should be on an off-duty night.

And yet Vomact had called. He had called an emergency higher than Space. There was no such thing. But Vomact had called it.

When Martel got there, he found about half the Scanners present, two dozen or so of them. He lifted the talking finger. Most of the Scanners were standing face to face, talking in pairs as they read lips. A few of the old, impatient ones were scribbling on their tablets and then thrusting the tablets into other people's faces. All the faces wore the dull dead relaxed look of a haberman. When Martel entered the room, he knew that most of the others laughed in the deep isolated privacy of their own minds, each thinking things it would be useless to express in formal words. It had been a long time since a Scanner showed up at a meeting cranched.

Vomact was not there: probably, thought Martel, he was still on the phone calling others. The light of the phone flashed on and off; the bell rang. Martel felt odd when he realized that, of all those present, he was the only one to hear that loud bell. It made him realize why ordinary people did not like to be around groups of habermans or Scanners. Martel looked around for company.

His friend Chang was there, busy explaining to some old and testy Scanner that he did not know why Vomact had called. Martel looked farther and saw Parizianski. He walked over, threading his way past the others with a dexterity that showed he could feel his feet from the inside, and did not have to watch them. Several of the others stared at him with their dead faces, and tried to smile. But they lacked full muscular control and their faces twisted into horrid masks. (Scanners usually knew better than to show expression on faces which they could no longer govern. Martel added to himself: I swear *I'll* never smile again unless I'm cranched.)

Parizianski gave him the sign of the talking finger. Looking face to face, he spoke:

'You come here cranched?'

Parizianski could not hear his own voice, so the words roared like the words on a broken and screeching phone; Martel was startled, but knew that the inquiry was well meant. No one could be better-natured than the burly Pole.

'Vomact called. Top emergency.'

'You told him you were cranched?'

'Yes.'

'He still made you come?'

'Yes.'

'Then all this – it is not for Space? You could not go Up-and-Out? You are like ordinary men?'

'That's right.'

'Then why did he call us?' Some pre-haberman habit made Parizianski wave his arms in inquiry. The hand struck the back of the old man behind them. The slap could be heard throughout the room, but only Martel heard it. Instinctively, he scanned Parizianski and the old Scanner, and they scanned him back. Only then did the old man ask why Martel had scanned him. When Martel explained that he was under the wire, the old man moved swiftly away to pass on the news that there was a cranched Scanner present at the Tie in.

Even this minor sensation could not keep the attention of most of the Scanners from the worry about the top emergency. One young man, who had scanned his first transit just the year before, dramatically interposed himself between Parizianski and Martel. He dramatically flashed his tablet at them: *Is Vmct mad?*

The older men shook their heads. Martel, remembering that it had not been too long that the young man had been haberman, mitigated the dead solemnity of the denial with a friendly smile. He spoke in a normal voice, saying, 'Vomact is the Senior of Scanners. I am sure that he could not go mad. Would he not see it on his boxes first?'

Martel had to repeat the question, speaking slowly and mouthing his words before the young Scanner could understand the comment. The young man tried to make his face smile, and twisted it into a comic mask. But he took up his tablet and scribbled: *Yr rght.*

Chang broke away from his friend and came over, his half-Chinese face gleaming in the warm evening. (It's strange, thought Martel, that more Chinese don't become Scanners. Or not so strange perhaps, if you think that they never fill their quota of habermans. Chinese love good living too much. The ones who do scan are all good ones.) Chang saw that Martel was cranched, and spoke with voice:

'You break precedents. Luci must be angry to lose you?'

'She took it well. Chang, that's strange.'

'What?'

'I'm cranched, and I can hear. Your voice sounds all right. How did you learn to talk like – like an ordinary person?'

'I practised with soundtracks. Funny you noticed it. I think I am the only Scanner in or between the Earths who can pass for an ordinary man. Mirrors and soundtracks. I found out how to act.'

'But you don't. . . ?'

'No. I don't feel, or taste, or hear, or smell things, any more than you do. Talking doesn't do me much good. But I notice that it cheers up the people around me.'

'It would make a difference in the life of Luci.'

Chang nodded sagely. 'My father insisted on it. He said, "You may be proud of being a Scanner. I am sorry you are not a man. Conceal your defects." So I tried. I wanted to tell the old boy about the Up-and-Out, and what we did here, but it did not matter. He said, "Airplanes were good enough for Confucius, and they are for me too." The old humbug! He tries so hard to be a Chinese when he can't even read Old Chinese. But he's got wonderful good sense, and for somebody going on 200 he certainly gets around.'

Martel smiled at the thought: 'In his airplane?'

Chang smiled back. This discipline of his facial muscles was amazing; a bystander would not think that Chang was a haberman, controlling his eyes, cheeks, and lips by cold intellectual control. The expression had the spontaneity of life. Martel felt a flash of envy for Chang when he looked at the dead cold faces of Parizianski and the others. He knew that he himself looked fine: but why shouldn't he? He was cranched. Turning to Parizianski he said, 'Did you see what Chang said about his father? The old boy uses an airplane.'

Parizianski made motions with his mouth, but the sounds meant nothing. He took up his tablet and showed it to Martel and Chang: *Bzz Bzz. Ha ha. Gd ol' boy.*

At that moment, Martel heard steps out in the corridor. He could not help looking toward the door. Other eyes followed the direction of his glance.

Vomact came in.

The group shuffled to attention in four parallel lines. They scanned one another. Numerous hands reached across to adjust the electrochemical controls on chestboxes which had begun to load up. One Scanner held out a broken finger which his counter-Scanner had discovered, and submitted it for treatment and splinting.

Vomact had taken out his Staff of Office. The cube at the top flashed red light through the room, the lines re-formed, and all Scanners gave the sign meaning, *Present and ready!*

Vomact countered with the stance signifying, *I am the Senior and take command.*

Talking fingers rose in the counter-gesture, *We concur and commit ourselves.*

Vomact raised his right arm, dropped the wrist as though it were broken, in a queer searching gesture, meaning: *Any men around? Any habermans not tied? All clear for the Scanners?*

Alone of all those present, the cranched Martel heard the queer rustle of feet as they all turned completely around without leaving position, looking sharply at one another and flashing their belt-lights into the dark corners of the great room. When again they faced Vomact, he made a further sign: *All clear. Follow my words.*

Martel noticed that he alone relaxed. The others could not know the meaning of relaxation with the minds blocked off up there in their skulls, connected only with the eyes, and the rest of the body connected with the mind only by controlling non-sensory nerves and the instrument boxes on their chests. Martel realized that, cranched as he was, he had expected to hear Vomact's voice: the Senior had been talking for some time. No sound escaped his lips. (Vomact never bothered with sounds.)

'. . . and when the first men to go Up-and-Out went to the moon, what did they find?'

'Nothing,' responded the silent chorus of lips.

'Therefore they went farther, to Mars and to Venus. The ships went out year by year, but they did not come back until the Year One of Space. Then did a ship come back with the First Effect. Scanners, I ask you, what is the First Effect?'

'No one knows. No one knows.'

'No one will ever know. Too many are the variables. By what do we know the First Effect?'

'By the Great Pain of Space,' came the chorus.

'And by what further sign?'

'By the need, oh, the need for death.'

Vomact again: 'And who stopped the need for death?'

'Henry Haberman conquered the First Effect, in the Year 83 of Space.'

'And, Scanners, I ask you, what did he do?'

'He made the habermans.'

'How, O Scanners, are habermans made?'

'They are made with the cuts. The brain is cut from the heart, the lungs. The brain is cut from the ears, the nose. The brain is cut from the mouth, the belly. The brain is cut from desire and pain. The brain is cut from the world. Save for the eyes. Save for the control of the living flesh.'

'And how, O Scanners, is flesh controlled?'

'By the boxes set in the flesh, the controls set in the chest, the signs made to rule the living body, the signs by which the body lives.'

'How does a haberman live and live?'

'The haberman lives by control of the boxes.'

'Whence come the habermans?'

Martel felt in the coming response a great roar of broken voices echoing through the room as the Scanners, habermans themselves, put sound behind their mouthings:

'Habermans are the scum of mankind. Habermans are the

weak, the cruel, the credulous, and the unfit. Habermans are the sentenced-to-more-than-death. Habermans live in the mind alone. They are killed for Space but they live for Space. They master the ships that connect the earths. They live in the Great Pain while ordinary men sleep in the cold, cold sleep of the transit.'

'Brothers and Scanners, I ask you now: are we habermans or are we not?'

'We are habermans in the flesh. We are cut apart, brain and flesh. We are ready to go to the Up-and-Out. All of us have gone through the haberman device.'

'We are habermans, then?' Vomact's eyes flashed and glittered as he asked the ritual question.

Again the chorused answer was accompanied by a roar of voices heard only by Martel: 'Habermans we are, and more, and more. We are the Chosen who are habermans by our own free will. We are the Agents of the Instrumentality of Mankind.'

'What must the others say to us?'

'They must say to us, "You are the bravest of the brave, the most skilful of the skilled. All mankind owes most honour to the Scanner, who unites the Earths of Mankind. Scanners are the protectors of the habermans. They are the judges in the Up-and-Out. They make men live in the place where men need desperately to die. They are the most honoured of mankind, and even the Chiefs of the Instrumentality are delighted to pay them homage!"'

Vomact stood more erect: 'What is the secret duty of the Scanner?'

'To keep secret our law, and to destroy the acquirers thereof.'

'How to destroy?'

'Twice to the *Overload*, back and *Dead*.'

'If habermans die, what the duty then?'

The Scanners all compressed their lips for answer. (Silence was the code.) Martel, who – long familiar with the code – was a little bored with the proceedings, noticed that Chang was breathing too heavily; he reached over and adjusted Chang's lung-control and received the thanks of Chang's eyes. Vomact observed the interruption and glared at them both. Martel relaxed, trying to imitate the dead cold stillness of the others. It was so hard to do, when you were cranched.

'If others die, what the duty then?' asked Vomact.

'Scanners together inform the Instrumentality. Scanners together accept the punishment. Scanners together settle the case.'

'And if the punishment be severe?'

'Then no ships go.'

'And if Scanners not be honoured?'

'Then no ships go.'

'And if a Scanner goes unpaid?'

'Then no ships go.'

'And if the Others and the Instrumentality are not in all ways at all times mindful of their proper obligation to the Scanners?'

'Then no ships go.'

'And what, O Scanners, if no ships go?'

'The Earths fall apart. The Wild comes back in. The Old Machines and the Beasts return.'

'What is the first known duty of a Scanner?'

'Not to sleep in the Up-and-Out.'

'What is the second duty of a Scanner?'

'To keep forgotten the name of fear.'

'What is the third duty of a Scanner?'

'To use the wire of Eustace Cranch only with care, only with moderation.' Several pair of eyes looked quickly at Martel before the mouthed chorus went on. 'To cranch only at home, only among friends, only for the purpose of remembering, of relaxing, or of begetting.'

'What is the word of the Scanner?'

'Faithful, though surrounded by death.'

'What is the motto of the Scanner?'

'Awake, though surrounded by silence.'

'What is the work of the Scanner?'

'Labour even in the heights of the Up-and-Out, loyalty even in the depths of the Earths.'

'How do you know a Scanner?'

'We know ourselves. We are dead, though we live. And we talk with the tablet and the nail.'

'What is this code?'

'This code is the friendly ancient wisdom of Scanners, briefly put that we may be mindful and be cheered by our loyalty to one another.'

At this point the formula should have run: 'We complete the code. Is there work or word for the Scanners?' But Vomact said, and he repeated:

'Top emergency. Top emergency.'

They gave him the sign, *Present and ready!*

He said, with every eye straining to follow his lips:

'Some of you know the work of Adam Stone?'

Martel saw lips move, saying: 'The Red Asteriod. The Other who lives at the edge of Space.'

'Adam Stone has gone to the Instrumentality, claiming success for his work. He says that he has found how to screen out the Pain of Space. He says that the Up-and-Out can be made safe for ordinary men to work in, to stay awake in. He says that there need be no more Scanners.'

Belt-lights flashed on all over the room as Scanners sought the right to speak. Vomact nodded to one of the older men. 'Scanner Smith will speak.'

Smith stepped slowly up into the light, watching his own feet. He turned so that they could see his face. He spoke: 'I say that this is a lie. I say that Stone is a liar. I say that the Instrumentality must not be deceived.'

He paused. Then, in answer to some question from the audience which most of the others did not see, he said:

'I invoke the secret duty of the Scanners.'

Smith raised his right hand for emergency attention:

'I say that Stone must die.'

Martel, still cranched, shuddered as he heard the boos, groans, shouts, squeaks, grunts and moans which came from the Scanners, who forgot noise in their excitement and strove to make their dead bodies talk to one another's deaf ears. Belt-lights flashed wildly all over the room. There was a rush for the rostrum and Scanners milled around at the top, vying for attention until Parizianski – by sheer bulk – shoved the others aside and down, and turned to mouth at the group.

'Brother Scanners, I want your eyes.'

The people on the floor kept moving, with their numb bodies jostling one another. Finally Vomact stepped up in front of

Parizianski, faced the others, and said:

'Scanners, be Scanners! Give him your eyes.'

Parizianski was not good at public speaking. His lips moved too fast. He waved his hands, which took the eyes of the others away from his lips. Nevertheless, Martel was able to follow most of the message:

'. . . can't do this. Stone may have succeeded. If he has succeeded, it means the end of the Scanners. It means the end of the habermans, too. None of us will have to fight in the Up-and-Out. We won't have anybody else going under the wire for a few hours or days of being human. Everybody will be Other. Nobody will have to cranch, never again. Men can be men. The habermans can be killed decently and properly, the way men were killed in the old days, without anybody keeping them alive. They won't have to work in the Up-and-Out! There will be no more Great Pain – think of it! No . . . more . . . Great . . . Pain! How do we know that Stone is a liar—' Lights began flashing directly into his eyes. (The rudest insult of Scanner to Scanner was this.)

Vomact again exercised authority. He stepped in front of Parizianski and said something which the others could not see. Parizianski stepped down from the rostrum. Vomact again spoke:

'I think that some of the Scanners disagree with our Brother Parizianski. I say that the use of the rostrum be suspended till we have had a chance for private discussion. In fifteen minutes I will call the meeting back to order.'

Martel looked around for Vomact when the Senior had rejoined the group on the floor. Finding the Senior, Martel wrote swift script on his tablet, waiting for a chance to thrust the tablet before the Senior's eyes. He had written: *Am crnchd. Rspctfly request prmissn lv now, stnd by fr orders.*

Being cranched did strange things to Martel. Most meetings that he attended seemed formal, hearteningly ceremonial, lighting up the dark inward eternities of habermanhood. When he was not cranched, he noticed his body no more than a marble bust notices its marble pedestal. He had stood with them before. He had stood with them effortless hours, while the long-winded ritual broke through the terrible loneliness behind his eyes, and made him feel that the Scanners, though a confraternity of the damned, were nonetheless forever honoured by the professional requirements of their mutilation.

This time, it was different. Coming cranched, and in full possession of smell-sound-taste-feeling, he reacted more or less as a normal man would. He saw his friends and colleagues as a lot of cruelly driven ghosts, posturing out the meaningless ritual of their indefeasible damnation. What difference did anything make, once you were a haberman? Why all this talk about habermans and Scanners? Habermans were criminals or heretics, and Scanners were gentlemen-volunteers, but they were all in the same fix – except that Scanners were deemed worthy of the short-time return of the cranching wire, while habermans were simply disconnected while the ships lay in port and were left suspended until they should be awakened, in some hour of emergency or trouble, to work out another spell of their damnation. It was a rare haberman that you saw on the street – someone of special merit or bravery, allowed to look at mankind from the terrible prison of his own mechanified body. And yet, what Scanner ever pitied a haberman? What Scanner ever honoured a haberman except perfunctorily in the line of duty? What had the Scanners as a guild and a class ever done for the habermans, except to murder them with a twist of the wrist whenever a haberman, too long beside a Scanner, picked up the tricks of the scanning trade and learned how to live at his own will, not the will the Scanners imposed? What could the Others, the ordinary men, know of what went on inside the ships? The Others slept in their cylinders, mercifully unconscious until they woke up on whatever other Earth they had consigned themselves to. What could the Others know of the men who had to stay alive within the ship?

What could any Other know of the Up-and-Out? What Other could look at the biting acid beauty of the stars in open Space? What could they tell of the Great Pain, which started quietly in the marrow, like an ache, and proceeded by the fatigue and nausea of each separate nerve cell, brain cell, touchpoint in the body, until life itself became a terrible aching hunger for silence and for death?

He was a Scanner. All right, he *was* a Scanner. He had been a Scanner from the moment when, wholly normal, he had stood in the sunlight before a Subchief of the Instrumentality, and had sworn:

'I pledge my honour and my life to Mankind. I sacrificed myself willingly for the welfare of Mankind. In accepting the perilous austere honour, I yield all my rights without exception to the Honourable Chiefs of the Instrumentality and to the Honoured Confraternity of Scanners.'

He had pledged.

He had gone into the haberman device.

He remembered his hell. He had not had such a bad one, even though it had seemed to last a hundred million years, all of them without sleep. He had learned to feel with his eyes. He had learned to see despite the heavy eyeplates set back of his eyeballs to insulate his eyes from the rest of him. He had learned to watch his skin. He still remembered the time he had noticed dampness on his shirt, and had pulled out his scanning mirror only to discover that he had worn a hole in his side by leaning against a vibrating machine. (A thing like that could not happen to him now; he was too adept at reading his own instruments.) He remembered the way that he had gone Up-and-Out, and the way that the Great Pain beat into him, despite the fact that his touch, smell, feeling and hearing were gone for all ordinary purposes. He remembered killing habermans, and keeping others alive, and standing for months beside the Honourable Scanner-Pilot while neither of them slept. He remembered going ashore on Earth Four, and remembered that he had not enjoyed it, and had realized on that day that there was no reward.

Martel stood among the other Scanners. He hated their awkwardness when they moved, their immobility when they stood still. He hated the queer assortment of smells which their bodies yielded unnoticed. He hated the grunts and groans and squawks which they emitted from their deafness. He hated them, and himself.

How could Luci stand him? He had kept his chestbox reading *Danger* for weeks while he courted her, carrying the cranch wire about with him most illegally, and going direct from one cranch to the other without worrying about the fact his indicators all crept up to the edge of *Overload*. He had wooed her without thinking of what would happen if she did say, 'Yes.' She had.

'And they lived happily ever after.' In old books they did, but how could they, in life? He had had eighteen days under the wire in the whole of the past year! Yet she had loved him. She still loved him. He knew it. She fretted about him through the long months that he was in the Up-and-Out. She tried to make home mean something to him even when he was haberman, make food pretty when it could not be tasted, make herself lovable when she could not be kissed – or might as well not, since a haberman body meant no more than furniture. Luci was patient.

And now, Adam Stone! (He let his tablet fade: how could he leave now?)

God bless Adam Stone!

Martel could not help feeling a little sorry for himself. No longer would the high keen call of duty carry him through 200 or so years of the Others' time, two million private eternities of his own. He could slouch and relax. He could forget High Space, and let the Up-and-Out be tended by Others. He could cranch as much as he dared. He could be almost normal – almost – for one year or five years or no years. But at least he could stay with Luci. He could go with her into the Wild, where there were Beasts and Old Machines still roving the dark places. Perhaps he would die in the excitement of the hunt, throwing spears at an ancient manshonyagger as it leapt from its lair, or tossing hot spheres at the tribesmen of the Unforgiven who still roamed the Wild. There was still life to live, still a good normal death to die, not the moving of a needle out in the silence and agony of Space!

He had been walking about restlessly. His ears were attuned to the sounds of normal speech, so that he did not feel like watching the mouthings of his brethren. Now they seemed to have come to a decision. Vomact was moving to the rostrum. Martel looked about for Chang, and went to stand beside him. Chang whispered:

'You're as restless as water in mid-air! What's the matter? De-cranching?'

They both scanned Martel, but the instruments held steady and showed no sign of the cranch giving out.

The great light flared in its call to attention. Again they formed

ranks. Vomact thrust his lean old face into the glare, and spoke:
'Scanners and Brothers, I call for a vote.' He held himself in the
stance which meant: *I am the Senior and take command.*

A belt-light flashed in protest.

It was old Henderson. He moved to the rostrum, spoke to
Vomact, and – with Vomact's nod of approval – turned full-face
to repeat his question:

'Who speaks for the Scanners Out in Space?'

No belt-light or hand answered.

Henderson and Vomact, face to face, conferred for a few
moments. Then Henderson faced them again:

'I yield to the Senior in command. But I do not yield to a
Meeting of the Confraternity. There are sixty-eight Scanners, and
only forty-seven present, of whom one is cranched and U.D. I
have therefore proposed that the Senior in command assume
authority only over an Emergency Committee of the Confraternity, not over a Meeting. Is that agreed and understood by the
Honourable Scanners?'

Hands rose in assent.

Chang murmured in Martel's ear, 'Lot of difference that
makes! Who can tell the difference between a meeting and a
committee?' Martel agreed with the words, but was even more
impressed with the way that Chang, while haberman, could
control his own voice.

Vomact resumed chairmanship: 'We now vote on the question
of Adam Stone.

'First, we can assume that he has not succeeded, and that his
claims are lies. We know that from our practical experiences as
Scanners. The Pain of Space is only part of Scanning' (But the
essential part, the basis of it all, thought Martel) 'and we can rest
assured that Stone cannot solve the problem of Space Discipline.'

'That tripe again,' whispered Chang, unheard save by Martel.

'The Space Discipline of our Confraternity has kept High
Space clean of war and dispute. Sixty-eight disciplined men control all High Space. We are removed by our oath and our haberman status from all Earthly passions.

'Therefore, if Adam Stone has conquered the Pain of Space,
so that Others can wreck our Confraternity and bring to Space

the trouble and ruin which afflicts Earths, I say that Adam Stone is wrong. If Adam Stone succeeds, Scanners live in vain!

'Secondly, if Adam Stone has not conquered the Pain of Space, he will cause great trouble in all the Earths. The Instrumentality and the Subchiefs may not give us as many habermans as we need to operate the ships of Mankind. There will be wild stories, and fewer recruits, and, worst of all, the Discipline of the Confraternity may relax if this kind of nonsensical heresy is spread around.

'Therefore, if Adam Stone has succeeded, he threatens the ruin of the Confraternity and should die.

'I move the death of Adam Stone.'

And Vomact made the sign, *The Honourable Scanners are pleased to vote.*

Martel grabbed wildly for his belt-light. Chang, guessing ahead, had his light out and ready; its bright beam, voting *No*, shone straight up at the ceiling. Martel got his light out and threw its beam upward in dissent. Then he looked around. Out of the forty-seven present, he could see only five or six glittering.

Two more lights went on. Vomact stood as erect as a frozen corpse. Vomact's eyes flashed as he stared back and forth over the group, looking for lights. Several more went on. Finally Vomact took the closing stance: *May it please the Scanners to count the vote.*

Three of the old men went up on the rostrum with Vomact. They looked over the room. (Martel thought: These damned ghosts are voting on the life of a real man, a live man! They have no right to do it. I'll tell the Instrumentality! But he knew that he would not. He thought of Luci and what she might gain by the triumph of Adam Stone: the heartbreaking folly of the vote was then almost too much for Martel to bear.)

All three of the tellers held up their hands in unanimous agreement on the sign of the number: *Fifteen against.*

Vomact dismissed them with a bow of courtesy. He turned and again took the stance: *I am the Senior and take command.*

Marvelling at his own daring, Martel flashed his belt-light on. He knew that any one of the bystanders might reach over and twist his heartbox to *Overload* for such an act. He felt Chang's hand reaching to catch him by the aircoat. But he eluded Chang's grasp and ran, faster than a Scanner should, to the platform. As he ran, he wondered what appeal to make. It was no use talking common sense. Not now. It had to be law.

He jumped up on the rostrum beside Vomact, and took the stance: *Scanners, an Illegality!*

He violated good custom while speaking, still in the stance: 'A Committee has no right to vote death by a majority vote. It takes two-thirds of a full Meeting.'

He felt Vomact's body lunge behind him, felt himself falling from the rostrum, hitting the floor, hurting his knees and his touch-aware hands. He was helped to his feet. He was scanned. Some Scanner he scarcely knew took his instruments and toned him down.

Immediately Martel felt more calm, more detached, and hated himself for feeling so.

He looked up at the rostrum. Vomact maintained the stance signifying: *Order!*

The Scanners adjusted their ranks. The two Scanners next to Martel took his arms. He shouted at them, but they looked away, and cut themselves off from communication altogether.

Vomact spoke again when he saw the room was quiet: 'A Scanner came here cranched. Honourable Scanners, I apologize for this. It is not the fault of our great and worthy Scanner and friend, Martel. He came here under orders. I told him not to decranch. I hoped to spare him an unnecessary haberman. We all know how happily Martel is married, and we wish his brave experiment well. I like Martel. I respect his judgement. I wanted him here. I knew you wanted him here. But he is cranched. He is in no mood to share in the lofty business of the Scanners. I therefore propose a solution which will meet all the requirements of fairness. I propose that we rule Scanner Martel out of order for his violation of rules. This violation would be inexcusable if Martel were not cranched.

'But at the same time, in all fairness to Martel, I further propose that we deal with the points raised so improperly by our worthy but disqualified brother.'

Vomact gave the sign, *The Honourable Scanners are pleased to vote.* Martel tried to reach his own belt-light; the dead strong hands held him tightly and he struggled in vain. One lone light shone high: Chang's, no doubt.

Vomact thrust his face into the light again: 'Having the approval of our worthy Scanners and present company for the general proposal, I now move that this Committee declare itself to have the full authority of a Meeting, and that this Committee further make me responsible for all misdeeds which this Committee may enact, to be held answerable before the next full Meeting, but not before any other authority beyond the closed and secret ranks of Scanners.'

Flamboyantly this time, his triumph evident, Vomact assumed the *vote* stance.

Only a few lights shone: far less, patently, than a minority of one-fourth.

Vomact spoke again. The light shone on his high calm forehead, on his dead relaxed cheekbones. His lean cheeks and chin were half-shadowed, save where the lower light picked up and spotlighted his mouth, cruel even in repose. (Vomact was said to be a descendant of some ancient lady who had traversed, in an illegitimate and inexplicable fashion, some hundreds of years of time in a single night. Her name, the Lady Vomact, has passed into legend; but her blood and her archaic lust for mastery lived on in the mute masterful body of her descendant. Martel could believe the old tales as he stared at the rostrum, wondering what untraceable mutatior. had left the Vomact kin as predators among Mankind.) Calling loudly with the movement of his lips, but still without sound, Vomact appealed:

'The honourable Committee is now pleased to reaffirm the sentence of death issued against the heretic and enemy, Adam Stone.' Again the *vote* stance.

Again Chang's light shone lonely in its isolated protest.

Vomact then made his final move:

'I call for the designation of the Senior Scanner present as the manager of the sentence. I call for authorization to him to appoint executioners, one or many, who shall make evident the will and majesty of Scanners. I ask that I be accountable for the deed, and not for the means. The deed is a noble deed, for the protection of Mankind and for the honour of the Scanners; but of the means it must be said that they are to be the best at hand, and no more. Who knows the true way to kill an Other, here on a crowded and watchful Earth? This is no mere matter of discharging a cylindered sleeper, no mere question of upgrading the needle of a haberman. When people die down here, it is not like the Up-and-Out. They die reluctantly. Killing within the Earth is not our usual business, O brothers and Scanners, as you know well. You must choose me to choose my agent as I see fit. Otherwise the common knowledge will become the common betrayal, whereas if I alone know the responsibility I alone could betray us, and you will not have far to look in case the Instrumentality comes searching.' (What about the killer you choose? thought Martel. He too will know unless – unless you silence him forever.)

Vomact went into the stance: *The Honourable Scanners are pleased to vote.*

One light of protest shone; Chang's, again.

Martel imagined that he could see a cruel joyful smile on Vomact's dead face – the smile of a man who knew himself righteous and who found his righteousness upheld and affirmed by militant authority.

Martel tried one last time to come free.

The dead hands held. They were locked like vices until their owners' eyes unlocked them: how else could they hold the piloting month by month?

Martel then shouted: 'Honourable Scanners, this is judicial murder.'

No ear heard him. He was cranched, and alone.

None the less, he shouted again: 'You endanger the Confraternity.'

Nothing happened.

The echo of his voice sounded from one end of the room to the other. No head turned. No eyes met his.

Martel realized that, as they paired for talk, the eyes of the Scanners averted him. He saw that no one desired to watch his speech. He knew that behind the cold faces of his friends there lay compassion or amusement. He knew that they knew him to be cranched – absurd, normal, man-like, temporarily no Scanner.

But he knew that in this matter the wisdom of Scanners was nothing. He knew that only a cranched Scanner could feel with his very blood the outrage and anger which deliberate murder would provoke among the Others. He knew that the Confraternity endangered itself, and knew that the most ancient prerogative of law was the monopoly of death. Even the ancient nations, in the times of the Wars, before the Beasts, before men went into the Up-and-Out – even the ancients had known this. How did they say it? *Only the state shall kill.* The states were gone but the Instrumentality remained, and the Instrumentality could not pardon things which occurred within the Earths but beyond its authority. Death in Space was the business, the right of the Scanners: how could the Instrumentality enforce its laws in a place where all men who wakened wakened only to die in the Great Pain? Wisely did the Instrumentality leave Space to the Scanners, wisely had the Confraternity not meddled inside the Earths. And now the Confraternity itself was going to step forth as an outlaw band, as a gang of rogues as stupid and reckless as the tribes of the Unforgiven!

Martel knew this because he was cranched. Had he been haberman, he would have thought only with his mind, not with his heart and guts and blood. How could the other Scanners know?

Vomact returned for the last time to the rostrum: *The Committee has met and its will shall be done.* Verbally he added: 'Senior among you, I ask your loyalty and your silence.'

At that point, the two Scanners let his arms go. Martel rubbed his numb hands, shaking his fingers to get the circulation back into the cold fingertips. With real freedom, he began to think of what he might still do. He scanned himself: the cranching held. He might have a day. Well, he could go even if haberman, but it would be inconvenient, having to talk with finger and tablet. He looked about for Chang. He saw his friend standing patient and immobile in a quiet corner. Martel moved slowly, so as not to attract any more attention to himself than could be helped. He faced Chang, moved until his face was in the light, and then articulated:

'What are we going to do? You're not going to let them kill

Adam Stone, are you? Don't you realize what Stone's work will
mean to us, if it succeeds? No more Scanners. No more habermans. No more Pain in the Up-and-Out. I tell you, if the others
were all cranched, as I am, they would see it in a human way, not
with the narrow crazy logic which they used in the Meeting. We've
got to stop them. How can we do it? What are we going to do?
What does Parizianski think? Who has been chosen?'

'Which question do you want me to answer?'

Martel laughed. (It felt good to laugh, even then; it felt like
being a man.) 'Will you help me?'

Chang's eyes flashed across Martel's face as Chang answered:
'No. No. No.'

'You won't help?'

'No.'

'Why not, Chang? Why not?'

'I am a Scanner. The vote has been taken. You would do the
same if you were not in this unusual condition.'

'I'm not in an unusual condition. I'm cranched. That merely
means that I see things the way that the Others would. I see the
stupidity. The recklessness. The selfishness. It is murder.'

'What is murder? Have you not killed? You are not one of the
Others. You are a Scanner. You will be sorry for what you are
about to do, if you do not watch out.'

'But why did you vote against Vomact, then? Didn't you, too,
see what Adam Stone means to all of us? Scanners will live in
vain. Thank God for that! Can't you see it?'

'No.'

'But you talk to me, Chang. You are my friend?'

'I talk to you. I am your friend. Why not?'

'But what are you going to do?'

'Nothing, Martel. Nothing.'

'Will you help me?'

'No.'

'Not even to save Stone?'

'No.'

'Then I will go to Parizianski for help.'

'It will do you no good.'

'Why not? He's more human than you, right now.'

'He will not help you, because he has the job. Vomact designated him to kill Adam Stone.'

Martel stopped speaking in mid-movement. He suddenly took the stance: *I thank you, brother, and I depart.*

At the window he turned and faced the room. He saw that Vomact's eyes were upon him. He gave the stance, *I thank you, brother, and I depart,* and added the flourish of respect which is shown when Seniors are present. Vomact caught the sign, and Martel could see the cruel lips move. He thought he saw the words 'Take good care of yourself' but did not wait to inquire. He stepped backward and dropped out the window.

Once below the window and out of sight, he adjusted his aircoat to a maximum speed. He swam lazily in the air scanning himself thoroughly, and adjusting his adrenal intake down. He then made the movement of release, and felt the cold air rush past his face like running water.

Adam Stone had to be at Chief Downport.

Adam Stone had to be there.

Wouldn't Adam Stone be surprised in the night? Surprised to meet the strangest of beings, the first renegade among Scanners. (Martel suddenly appreciated that it was of himself he was thinking. Martel, the Traitor to Scanners! That sounded strange and bad. But what of Martel, the Loyal to Mankind? Was that no compensation? And, if he won, he won Luci. If he lost, he lost nothing – an unconsidered and expendable haberman. It happened to be himself. But, in contrast to the immense reward, to Mankind, to the Confraternity, to Luci, what did that matter?)

Martel thought to himself: 'Adam Stone will have two visitors tonight. Two Scanners, who are the friends of one another.' He hoped that Parizianski was still his friend.

'And the world', he added, 'depends on which of us gets there first.'

Multifaceted in their brightness, the lights of Chief Downport began to shine through the mist ahead. Martel could see the outer towers of the city and glimpsed the phosphorescent periphery which kept back the Wild, whether Beasts, Machines or the Unforgiven.

Once more Martel invoked the lords of his chance: 'Help me to pass for an Other!'

Within the Downport, Martel had less trouble than he thought. He draped his aircoat over his shoulder so that it concealed the instruments. He took up his scanning mirror, and made up his face from the inside, by adding tone and animation to his blood and nerves until the muscles of his face glowed and the skin gave out a healthy sweat. That way he looked like an ordinary man who had just completed a long night flight.

After straightening out his clothing, and hiding his tablet within his jacket, he faced the problem of what to do about the talking finger. If he kept the nail, it would show him to be a Scanner. He would be respected but he would be identified. He might be stopped by the guards whom the Instrumentality had undoubtedly set around the person of Adam Stone. If he broke the nail— But he couldn't! No Scanner in the history of the Confraternity had ever willingly broken his nail. That would be Resignation, and there was no such thing. The only way *out* was in the Up-and-Out! Martel put his finger to his mouth and bit off the nail. He looked at the now-queer finger, and sighed to himself.

He stepped toward the city gate, slipping his hand into his jacket and running up his muscular strength to four times normal. He started to scan, and then realized that his instruments were masked. *Might as well take all the chances at once*, he thought.

The watcher stopped him with a searching wire. The sphere thumped suddenly against Martel's chest.

'Are you a man?' said the unseen voice. (Martel knew that as a Scanner in haberman condition his own field-charge would have illuminated the sphere.)

'I am a man.' Martel knew that the timbre of his voice had been good; he hoped that it would not be taken for that of a manshonyagger or a Beast or an Unforgiven one, who with mimicry sought to enter the cities and ports of Mankind.

'Name, number, rank, purpose, function, time departed.'

'Martel.' He had to remember his old number, not Scanner 34. 'Sunward 4234, 782nd Year of Space. Rank, rising Subchief.' That was no lie, but his substantive rank. 'Purpose, personal and lawful within the limits of this city. No function of the Instrumentality. Departed Chief Outport 2019 hours.' Everything now depended on whether he was believed or would be checked against Chief Outport.

The voice was flat and routine: 'Time desired within the city.'

Martel used the standard phrase: 'Your honourable sufferance is requested.'

He stood in the cool night air, waiting. Far above him, through a gap in the mist, he could see the poisonous glittering in the sky of Scanners. The stars are my enemies, he thought: I have mastered the stars but they hate me. Ho, that sounds ancient! Like a book. Too much cranching.

The voice returned: 'Sunward 4234 dash 782 rising Subchief Martel, enter the lawful gates of the city. Welcome. Do you desire food, raiment, money, or companionship?' The voice had no hospitality in it, just business. This was certainly different from entering a city in a Scanner's role! Then the petty officers came out, and threw their belt-lights in their fretful faces, and mouthed their words with preposterous deference, shouting against the stone deafness of Scanners' ears. So that was the way that a Subchief was treated: matter of fact, but not bad. Not bad.

Martel replied: 'I have that which I need, but beg of the city a favour. My friend Adam Stone is here. I desire to see him, on urgent and personal lawful affairs.'

The voice replied: 'Did you have an appointment with Adam Stone?'

'No.'

'The city will find him. What is his number?'

'I have forgotten it.'

'You have forgotten it? Is not Adam Stone a Magnate of the Instrumentality? Are you truly his friend?'

'Truly.' Martel let a little annoyance creep into his voice. 'Watcher, doubt me and call your Subchief.'

'No doubt implied. Why do you not know the number? This must go into the record,' added the voice.

'We were friends in childhood. He had crossed the—' Martel started to say 'the Up-and-Out' and remembered that the phrase was current only among Scanners. 'He has leapt from Earth to Earth, and has just now returned. I knew him well and I seek him out. I have word of his kith. May the Instrumentality protect us!'

'Heard and believed. Adam Stone will be searched.'

At a risk, though a slight one, of having the sphere sound an alarm for *non-human*, Martel cut in on his Scanner speaker within his jacket. He saw the trembling needle of light await his words and he started to write on it with his blunt finger. That won't work, he thought, and had a moment's panic until he found his comb, which had a sharp enough tooth to write. He wrote: 'Emergency none. Martel Scanner calling Parizianski Scanner.'

The needle quivered and the reply glowed and faded out: 'Parizianski Scanner on duty and D.C. Calls taken by Scanner Relay.'

Martel cut off his speaker.

Parizianski was somewhere around. Could he have crossed the direct way, right over the city wall, setting off the alert, and invoking official business when the petty officers overtook him in mid-air? Scarcely. That meant that a number of other Scanners must have come in with Parizianski, all of them pretending to be in search of a few of the tenuous pleasures which could be enjoyed by a haberman, such as the sight of the newspictures or the viewing of beautiful women in the Pleasure Gallery. Parizianski was around, but he could not have moved privately, because Scanner Central registered him on duty and recorded his movements city by city.

The voice returned. Puzzlement was expressed in it. 'Adam Stone is found and awakened. He has asked pardon of the Honourable, and says he knows no Martel. Will you see Adam Stone in the morning? The city will bid you welcome.'

Martel ran out of resources. It was hard enough mimicking a man without having to tell lies in the guise of one. Martel could only repeat: 'Tell him I am Martel. The husband of Luci.'

'It will be done.'

Again the silence, and the hostile stars, and the sense that Parizianski was somewhere near and getting nearer; Martel felt his heart beating faster. He stole a glimpse at his chestbox and set his heart down a point. He felt calmer, even though he had not been able to scan with care.

The voice this time was cheerful, as though an annoyance had been settled: 'Adam Stone consents to see you. Enter Chief Downport, and welcome.'

The little sphere dropped noiselessly to the ground and the wire whispered away into the darkness. A bright arc of narrow light rose from the ground in front of Martel and swept through the city to one of the higher towers – apparently a hostel, which Martel had never entered. Martel plucked his aircoat to his chest for ballast, stepped heel-and-toe on the beam, and felt himself whistle through the air to an entrance window which sprang up before him as suddenly as a devouring mouth.

A tower guard stood in the doorway. 'You are awaited, sir. Do you bear weapons, sir?'

'None,' said Martel, grateful that he was relying on his own strength.

The guard led him past the check-screen. Martel noticed the quick flight of a warning across the screen as his instruments registered and identified him as a Scanner. But the guard had not noticed it.

The guard stopped at a door. 'Adam Stone is armed. He is lawfully armed by authority of the Instrumentality and by the liberty of this city. All those who enter are given warning.'

Martel nodded in understanding at the man and went in.

Adam Stone was a short man, stout and benign. His grey hair rose stiffly from a low forehead. His whole face was red and merry-looking. He looked like a jolly guide from the Pleasure Gallery, not like a man who had been at the edge of the Up-and-Out, fighting the Great Pain without haberman protection.

He stared at Martel. His look was puzzled, perhaps a little annoyed, but not hostile.

Martel came to the point. 'You do not know me. I lied. My name is Martel, and I mean you no harm. But I lied. I beg the honourable gift of your hospitality. Remain armed. Direct your weapon against me—'

Stone smiled: 'I am doing so,' and Martel noticed the small

wirepoint in Stone's capable plump hand.

'Good. Keep on guard against me. It will give you confidence in what I shall say. But do, I beg you, give us a screen of privacy. I want no casual lookers. This is a matter of life and death.'

'First: whose life and death?' Stone's face remained calm, his voice even.

'Yours, and mine, and the worlds'.'

'You are cryptic, but I agree.' Stone called through the doorway: 'Privacy, please.' There was a sudden hum, and all the little noises of the night quickly vanished from the air of the room.

Said Adam Stone: 'Sir, who are you? What brings you here?'

'I am Scanner 34.'

'You a Scanner? I don't believe it.'

For answer, Martel pulled his jacket open, showing his chestbox. Stone looked up at him, amazed. Martel explained:

'I am cranched. Have you never seen it before?'

'*Not with men.* On animals. Amazing! But – what do you want?'

'The truth. Do you fear me?'

'Not with this,' said Stone, grasping the wirepoint. 'But I shall tell you the truth.'

'Is it true that you have conquered the Great Pain?'

Stone hesitated, seeking words for an answer.

'Quick, can you tell me how you have done it, so that I may believe you?'

'I have loaded the ships with life.'

'Life?'

'Life. I don't know what the Great Pain is, but I did find that in the experiments, when I sent out masses of animals or plants, the life in the centre of the mass lived longest. I built ships – small ones, of course – and sent them out with rabbits, with monkeys—'

'Those are Beasts?'

'Yes. With small Beasts. And the Beasts came back unhurt. They came back because the walls of the ships were filled with life. I tried many kinds, and finally found a sort of life which lives in the waters. Oysters. Oyster-beds. The outermost oysters died in the Great Pain. The inner ones lived. The passengers were unhurt.'

'But they were Beasts?'

'Not only Beasts. Myself.'

'You!'

'I came through Space alone. Through what you call the Up-and-Out, alone. Awake and sleeping. I am unhurt. If you do not believe me, ask your brother Scanners. Come and see my ship in the morning. I will be glad to see you then, along with your brother Scanners. I am going to demonstrate before the Chiefs of the Instrumentality.'

Martel repeated his question: 'You came here alone?'

Adam Stone grew testy: 'Yes, alone. Go back and check your Scanner's register if you do not believe me. You never put me in a bottle to cross Space.'

Martel's face was radiant. 'I believe you now. It is true. No more Scanners. No more habermans. No more cranching.'

Stone looked significantly toward the door.

Martel did not take the hint. 'I must tell you that—'

'Sir, tell me in the morning. Go enjoy your cranch. Isn't it supposed to be pleasure? Medically I know it well. But not in practice.'

'It is pleasure. It's normality – for a while. But listen. The Scanners have sworn to destroy you, and your work.'

'What!'

'They have met and have voted and sworn. You will make Scanners unnecessary, they say. You will bring the ancient wars back to the world, if scanning is lost and the Scanners live in vain!'

Adam Stone was nervous but kept his wits about him: 'You're a Scanner. Are you going to kill me – or try?'

'No, you fool. I have betrayed the Confraternity. Call guards the moment I escape. Keep guards around you. I will try to intercept the killer.'

Martel saw a blur in the window. Before Stone could turn, the wirepoint was whipped out of his hand. The blur solidified and took form as Parizianski.

Martel recognized what Parizianski was doing: *High speed.*

Without thinking of his cranch, he thrust his hand to his chest, set himself up to *High speed* too. Waves of fire, like the Great Pain, but hotter, flooded over him. He fought to keep his face readable as he stepped in front of Parizianski and gave the sign, *Top emergency*.

Parizianski spoke, while the normally moving body of Stone stepped away from them as slowly as a drifting cloud: 'Get out of my way. I am on a mission.'

'I know it. I stop you here and now. Stop. Stop. Stop. Stone is right.'

Parizianski's lips were barely readable in the haze of pain which flooded Martel. (He thought: God, God, God of the ancients! Let me hold on! Let me live under Overload just long enough!) Parizianski was saying: 'Get out of my way. By order of the Confraternity, get out of my way!' And Parizianski gave the sign, *Help I demand in the name of my duty!*

Martel choked for breath in the syrup-like air. He tried one last time: 'Parizianski, friend, friend, my friend. Stop. Stop.' (No Scanner had ever murdered Scanner before.)

Parizianski made the sign: *You are unfit for duty, and I will take over.*

Martel thought, For the first time in the world! as he reached over and twisted Parizianski's brainbox up to *Overload*. Parizianski's eyes glittered in terror and understanding. His body began to drift down toward the floor.

Martel had just strength enough to reach his own chestbox. As he faded into haberman or death, he knew not which, he felt his fingers turning on the control of speed, turning down. He tried to speak, to say, 'Get a Scanner, I need help, get a Scanner. . . .'

But the darkness rose about him, and the numb silence clasped him.

Martel awakened to see the face of Luci near his own.

He opened his eyes wider, and found that he was hearing – the sound of her happy weeping, the sound of her chest as she caught the air back into her throat.

He spoke weakly: 'Still cranched? Alive?'

Another face swam into the blur beside Luci's. It was Adam Stone. His deep voice rang across immensities of space before coming to Martel's hearing. Martel tried to read Stone's lips, but could not make them out. He went back to listening to the voice:

'. . . not cranched. Do you understand me? Not cranched!'

Martel tried to say: 'But I can hear! I can feel!' The others got his sense if not his words.

Adam Stone spoke again:

'You have gone back through the haberman. I put you back first. I didn't know how it would work in practice, but I had the theory all worked out. You don't think the Instrumentality would waste the Scanners, do you? You go back to normality. We are letting the habermans die as fast as the ships come in. They don't need to live any more. But we are restoring the Scanners. You are the first. Do you understand? You are the first. Take it easy, now.'

Adam Stone smiled. Dimly, behind Stone, Martel thought that he saw the face of one of the Chiefs of the Instrumentality. That face, too, smiled at him, and then both faces disappeared upward and away.

Martel tried to lift his head, to scan himself. He could not. Luci stared at him, calming herself, but with an expression of loving perplexity. She said, 'My darling husband! You're back again, to stay!'

Still, Martel tried to see his box. Finally he swept his hand across his chest with a clumsy motion. There was nothing there. The instruments were gone. He was back to normality but still alive.

In the deep weak peacefulness of his mind, another troubling thought took shape. He tried to write with his finger, the way that Luci wanted him to, but he had neither pointed fingernail nor Scanner's tablet. He had to use his voice. He summoned up his strength and whispered:

'Scanners?'

'Yes, darling? What is it?'

'Scanners?'

'Scanners. Oh, yes, darling, they're all right. They had to arrest some of them for going into *High speed* and running away. But the Instrumentality caught them all – all those on the ground – and they're happy now. Do you know, darling,' she laughed,

Her face turned sad. She looked at him earnestly and said:
'I might as well tell you now. You'll worry otherwise. There has
been one accident. Only one. When you and your friend called on
Adam Stone, your friend was so happy that he forgot to scan,
and he let himself die of *Overload*.'

'Called on Stone?'

'Yes. Don't you remember? Your friend.'

He still looked surprised, so she said:

'Parizianski.'

'some of them didn't want to be restored to normality. But Stone
and the Chiefs persuaded them.'

'Vomact?'

'He's fine, too. He's staying cranched until he can be restored.
Do you know, he has arranged for Scanners to take new jobs.
You're all to be Deputy Chiefs for Space. Isn't that nice? But
he got himself made Chief for Space. You're all going to be pilots,
so that your fraternity and guild can go on. And Chang's getting
changed right now. You'll see him soon.'

Ray Bradbury

The pedestrian

To enter out into that silence that was the city at eight o'clock of a misty evening in November, to put your feet upon that buckling concrete walk, to step over grassy seams and make your way, hands in pockets, through the silences, that was what Mr Leonard Mead most dearly loved to do. He would stand upon the corner of an intersection and peer down long moonlit avenues of sidewalk in four directions, deciding which way to go, but it really made no difference; he was alone in this world of A.D. 2131, or as good as alone, and with a final decision made, a path selected, he would stride off sending patterns of frosty air before him like the smoke of a cigar.

Sometimes he would walk for hours and miles and return only at midnight to his house. And on his way he would see the cottages and homes with their dark windows, and it was not unequal to walking through a graveyard, because only the faintest glimmers of firefly light appeared in flickers behind the windows. Sudden grey phantoms seemed to manifest themselves upon inner room walls where a curtain was still undrawn against the night, or there were whisperings and murmurs where a window in a tomb-like building was still open.

Mr Leonard Mead would pause, cock his head, listen, look, and march on, his feet making no noise on the lumpy walk. For a long while now the sidewalks had been vanishing under flowers and grass. In ten years of walking by night or day, for thousands of miles, he had never met another person walking, not one in all that time.

He now wore sneakers when strolling at night, because the dogs in intermittent squads would parallel his journey with barkings if he wore hard heels, and lights might click on and faces appear, and an entire street be startled by the passing of a lone figure, himself, in the early November evening.

On this particular evening he began his journey in a westerly direction, toward the hidden sea. There was a good crystal frost in the air; it cut the nose going in and made the lungs blaze like a Christmas tree inside; you could feel the cold light going on and off, all the branches filled with invisible snow. He listened to the faint push of his soft shoes through autumn leaves with satisfaction, and whistled a cold quiet whistle between his teeth, occasionally picking up a leaf as he passed, examining its skeletal pattern in the infrequent lamplights as he went on, smelling its rusty smell.

'Hello, in there,' he whispered to every house on every side as he moved. 'What's up tonight on Channel 4, Channel 7, Channel 9? Where are the cowboys rushing, and do I see the United States Cavalry over the next hill to the rescue?'

The street was silent and long and empty, with only his shadow moving like the shadow of a hawk in mid-country. If he closed his eyes and stood very still, frozen, he imagined himself upon the centre of a plain, a wintry windless Arizona country with no house in a thousand miles, and only dry river-beds, the streets, for company.

'What is it now?' he asked the houses, noticing his wristwatch. 'Eight-thirty p.m. Time for a dozen assorted murders? A quiz? A revue? A comedian falling off the stage?'

Was that a murmur of laughter from within a moon-white house? He hesitated, but went on when nothing more happened. He stumbled over a particularly uneven section of walk as he came to a clover-leaf intersection which stood silent where two main highways crossed the town. During the day it was a thunderous surge of cars, the gas stations open, a great insect rustling and ceaseless jockeying for position as the scarab beetles, a faint incense puttering from their exhausts, skimmed homeward to the far horizons. But now these highways, too, were like streams in a dry season, all stone and bed and moon radiance.

He turned back on a side street, circling around toward his home. He was within a block of his destination when the lone car turned a corner quite suddenly and flashed a fierce white cone of light upon him. He stood entranced, not unlike a night moth, stunned by the illumination and then drawn toward it.

A metallic voice called to him:
'Stand still. Stay where you are! Don't move!'
He halted.
'Put up your hands.'
'But—' he said.
'Your hands up! Or we'll shoot!'

The police, of course, but what a rare, incredible thing; in a city of three million, there was only one police car left. Ever since a year ago, 2130, the election year, the force had been cut down from three cars to one. Crime was ebbing; there was no need now for the police, save for this one lone car wandering and wandering the empty streets.

'Your name?' said the police car in a metallic whisper. He couldn't see the men in it for the bright light in his eyes.

'Leonard Mead,' he said.

'Speak up!'

'Leonard Mead!'

'Business or profession?'

'I guess you'd call me a writer.'

'No profession,' said the police car, as if talking to itself. The light held him fixed like a museum specimen, needle thrust through chest.

'You might say that,' said Mr Mead. He hadn't written in years. Magazines and books didn't sell any more. Everything went on in the tomb-like houses at night now, he thought, continuing his fancy. The tombs, ill-lit by television light, where the people sat like the dead, the grey or multi-coloured lights touching their expressionless faces but never really touching *them*.

'No profession,' said the phonograph voice, hissing. 'What are you doing out?'

'Walking,' said Leonard Mead.

'Walking!'

'Just walking,' he said, simply, but his face felt cold.

'Walking, just walking, walking?'

'Yes, sir.'

'Walking where? For what?'

'Walking for air. Walking to *see*.'

'Your address!'

'Eleven South St James Street.'

'And there is air *in* your house, you have an air-*conditioner*, Mr Mead?'

'Yes.'

'And you have a viewing screen in your house to see with?'

'No.'

'No?' There was a crackling quiet that in itself was an accusation.

'Are you married, Mr Mead?'

'No.'

'Not married,' said the police voice behind the fiery beam. The moon was high and clear among the stars and the houses were grey and silent.

'Nobody wanted me,' said Leonard Mead, with a smile.

'Don't speak unless you're spoken to!'

Leonard Mead waited in the cold night.

'Just walking, Mr Mead?'

'Yes.'

'But you haven't explained for what purpose.'

'I explained: for air and to see, and just to walk.'

'Have you done this often?'

'Every night for years.'

The police car sat in the centre of the street with its radio throat faintly humming.

'Well, Mr Mead,' it said.

'Is that all?' he asked politely.

'Yes,' said the voice. 'Here.' There was a sigh, a pop. The back door of the police car sprang wide. 'Get in.'

'Wait a minute, I haven't done anything!'

'Get in.'

'I protest!'

'Mr Mead.'

He walked like a man suddenly drunk. As he passed the front window of the car he looked in. As he had expected, there was no one in the front seat, no one in the car at all.

'Get in.'

He put his hand to the door and peered into the back seat, which was a little cell, a little black jail with bars. It smelled of rivited steel. It smelled of harsh antiseptic; it smelled too clean and hard and metallic. There was nothing soft there.

'Now, if you had a wife to give you an alibi,' said the iron voice. 'But—'

'Where are you taking me?'

The car hesitated, or rather gave a faint whirring click, as if information, somewhere, was dropping card by punch-slotted card under electric eyes. 'To the Psychiatric Centre for Research on Regressive Tendencies.'

He got in. The door shut with a soft thud. The police car rolled through the night avenues, flashing its dim lights ahead.

They passed one house on one street a moment later, one house in an entire city of houses that were dark, but this one particular house had all its electric lights brightly lit, every window a loud yellow illumination, square and warm in the cool darkness.

'That's *my* house,' said Leonard Mead.

No one answered him.

The car moved down the empty river-bed streets and off away, leaving the empty streets with the empty sidewalks, and no sound and no motion all the rest of the chill November night.

Richard Matheson
The last day

He woke up and the first thing he thought was – *the last night is gone.*

He had slept through half of it.

He lay there on the floor and looked up at the ceiling. The walls still glowed reddish from the outside light. There was no sound in the living-room but that of snoring.

He looked around.

There were bodies sprawled out all over the room. They were on the couch, slumped on chairs, curled up on the floor. Some were covered with rugs. Two of them were naked.

He raised up on one elbow and winced at the shooting pains in his head. He closed his eyes and held them tightly shut for a moment. Then he opened them again. He ran his tongue over the inside of his dry mouth. There was still a stale taste of liquor and food in his mouth.

He rested on his elbow as he looked around the room again, his mind slowly registering the scene.

Nancy and Bill lying in each other's arms, both naked. Norman curled up in an armchair, his thin face taut as he slept. Mort and Mel lying on the floor, covered with dirty throw-rugs. Both snoring. Others on the floor.

Outside the red glow.

He looked at the window and his throat moved. He blinked. He looked down over his long body. He swallowed again.

I'm alive, he thought, and it's all true.

He rubbed his eyes. He took a deep breath of the dead air in the apartment.

He knocked over a glass as he struggled to his feet. The liquor and soda sloshed over the rug and soaked into the dark blue weave.

He looked around at the other glasses, broken, kicked over, hurled against the wall. He looked at the bottles all over, all empty.

He stood staring around the room. He looked at the record player overturned, the albums all strewn around, jagged pieces of records in crazy patterns on the rug.

He remembered.

It was Mort who had started it the night before. He had suddenly rushed to the playing record machine and shouted drunkenly:

'What the hell is music any more! Just a lot of noise!'

And he had driven the point of his shoe against the front of the record player and knocked it against the wall. He had lurched over and down on his knees. He had struggled up with the player in his beefy arms and heaved the entire thing over on its back and kicked it again.

'The hell with music!' he had yelled. 'I hate the crap anyway!'

Then he'd started to drag records out of their albums and their envelopes and snap them over his kneecap.

'Come on!' he'd yelled to everybody. 'Come on!'

And it had caught on. The way all crazy ideas had caught on in those last few days.

Mel had jumped up from making love to a girl. He had flung records out of the windows, scaling them far across the street. And Charlie had put aside his gun for a moment to stand at the windows too and try to hit people in the street with thrown records.

Richard had watched the dark saucers bounce and shatter on the sidewalks below. He'd even thrown one himself. Then he'd just turned away and let the others rage. He'd taken Mel's girl into the bedroom and had relations with her.

He thought about that as he stood waveringly in the reddish light of the room.

He closed his eyes a moment.

Then he looked at Nancy and remembered taking her too sometime in the jumble of wild hours that had been yesterday and last night.

She looked vile now, he thought. She'd always been an animal.

Before, though, she'd had to veil it. Now, in the final twilight of everything she could revel in the only thing she'd ever really cared about.

He wondered if there were any people left in the world with real dignity. The kind that was still there when it no longer was necessary to impress people with it.

He stepped over the body of a sleeping girl. She had on only a slip. He looked down at her tangled hair, at her red lips smeared, the tight unhappy frown printed on her face.

He glanced into the bedroom as he passed it. There were three girls and two men in the bed.

He found the body in the bathroom.

It was thrown carelessly in the tub and the shower curtain torn down to cover it. Only the legs showed, dangling ridiculously over the front rim of the tub.

He drew back the curtain and looked at the blood-soaked shirt, at the white, still face.

Charlie.

He shook his head, then turned away and washed his face and hands at the sink. It didn't matter. Nothing mattered. As a matter of fact, Charlie was one of the lucky ones now. A member of the legion who had put their heads into ovens or cut their wrists or taken pills or done away with themselves in the accepted fashions of suicide.

As he looked at his tired face in the mirror he thought of cutting his wrists. But he knew he couldn't. Because it took more than just despair to incite self-destruction.

He took a drink of water. Lucky, he thought, there's still water running. He didn't suppose there was a soul left to run the water system. Or the electric system or the gas system or the telephone system or any system for that matter.

What fool would work on the last day of the world?

Spencer was in the kitchen when Richard went in.

He was sitting in his shorts at the table looking at his hands. On the stove some eggs were frying. The gas was working, then, too, Richard thought.

'Hello,' he said to Spencer.

Spencer grunted without looking up. He stared at his hands. Richard let it go. He turned the gas down a little. He took bread out of the cupboard and put it in the electric toaster. But the toaster didn't work. He shrugged and forgot about it.

'What time is it?'

Spencer was looking at him with the question.

Richard looked at his watch.

'It stopped,' he said.

They looked at each other.

'Oh,' Spencer said. Then he asked, 'What day is it?'

Richard thought. 'Sunday, I think,' he said.

'I wonder if people are at church,' Spencer said.

'Who cares?'

Richard opened the refrigerator.

'There aren't any more eggs,' Spencer said.

Richard shut the door.

'No more eggs,' he said dully. 'No more chickens. No more anything.'

He leaned against the wall with a shuddering breath and looked out the window at the red sky.

Mary, he thought. Mary, who I should have married. Who I let go. He wondered where she was. He wondered if she were thinking about him at all.

Norman came trudging in, groggy with sleep and hangover. His mouth hung open. He looked dazed.

'Morning,' he slurred.

'Good morning, merry sunshine,' Richard said, without mirth.

Norman looked at him blankly. Then he went over to the sink and washed out his mouth. He spit the water down the drain.

'Charlie's dead,' he said.

'I know,' Richard said.

'Oh. When did it happen?'

'Last night,' Richard told him. 'You were unconscious. You remember how he kept saying he was going to shoot us all? Put us out of our misery?'

'Yeah,' Norman said. 'He put the muzzle against my head. He said feel how cool it is.'

'Well, he got in a fight with Mort,' Richard said. 'The gun went off.' He shrugged. 'That was it.'

They looked at each other without expression.

Then Norman turned his head and looked out the window.

'It's still up there,' he muttered.

They looked up at the great flaming ball in the sky that crowded out the sun, the moon, the stars.

Norman turned away, his throat moving. His lips trembled and he clamped them together.

'Jesus,' he said. 'It's *today*.'

He looked up at the sky again.

'Today,' he repeated. '*Everything*.'

'Everything,' said Richard.

Spencer got up and turned off the gas. He looked down at the eggs for a moment. Then he said:

'What the hell did I fry these for?'

He dumped them into the sink and they slid greasily over the white surface. The yolks burst and spurted smoking, yellow fluid over the enamel.

Spencer bit his lips. His face grew hard.

'I'm taking her again,' he said suddenly.

He pushed past Richard and dropped his shorts off as he turned the corner into the hallway.

'There goes Spencer,' Richard said.

Norman sat down at the table. Richard stayed at the wall.

In the living-room they heard Nancy suddenly call out at the top of her strident voice.

'Hey, wake up, everybody! Watch me do it! Watch me, everybody, *watch me!*'

Norman looked at the kitchen doorway for a moment. Then something gave inside of him and he slumped his head forward on his arms on the table. His thin shoulders shook.

'I did it too,' he said brokenly. 'I did it too. Oh, God, what did I come here for?'

'Sex,' Richard said. 'Like all the rest of us. You thought you could end your life in carnal, drunken bliss.'

Norman's voice was muffled.

'I can't die like that,' he sobbed. 'I can't.'

'A couple of billion people are doing it,' Richard said. 'When the sun hits us, they'll still be at it. What a sight.'

The thought of a world's people indulging themselves in one last orgy of animalism made him shudder. He closed his eyes and pressed his forehead against the wall and tried to forget.

But the wall was warm.

Norman looked up from the table.

'Let's go home,' he said.

Richard looked at him. 'Home?' he said.

'To our parents. My mother and father. Your mother.'

Richard shook his head.

'I don't want to,' he said.

'But I can't go alone.'

'Why?'

'Because . . . I can't. You know the streets are full of guys just *killing* everybody they meet.'

Richard shrugged.

'Why don't you?' Norman asked.

'I don't want to see her.'

'Your *mother*?'

'Yes.'

'You're crazy,' Norman said. 'Who else is there to . . . .'

'No.'

He thought of his mother at home waiting for him. Waiting for him on the last day. And it made him ill to think of him delaying, of maybe never seeing her again.

But he kept thinking: How can I go home and have her try to make me pray? Try to make me read from the Bible, spend these last hours in a muddle of religious absorption?

He said it again for himself.

'*No.*'

Norman looked lost. His chest shook with a swallowed sob.

'I want to see my mother,' he said.

'Go ahead,' Richard said casually.

But his insides were twisting themselves into knots. To never see her again. Or his sister and her husband and her daughter.

Never to see any of them again.

He sighed. It was no use fighting it. In spite of everything, Norman was right. Who else was there in the world to turn to?

In a wide world, about to be burned, was there any other person who loved him above all others?

'Oh . . . all right,' he said. 'Come on. Anything to get out of this place.'

The apartment house hall smelled of vomit. They found the janitor dead drunk on the stairs. They found a dog in the foyer with its head kicked in.

They stopped as they came out of the entrance of the building.

Instinctively they looked up.

At the red sky, like molten slag. At the fiery wisps that fell like hot raindrops through the atmosphere. At the gigantic ball of flame that kept coming closer and closer that blotted out the universe.

They lowered their watering eyes. It hurt to look. They started walking along the street. It was very warm.

'December,' Richard said. 'It's like the tropics.'

As they walked along in silence, he thought of the tropics, of the poles, of all the world's countries he would never see. Of all the things he would never do.

Like hold Mary in his arms and tell her, as the world was ending, that he loved her very much and was not afraid.

'*Never*,' he said, feeling himself go rigid with frustration.

'What?' Norman said.

'Nothing. Nothing.'

As they walked, Richard felt something heavy in his jacket pocket. It bumped against his side. He reached in and drew out the object.

'What's that?' Norman asked.

'Charlie's gun,' Richard said. 'I took it last night so nobody else would get hurt.'

His laughter was harsh.

'So nobody else would get killed,' he said bitterly. 'Jesus, I ought to be on the stage.'

He was about to throw it away when he changed his mind. He slid it back into his pocket.

'I may need it,' he said.

Norman wasn't listening.

'Thank God nobody stole my car. Oh. . . !'
Somebody had thrown a rock through the windshield.
'What's the difference?' Richard said.
'I . . . none, I suppose.'
They got into the front seat and brushed the glass off the
cushion. It was stuffy in the car. Richard pulled off his jacket and
threw it out. He put the gun in his side pants pocket.

As Norman drove downtown, they passed people in the street.
Some were running around wildly, as if they were searching for
something. Some were fighting with each other. Strewn all over
the sidewalks were bodies of people who had leaped from windows
and been struck down by speeding cars. Buildings were on fire,
windows shattered from the explosions of unlit gas jets.

There were people looting stores.

'What's the matter with them?' Norman asked miserably. 'Is
that how they want to spend their last day?'

'Maybe that's how they spent their whole life,' Richard
answered.

He leaned against the door and gazed at the people they passed.
Some of them waved at him. Some cursed and spat. A few threw
things at the speeding car.

'People die the way they lived,' he said. 'Some good, some bad.'

'*Look out!*'

Norman cried out as a car came careering down the street on
the wrong side. Men and women hung out of the window shouting and singing and waving bottles.

Norman twisted the wheel violently and they missed the car by
inches.

'Are they crazy!' he said.

Richard looked out through the back window. He saw the car
skid, saw it get out of control and go crashing into a store front
and turn over on its side, the wheels spinning crazily.

He turned back front without speaking. Norman kept looking
ahead grimly, his hands on the wheel, white and tense.

Another intersection.

A car came speeding across their path. Norman jammed on the
brakes with a gasp. They crashed against the dashboard, getting
their breath knocked out.

Then, before Norman could get the car started again, a gang of teenage boys with knives and clubs came dashing into the intersection. They'd been chasing the other car. Now they changed direction and flung themselves at the car that held Norman and Richard.

Norman threw the car into first and gunned across the street.

A boy jumped on the back of the car. Another tried for the running-board, missed and went spinning over the street. Another jumped on the running-board and grabbed the door handle. He slashed at Richard with a knife.

'Gonna kill ya bastids!' yelled the boy. 'Sonsabitches!'

He slashed again and tore open the back of the seat as Richard jerked his shoulder to the side.

'Get out of here!' Norman screamed, trying to watch the boy and the street ahead at the same time.

The boy tried to open the door as the car wove wildly up Broadway. He slashed again but the car's motion made him miss.

'I'll *get ya!*' he screamed in a fury of brainless hate.

Richard tried to open the door and knock the boy off, but he couldn't. The boy's twisted white face thrust in through the window. He raised his knife.

Richard had the gun now. He shot the boy in the face.

The boy flung back from the car with a dying howl and landed like a sack of rocks. He bounced once, his left leg kicked and then he lay still.

Richard twisted around.

The boy on the back was still hanging on, his crazed face pressed against the back window. Richard saw his mouth moving as the boy cursed.

'Shake him off!' he said.

Norman headed for the sidewalk, then suddenly veered back into the street. The boy hung on. Norman did it again. The boy still clung to the back.

Then on the third time he lost his grip and went off. He tried to run along the street but his momentum was too great and he went leaping over the kerb and crashing into a plate-glass window, arms stuck up in front of him to ward off the blow.

They sat in the car, breathing heavily. They didn't talk for a long while. Richard flung the gun out of the window and watched it clatter on the concrete and bounce off a hydrant. Norman started to say something about it, then stopped.

The car turned into Fifth Avenue and started downtown at sixty miles an hour. There weren't many cars.

They passed churches. People were packed inside them. They overflowed out on to the steps.

'Poor fools,' Richard muttered, his hands still shaking.

Norman took a deep breath.

'I wish I was a poor fool,' he said. 'A poor fool who could believe in something.'

'Maybe,' Richard said. Then he added, 'I'd rather spend the last day believing what I think is true.'

'The last day,' Norman said. 'I. . . .'

He shook his head. 'I can't believe it,' he said. 'I read the papers. I see that . . . thing up there. I know it's going to happen. But, God! The *end*?'

He looked at Richard for a split second.

'Nothing afterward?' he said.

Richard said, 'I don't know.'

At 14th Street, Norman drove to the East Side, then sped across the Manhattan Bridge. He didn't stop for anything, driving around bodies and wrecked cars. Once he drove over a body and Richard saw his face twitch as the wheel rolled over the dead man's leg.

'They're all lucky,' Richard said. 'Luckier than we are.'

They stopped in front of Norman's house in downtown Brooklyn. Some kids were playing ball in the street. They didn't seem to realize what was happening. Their shouts sounded very loud in the silent street. Richard wondered if their parents knew where the children were. Or cared.

Norman was looking at him.

'Well. . . ?' he started to say.

Richard felt his stomach muscles tightening. He couldn't answer.

'Would you . . . like to come in for a minute?' Norman asked.

Richard shook his head.

'No,' he said. 'I better get home. I . . . should see her. My mother, I mean.'

'Oh.'

Norman nodded. Then he straightened up. He forced a momentary calm over himself.

'For what it's worth, Dick,' he said, 'I consider you my best friend and. . . .'

He faltered. He reached out and gripped Richard's hand. Then he pushed out of the car, leaving the keys in the ignition.

'So long,' he said hurriedly.

Richard watched his friend run around the car and move for the apartment house. When he had almost reached the door, Richard called out.

'Norm!'

Norman stopped and turned. The two of them looked at each other. All the years they had known each other seemed to flicker between them.

Then Richard managed to smile. He touched his forehead in a last salute.

'So long, Norm,' he said.

Norman didn't smile. He pushed through the door and was gone.

Richard looked at the door for a long time. He started the motor. Then he turned it off again thinking that Norman's parents might not be home.

After a while he started it again and began the trip home.

As he drove he kept thinking.

The closer he got to the end, the less he wanted to face it. He wanted to end it now. Before the hysterics started.

Sleeping-pills, he decided. It was the best way. He had some at home. He hoped there were enough left. There might not be any left in the corner drugstore. There'd been a rush for sleeping-pills during those last few days. Entire families took them together.

He reached the house without event. Overhead the sky was an incandescent crimson. He felt the heat on his face like waves from a distant oven. He breathed in the heated air.

He unlocked the front door and walked in slowly.

I'll probably find her in the front room, he thought. Surrounded by her books, praying, exhorting invisible powers to succour her as the world prepared to fry itself.

She wasn't in the front room.

He searched the house. And, as he did so, his heart began to beat quickly and, when he knew she really wasn't there, he felt a great hollow feeling in his stomach. He knew that his talk about not wanting to see her had been just talk. He loved her. And she was the only one left now.

He searched for a note in her room, in his, in the living-room.

'Mom,' he said, 'Mom, where are you?'

He found the note in the kitchen. He picked it up from the table.

Richard, Darling.

I'm at your sister's house. Please come there. Don't make me spend the last day without you. Don't make me leave this world without seeing your dear face again. Please.

The last day.

There it was in black and white. And, of all people, it had been his mother to write down the words. She who had always been so sceptical of his taste for material science. Now admitting that science's last prediction.

Because she couldn't doubt any more. Because the sky was filled with flaming evidence and no one could doubt any more.

The whole world going. The staggering detail of evolutions and revolutions, of strifes and clashes, of endless continuities of centuries streaming back into the clouded past, of rocks and trees and animals and men. All to pass. In a flash, in a moment. The pride, the vanity of man's world incinerated by a freak of astronomical disorder.

What point was there to all of it, then? None, none at all. Because it was all ending.

He got sleeping-pills from the medicine cabinet and left. He drove to his sister's house, thinking about his mother as he passed through the streets littered with everything from empty bottles to dead people.

If only he didn't dread the thought of arguing with his mother on this last day. Of disputing with her about her God and her conviction.

He made up his mind not to argue. He'd force himself to make their last day a peaceful one. He would accept her simple devotion and not hack at her faith any more.

The front door was locked at Grace's house. He rang the bell and, after a moment, heard hurried steps inside.

He heard Ray shout inside, 'Don't open it, Mom! It may be that gang again!'

'It's Richard, I know it is!' his mother called back.

Then the door was open and she was embracing him and crying happily.

He didn't speak. Finally he said softly:

'Hello, Mom.'

His niece Doris played all afternoon in the front room, while Grace and Ray sat motionless in the living-room looking at her.

If I were with Mary, Richard kept thinking. If only we were together today. Then he thought they might have had children. And he would have to sit like Grace and know that the few years his child lived would be its only years.

The sky grew brighter as evening approached. It flowed with violent crimson currents. Doris stood quietly at the window and looked at it. She hadn't laughed all day or cried. And Richard thought to himself – she *knows*.

And thought, too, that at any moment his mother would ask them all to pray together. To sit and read the Bible and hope for divine charity.

But she didn't say anything. She smiled. She made supper. Richard stood with her in the kitchen as she made supper.

'I may not wait,' he told her. 'I . . . may take sleeping-pills.'

'Are you afraid, son?' she asked.

'Everybody is afraid,' he said.

She shook her head. 'Not everybody,' she said.

Now, he thought, it's coming. That smug look, the opening line.

She gave him a dish with the vegetable and they all sat down to eat.

During supper none of them spoke except to ask for food. Doris never spoke once. Richard sat looking at her from across the table.

He thought about the night before. The crazy drinking, the fighting, the carnal abuses. He thought of Charlie dead in the bathtub. Of the apartment in Manhattan. Of Spencer driving himself into a frenzy of lust as the climax of his life. Of the boy lying dead in the New York gutter with a bullet in his brain.

They all seemed very far away. He could almost believe it had all never happened. Could almost believe that this was just another evening meal with his family.

Except for the cherry glow that filled the sky and flooded in through the windows like an aura from some fantastic fireplace.

Near the end of the meal Grace went and got a box. She sat down at the table with it and opened it. She took out white pills. Doris looked at her, her large eyes searching.

'This is dessert,' Grace told her. 'We're all going to have white candy for dessert.'

'Is it peppermint?' Doris asked.

'Yes,' Grace said. 'It's peppermint.'

Richard felt his scalp crawling as Grace put pills in front of Doris. In front of Ray.

'We haven't enough for all of us,' she said to Richard.

'I have my own,' he said.

'Have you enough for Mom?' she asked.

'I won't need any,' her mother said.

In his tenseness, Richard almost shouted at her. Shouted: Oh, stop being so damned noble! But he held himself. He stared in fascinated horror at Doris holding the pills in her small hand.

'This isn't peppermint,' she said. 'Momma, this isn't—'

'*Yes it is.*' Grace took a deep breath. 'Eat it, darling.'

Doris put one in her mouth. She made a face. Then she spit it into her palm.

'It *isn't* peppermint,' she said, upset.

Grace threw up her head and buried her teeth in the white knuckles. Her eyes moved frantically to Ray.

'Eat it, Doris,' Ray said. 'Eat it, it's good.'

Doris started to cry. 'No, I don't like it.'

'*Eat it!*'

Ray turned away suddenly, his body shaking. Richard tried to think of some way to make her eat the pills but he couldn't.

Then his mother spoke.

'We'll play a game, Doris,' she said. 'We'll see if you can swallow all the candy before I count ten. If you do, I'll give you a dollar.'

Doris sniffed. 'A dollar?' she said.

Richard's mother nodded.

'One,' she said.

Doris didn't move.

'Two,' said Richard's mother. 'A *dollar*. . . .'

Doris brushed aside a tear. 'A . . . whole dollar?'

'Yes, darling. Three, four, hurry up.'

Doris reached for the pills.

'Five . . . six . . . seven. . . .'

Grace had her eyes shut tightly. Her cheeks were white.

'Nine . . . ten. . . .'

Richard's mother smiled but her lips trembled and there was a glistening in her eyes.

'There,' she said cheerfully. 'You've won the game.'

Grace suddenly put pills into her mouth and swallowed them in fast succession. She looked at Ray. He reached out one trembling hand and swallowed his pills. Richard put his hand in his pocket for his pills but took it out again. He didn't want his mother to watch him take them.

Doris got sleepy almost immediately. She yawned and couldn't keep her eyes open. Ray picked her up and she rested against his shoulder, her small arms around his neck. Grace got up and the three of them went back into the bedroom.

Richard sat there while his mother went back and said goodbye to them. He sat staring at the white tablecloth and the remains of food.

When his mother came back she smiled at him.

'Help me with the dishes,' she said.

'The. . . ?' he started. Then he stopped. What difference did it make what they did?

He stood with her in the red-lit kitchen, feeling a sense of sharp unreality as he dried the dishes they would never use again and put them in the closet that would be no more in a matter of hours.

He kept thinking about Ray and Grace in the bedroom. Finally he left the kitchen without a word and went back. He opened the door and looked in. He looked at the three of them for a long time. Then he shut the door again and walked slowly back to the kitchen. He stared at his mother.

'They're. . . .'

'All right,' his mother said.

'Why didn't you say anything to them?' he asked her. 'How come you let them do it without saying anything?'

'Richard,' she said, 'everyone has to make his own way on this day. No one can tell others what to do. Doris was their child.'

'And I'm yours. . . ?'

'You're not a child any longer,' she said.

He finished up the dishes, his fingers numb and shaking.

'Mom, about last night,' he said.

'I don't care about it,' she said.

'But. . . .'

'It doesn't matter,' she said. 'This part is ending.'

Now, he thought, almost with pain. *This* part. Now she would talk about afterlife and heaven and reward for the just and eternal penitence for the sinning.

She said, 'Let's go out and sit on the porch.'

He didn't understand. He walked through the quiet house with her. He sat next to her on the porch steps and thought. I'll never see Grace again. Or Doris. Or Norman or Spencer or Mary or anybody. . . .

He couldn't take it all in. It was too much. All he could do was sit there woodenly and look at the red sky and the huge sun about to swallow them. He couldn't even feel nervous any more. Fears were blunted by endless repetition.

'Mom,' he said after a while, 'why . . . why haven't you spoken about religion to me? I know you must want to.'

She looked at him and her face was very gentle in the red glow.

'I don't have to, darling,' she said. 'I know we'll be together when this is over. You don't have to believe it. I'll believe for both of us.'

And that was all. He looked at her, marvelling at her confidence and her strength.

'If you want to take those pills now,' she said, 'it's all right. You can go to sleep in my lap.'

He felt himself tremble. 'You wouldn't mind?'

'I want you to do what you think is best.'

He didn't know what to do until he thought of her sitting there alone when the world ended.

'I'll stay with you,' he said impulsively.

She smiled.

'If you change your mind,' she said, 'you can tell me.'

They were quiet for a while. Then she said:

'It is pretty.'

'*Pretty?*' he asked.

'Yes,' she said. 'God closes a bright curtain on our play.'

He didn't know. But he put his arm around her shoulders and she leaned against him. And he did know one thing.

They sat there in the evening of the last day. And, though there was no actual point to it, they loved each other.

Jerome Bixby
The holes around Mars

Spaceship crews should be selected on the basis of their non-irritating qualities as individuals. No chronic complainers, no hypochondriacs, no bugs on cleanliness – particularly, no one-man parties. I speak from bitter experience.

Because on the first expedition to Mars, Hugh Allenby damned near drove us nuts with his puns. We finally got so we just ignored them.

But no one can ignore that classic last one – it's written right into the annals of astronomy, and it's there to stay.

Allenby, in command of the expedition, was first to set foot outside the ship. As he stepped down from the airlock of the *Mars I*, he placed that foot on a convenient rock, caught the toe of his weighted boot in a hole in the rock, wrenched his ankle and smote the ground with his pants.

Sitting there, eyes pained behind the transparent shield of his oxygen-mask, he stared at the rock.

It was about five feet high. Ordinary granite – no special shape – and several inches below its summit, running straight through it in a north-easterly direction, was a neat round four-inch hole.

'I'm *upset* by the *hole* thing,' he grunted.

The rest of us scrambled out of the ship and gathered around his plump form. Only one or two of us winced at his miserable double pun.

'Break anything, Hugh?' asked Burton, our pilot, kneeling beside him.

'Get out of my way, Burton,' said Allenby. 'You're obstructing my view.'

Burton blinked. A man constructed of long bones and caution, he angled out of the way, looking around to see what he was obstructing view *of*.

He saw the rock and the round hole through it. He stood very still. So did the rest of us.

'Well, I'll be damned,' said Janus, our photographer. 'A hole.'

'In a rock,' added Gonzales, our botanist.

'Round,' said Randolph, our biologist.

'An *artefact*,' finished Allenby softly.

Burton helped him to his feet. Silently we gathered around the rock.

Janus bent down and put an eye to one end of the hole. I bent down and looked through the other end. We squinted at each other.

As mineralogist, I was expected to opinionate. 'Not drilled,' I said slowly. 'Not chipped. Not melted. Certainly not eroded.'

I heard a rasping sound by my ear and straightened. Burton was scratching a thumbnail along the rim of the hole. 'Weathered,' he said. 'Plenty old. But I'll bet it's a perfect circle, if we measure.'

Janus was already fiddling with his camera, testing the co-operation of the tiny distant sun with a light-meter.

'Let us see *weather* it is or not,' Allenby said.

Burton brought out a steel tape-measure. The hole was four and three-eighths inches across. It was perfectly circular and about sixteen inches long. And four feet above the ground.

'But why?' said Randolph. 'Why should anyone bore a four-inch tunnel through a rock way out in the middle of the desert?'

'Religious symbol,' said Janus. He looked around, one hand on his gun. 'We'd better keep an eye out – maybe we've landed on sacred ground or something.'

'A totem *hole*, perhaps,' Allenby suggested.

'Oh, I don't know,' Randolph said – to Janus, not Allenby. As I've mentioned, we always ignored Allenby's puns. 'Note the lack of ornamentation. Not at all typical of religious articles.'

'On Earth,' Gonzales reminded him. 'Besides, it might be utilitarian, not symbolic.'

'Utilitarian, how?' asked Janus.

'An altar for snakes,' Burton said dryly.

'Well,' said Allenby, 'you can't deny that it has its *holy* aspects.'

'Get your hand away, will you, Peters?' asked Janus.

I did. When Janus's camera had clicked, I bent again and peered through the hole. 'It sights on that low ridge over there,' I said. 'Maybe it's some kind of surveying set-up. I'm going to take a look.'

'Careful,' warned Janus. 'Remember, it may be sacred.'

As I walked away, I heard Allenby say, 'Take some scrapings from the inside of the hole, Gonzales. We might be able to determine if anything is kept in it. . . .'

One of the stumpy, purplish, barrel-type cacti on the ridge had a long vertical bite out of it – as if someone had carefully carved out a narrow U-shaped section from the top down, finishing the bottom of the U in a neat semicircle. It was as flat and clean-cut as the inside surface of a horseshoe magnet.

I hollered. The others came running. I pointed.

'Oh, my God!' said Allenby. 'Another one.'

The pulp of the cactus in and around the U-hole was dried and dead-looking.

Silently Burton used his tape-measure. The hole measured four and three-eighths inches across. It was eleven inches deep. The semicircular bottom was about a foot above the ground.

'This ridge,' I said, 'is about three feet higher than where we landed the ship. I bet the hole in the rock and the hole in this cactus are on the same level.'

Gonzales said slowly, 'This was not done all at once. It is a result of periodic attacks. Look here and here. These overlapping depressions along the outer edges of the hole' – he pointed – 'on this side of the cactus. They are the signs of repeated impact. And the scallop effect on *this* side, where whatever made the hole emerged. There are juices still oozing – not at the point of impact, where the plant is desiccated, but below, where the shock was transmitted—'

A distant shout turned us around. Burton was at the rock, beside the ship. He was bending down, his eye to the far side of the mysterious hole.

He looked for another second, then straightened and came toward us at a lope.

'They line up,' he said when he reached us. 'The bottom of the hole in the cactus is right in the middle when you sight through the hole in the rock.'

'As if somebody came around and whacked the cactus regularly,' Janus said, looking around warily.

'To keep the line of sight through the holes clear?' I wondered. 'Why not just remove the cactus?'

'Religious,' Janus explained.

The gauntlet he had discarded lay ignored on the ground, in the shadow of the cactus. We went on past the ridge toward an outcropping of rock about a hundred yards farther on. We walked silently, each of us wondering if what we half-expected would really be there.

It was. In one of the tall, weathered spires in the outcropping, some ten feet below its peak and four feet above the ground, was a round four-inch hole.

Allenby sat down on a rock, nursing his ankle, and remarked that anybody who believed this crazy business was really happening must have holes in the rocks in his head.

Burton put his eye to the hole and whistled. 'Sixty feet long if it's an inch,' he said. 'The other end's just a pinpoint. But you can see it. The damn thing's perfectly straight.'

I looked back the way we had come. The cactus stood on the ridge, with its U-shaped bite, and beyond was the ship, and beside it the perforated rock.

'If we surveyed,' I said, 'I bet the holes would all line up right to the last millimetre.'

'But', Randolph complained, 'why would anybody go out and bore holes in things all along a line through the desert?'

'Religious,' Janus muttered. 'It doesn't *have* to make sense.'

We stood there by the outcropping and looked out along the wide, red desert beyond. It stretched flatly for miles from this point, south toward Mars' equator – dead, sandy wastes, crisscrossed by the 'canals', which we had observed while landing to be great straggly patches of vegetation, probably strung along underground waterflows.

BLONG-G-G-G . . . st-st-st . . . .

We jumped half out of our skins. Ozone bit at our nostrils. Our hair stirred in the electrical uproar.

'L-look,' Janus chattered, lowering his smoking gun.

About forty feet to our left, a small rabbity creature poked its head from behind a rock and stared at us in utter horror.

Janus raised his gun again.

'Don't bother,' said Allenby tiredly. 'I don't think it intends to attack.'

'But—'

'I'm sure it isn't a Martian with religious convictions.'

Janus wet his lips and looked a little shamefaced. 'I guess I'm kind of taut.'

'That's what I *taut*,' said Allenby.

The creature darted from behind its rock and, looking at us over its shoulder, employed six legs to make small but very fast tracks.

We turned out attention again to the desert. Far out, black against Mars' azure horizon, was a line of low hills.

'Shall we go look?' asked Burton, eyes gleaming at the mystery.

Janus hefted his gun nervously. It was still crackling faintly from the discharge. 'I say let's get back to the ship!'

Allenby sighed. 'My leg hurts.' He studied the hills. 'Give me the field-glasses.'

Randolph handed them over. Allenby put them to the shield of his mask and adjusted them.

After a moment he sighed again. 'There's a hole. On a plane surface that catches the Sun. A lousy, damned, round, little, impossible hole.'

'Those hills', Burton observed, 'must be thousands of feet thick.'

The argument lasted all the way back to the ship.

Janus, holding out for his belief that the whole thing was of religious origin, kept looking around for Martians as if he expected them to pour screaming from the hills.

Burton came up with the suggestion that perhaps the holes had been made by a disintegrator-ray.

'It's possible,' Allenby admitted. 'This might have been the scene of some great battle—'

'With only one such weapon?' I objected.

Allenby swore as he stumbled. 'What do you mean?'

'I haven't seen any other lines of holes – only the one. In a battle, the whole joint should be cut up.'

That was good for a few moments' silent thought. Then Allenby said, 'It might have been brought out by one side as a last resort. Sort of an ace in the hole.'

I resisted the temptation to mutiny. 'But would even one such weapon, in battle, make only *one* line of holes? Wouldn't it be played in an arc against the enemy? You know it would.'

'Well—'

'Wouldn't it cut slices out of the landscape, instead of boring holes? And wouldn't it sway or vibrate enough to make the holes miles away from it something less than perfect circles?'

'It could have been very firmly mounted.'

'Hugh, does that sound like a practical weapon to you?'

Two seconds of silence. 'On the other hand,' he said, 'instead of a war, the whole thing might have been designed to frighten some primitive race – or even some kind of beast – the *hole* out of here. A demonstration.'

'Religious,' Janus grumbled, still looking around.

We walked on, passing the cactus on the low ridge.

'Interesting,' said Gonzales. 'The evidence that whatever causes the phenomenon has happened again and again. I'm afraid that the war theory—'

'Oh, my God!' gasped Burton.

We stared at him.

'The ship,' he whispered. 'It's right in line with the holes! If whatever made them is still in operation. . . .'

'Run,' yelled Allenby, and we ran like fiends.

We got the ship into the air, out of line with the holes to what we fervently hoped was safety, and then we realized we were admitting our fear that the mysterious hole-maker might still be lurking around.

Well, the evidence was all for it, as Gonzales had reminded us – that cactus had been oozing.

We cruised at twenty thousand feet and thought it over.

Janus, whose only training was in photography, said, 'Some kind of omnivorous animal? Or bird? Eats rocks and everything?'

'I will not totally discount the notion of such an animal,' Randolph said. 'But I will resist to the death the suggestion that it forages with geometric precision.'

After a while, Allenby said, 'Land, Burton. By that "canal".'

Lots of plant life – fauna, too. We'll do a little collecting.'

Burton set us down feather-light at the very edge of the sprawl-ing flat expanse of vegetation, commenting that the scene reminded him of his native Texas pear-flats.

We wandered in the chilly air, each of us except Burton pur-suing his speciality. Randolph relentlessly stalked another of the rabbity creatures. Gonzales was carefully digging up plants and stowing them in jars. Janus was busy with his cameras, recording every aspect of Mars transferable to film. Allenby walked around, helping anybody who needed it. An astronomer, he'd done half his work on the way to Mars and would do the other half on the return trip. Burton lounged in the Sun, his back against a ship's fin, and played chess with Allenby, who was calling out his moves in a bull roar. I grubbed for rocks.

My search took me farther and farther away from the others – all I could find around the 'canal' was gravel, and I wanted to chip at some big stuff. I walked toward a long rise a half-mile or so away, beyond which rose an enticing array of house-sized boulders.

As I moved out of earshot, I heard Randolph snarl, 'Burton, *will* you stop yelling, "Kt to B-2 and check"? Every time you open your yap, this critter takes off on me.'

Then I saw the groove.

It started right where the ground began to rise – a thin, shallow, curve-bottomed groove in the dirt at my feet, about half an inch across, running off straight toward higher ground.

With my eyes glued to it, I walked. The ground slowly rose. The groove deepened, widened – now it was about three inches across, about one and a half deep.

I walked on, holding my breath. Four inches wide. Two inches deep.

The ground rose some more. Four and three-eighths inches wide. I didn't have to measure it – I *knew*.

Now, as the ground rose, the edges of the groove began to curve inward over the groove. They touched. No more groove.

The ground had risen, the groove had stayed level and gone underground.

Except that now it wasn't a groove. It was a round tunnel.

A hole.

A few paces farther on, I thumped the ground with my heel where the hole ought to be. The dirt crumbled, and there was the little dark tunnel, running straight in both directions.

I walked on, the ground falling away gradually again. The entire process was repeated in reverse. A hairline appeared in the dirt – widened – became lips that drew slowly apart to reveal the neat straight four-inch groove – which shrank as slowly to a shallow line of the ground – and vanished.

I looked ahead of me. There was one low ridge of ground between me and the enormous boulders. A neat four-inch semi-circle was bitten out of the very top of the ridge. In the house-sized boulder directly beyond was a four-inch hole.

Allenby winced and called the others when I came back and reported.

'The mystery *deepens*,' he told them. He turned to me. 'Lead on, Peters. You're temporary *drill* leader.'

Thank God he didn't say *Fall in*.

The holes went straight through the nest of boulders – there'd be a hole in one and, ten or twenty feet farther on in the next boulder, another hole. And then another, and another – right through the nest in a line. About thirty holes in all.

Burton, standing by the boulder I'd first seen, flashed his flashlight into the hole. Randolph, clear on the other side of the jumbled nest, eye to hole, saw it.

Straight as a string!

The ground sloped away on the far side of the nest – no holes were visible in that direction – just miles of desert. So, after we'd stared at the holes for a while and they didn't go away, we headed back for the canal.

'Is there any possibility', asked Janus, as we walked, 'that it could be a natural phenomenon?'

'There are no straight lines in nature,' Randolph said, a little shortly. 'That goes for a bunch of circles in a straight line. And for perfect circles, too.'

'A planet is a circle,' objected Janus.

'An oblate spheroid,' Allenby corrected.

'A planet's orbit—'

'An ellipse.'

Janus walked a few steps, frowning. Then he said, 'I remember reading that there *is* something darned near a perfect circle in nature,' He paused a moment. 'Potholes.' And he looked at me, as mineralogist, to corroborate.

'What kind of potholes?' I asked cautiously. 'Do you mean where part of a limestone deposit has dissol—'

'No. I once read that when a glacier passes over a hard rock that's lying on some softer rock it grinds the hard rock down into the softer, and both of them sort of wear down to fit together, and it all ends up with a round hole in the soft rock.'

'Probably neither stone', I told Janus, 'would be homogenous. The softer parts would abrade faster in the soft stone. The end result wouldn't be a perfect circle.'

Janus's face fell.

'Now,' I said, 'would anyone care to define this term "perfect circle" we're throwing around so blithely? Because such holes as Janus describes are often pretty damned round.'

Randolph said, 'Well. . . .'

'It is settled, then,' Gonzales said, a little sarcastically. 'Your discussion, gentlemen, has established that the long, horizontal holes we have found were caused by glacial action.'

'Oh, no,' Janus argued seriously. 'I once read that Mars never had any glaciers.'

All of us shuddered.

Half an hour later, we spotted more holes, about a mile down the 'canal', still on a line, marching along the desert, through cacti, rocks, hills, even through one edge of the low vegetation of the 'canal' for thirty feet or so. It was the damnedest thing to bend down and look straight through all that curling, twisting growth – a round tunnel from either end.

We followed the holes for about a mile, to the rim of an enormous saucer-like valley that sank gradually before us until, miles away, it was thousands of feet deep. We stared out across it, wondering about the other side.

Allenby said determinedly, 'We'll burrow to the *bottom* of these holes, once and for all. Back to the ship, men!'

We hiked back, climbed in and took off.

At an altitude of fifty feet, Burton lined the nose of the ship on the most recent line of holes and we flew out over the valley.

On the other side was a range of hefty hills. The holes went through them. Straight through. We would approach one hill – Burton would manipulate the front viewscreen until we spotted the hole – we would pass over the hill and spot the other end of the hole in the rear screen.

One hole was 280 miles long.

Four hours later, we were halfway around Mars.

Randolph was sitting by a side port, chin on one hand, his eyes unbelieving. 'All around the planet,' he kept repeating. 'All around the planet....'

'Halfway at least,' Allenby mused. 'And we can assume that it continues in a straight line, through anything and everything that gets in its way. ....' He gazed out the front port at the uneven blue-green haze of a 'canal' off to our left. 'For the love of Heaven, why?'

Then Allenby fell down. We all did.

Burton had suddenly slapped at the control board, and the ship braked and sank like a plugged duck. At the last second, Burton propped up the nose with a short burst, the ten-foot wheels hit desert sand and in 500 yards we had jounced to a stop.

Allenby got up from the floor. 'Why did you do that?' he asked Burton politely, nursing a bruised elbow.

Burton's nose was almost touching the front port. 'Look!' he said, and pointed.

About two miles away, the Martian village looked like a handful of yellow marbles flung on the desert.

We checked our guns. We put on our oxygen masks. We checked our guns again. We got out of the ship and made sure the damned airlock was locked.

An hour later, we crawled inch by painstaking inch up a high sand dune and poked our heads over the top.

The Martians were runts – the tallest of them less than five feet tall – and skinny as a pencil. Dried-up and brown, they wore loin-cloths of woven fibre.

They stood among the dusty-looking inverted-bowl buildings of their village, and every one of them was looking straight up at us with unblinking brown eyes.

The six safeties of our six guns clicked off like a rattle of dice. The Martians stood there and gawped.

'Probably a highly developed sense of hearing in this thin atmosphere,' Allenby murmured. 'Heard us coming.'

'They thought that landing of Burton's was an earthquake,' Randolph grumbled sourly.

'Marsquake,' corrected Janus. One look at the village's scrawny occupants seemed to have convinced him that his life was in no danger.

Holding the Martians covered, we examined the village from atop the thirty-foot dune.

The dome-like buildings were constructed of something that looked like adobe. No windows – probably built with sandstorms in mind. The doors were about halfway up the sloping sides, and from each door a stone ramp wound down around the house to the ground – again with sandstorms in mind, no doubt, so drifting dunes would not block the entrances.

The centre of the village was a wide street, a long sandy area some thirty feet wide. On either side of it, the houses were scattered at random, as if each Martian had simply hunted for a comfortable place to sit and then built a house around it.

'Look,' whispered Randolph.

One Martian had stepped from a group situated on the far side of the street from us. He started to cross the street, his round brown eyes on us, his small bare feet plodding sand, and we saw that in addition to a loincloth he wore jewelry – a hammered metal ring, a bracelet on one skinny ankle. The Sun caught a copperish gleam on his bald narrow head, and we saw a band of metal there, just above where his eyebrows should have been.

'The super-chief,' Allenby murmured. 'Oh, *shaman* me!'

As the bejewelled Martian approached the centre of the street, he glanced briefly at the ground at his feet. Then he raised his head, stepped with dignity across the exact centre of the street and came on towards us, passing the dusty-looking buildings of his realm and the dusty-looking groups of his subjects.

He reached the slope of the dune we lay on, paused – and raised small hands over his head, palms toward us.

'I think', Allenby said, 'that an anthropologist would give odds on that gesture meaning peace.'

He stood up, holstered his gun – without buttoning the flap – and raised his own hands over his head. We all did.

The Martian language consisted of squeaks.

We made friendly noises, the chief squeaked and pretty soon we were the centre of a group of wide-eyed Martians, none of whom made a sound. Evidently no one dared peep while the chief spoke – very likely the most articulate Martians simply squeaked themselves into the job. Allenby, of course, said they just *squeaked by*.

He was going through the business of drawing concentric circles in the sand, pointing at the third orbit away from the Sun and thumping his chest. The crowd around us kept growing as more Martians emerged from the dome buildings to see what was going on. Down the winding ramps of the buildings on our side of the wide, sandy street they came – and from the buildings on the other side of the street, plodding through the sand, blinking brown eyes at us, not making a sound.

Allenby pointed at the third orbit and thumped his chest. The chief squeaked and thumped his own chest and pointed at the copperish band around his head. Then he pointed at Allenby.

'I seem to have conveyed to him', Allenby said dryly, 'the fact that I'm chief of our party. Well, let's try again.'

He started over on the orbits. He didn't seem to be getting any place, so the rest of us watched the Martians instead. A last handful was straggling across the wide street.

'Curious,' said Gonzales. 'Note what happens when they reach the centre of the street.'

Each Martian, upon reaching the centre of the street, glanced at his feet – just for a moment – without even breaking stride. And then came on.

'What can they be looking at?' Gonzales wondered.

'The chief did it too,' Burton mused. 'Remember when he first came toward us?'

We all stared intently at the middle of the street. We saw absolutely nothing but sand.

The Martians milled around us and watched Allenby and his orbits. A Martian child appeared from between two buildings across the street. On six-inch legs, it started across, got halfway, glanced downward – and came on.

'I don't get it,' Burton said. 'What in hell are they *looking* at?'

The child reached the crowd and squeaked a thin, high note.

A number of things happened at once.

Several members of the group around us glanced down, and along the edge of the crowd nearest the centre of the street there was a mild stir as individuals drifted off to either side. Quite casually – nothing at all urgent about it. They just moved concertedly to get farther away from the centre of the street, not taking their interested gaze off us for one second in the process.

Even the chief glanced up from Allenby's concentric circles at the child's squeak. And Randolph, who had been fidgeting uncomfortably and paying very little attention to our conversation, decided that he must answer Nature's call. He moved off into the dunes surrounding the village. Or, rather, he started to move.

The moment he set off across the wide street, the little Martian chief was in front of him, brown eyes wide, hands out before him as if to thrust Randolph back.

Again six safeties clicked. The Martians didn't even blink at the sudden appearance of our guns. Probably the only weapon they recognized was a club, or maybe a rock.

'What can the matter be?' Randolph said.

He took another step forward. The chief squeaked and stood his ground. Randolph had to stop or bump into him. Randolph stopped.

The chief squeaked, looking right into the bore of Randolph's gun.

'Hold still,' Allenby told Randolph, 'till we know what's up.'

Allenby made an interrogative sound at the chief. The chief squeaked and pointed at the ground. We looked. He was pointing at his shadow.

Randolph stirred uncomfortably.

'Hold still,' Allenby warned him, and again he made the questioning sound.

The chief pointed up the street. Then he pointed down the street. He bent to touch his shadow, thumping it with thin fingers. Then he pointed at the wall of a house nearby.

We all looked.

Straight lines had been painted on the curved brick-coloured wall, up and down and across, to form many small squares about four inches across. In each square was a bit of squiggly writing, in blackish paint, and a small wooden peg jutting out from the wall.

Burton said, 'Looks like a damn crossword puzzle.'

'Look,' said Janus. 'In the lower right corner – a metal ring hanging from one of the pegs.'

And that was all we saw on the wall. Hundreds of squares with figures in them – a small peg set in each – and a ring hanging on one of the pegs.

'You know what?' Allenby said slowly. 'I think it's a calendar! Just a second – thirty squares wide by twenty-two high – that's six hundred and sixty. And that bottom line has twenty-six – twenty-*seven* squares. Six hundred and eighty-seven squares in all. That's how many days there are in the Martian year!'

He looked thoughtfully at the metal ring. 'I'll bet that ring is hanging from the peg in the square that represents *today*. They must move it along every day, to keep track. . . .'

'What's a calendar got to do with my crossing the street?' Randolph asked in a pained tone.

He started to take another step. The chief squeaked as if it were a matter of desperate concern that he make us understand. Randolph stopped again and swore impatiently.

Allenby made his questioning sound again.

The chief pointed emphatically at his shadow, then at the communal calendar – and we could see now that he was pointing at the metal ring.

Burton said slowly, 'I think he's trying to tell us that this is *today*. And such and such a *time* of day. I bet he's using his shadow as a sundial.'

'Perhaps,' Allenby granted.

Randolph said, 'If this monkey doesn't let me go in another minute—'

The chief squeaked, eyes concerned.

'Stand still,' Allenby ordered. 'He's trying to warn you of some danger.'

The chief pointed down the street again and, instead of squealing, revealed that there was another sound at his command. He said, 'Whoooooosh!'

We all stared at the end of the street.

Nothing! Just the wide avenue between the houses, and the high sand dune down at the end of it, from which we had first looked upon the village.

The chief described a large circle with one hand, sweeping the hand above his head, down to his knees, up again, as fast as he could. He pursed his monkey-lips and said, 'Whooooooooosh!' And made the circle again.

A Martian emerged from the door in the side of a house across the avenue and blinked at the Sun, as if he had just awakened. Then he saw what was going on below and blinked again, this time in interest. He made his way down around the winding ramp and started to cross the street.

About halfway, he paused, eyed the calendar on the house wall, glanced at his shadow. Then he got down on his hands and knees and *crawled* across the middle of the street. Once past the middle, he rose, walked the rest of the way to join one of the groups and calmly stared at us along with the rest of them.

'They're all crazy,' Randolph said disgustedly. 'I'm going to cross that street!'

'Shut up. So it's a certain time of a certain day,' Allenby mused. 'And, from the way the chief is acting, he's afraid for you to cross the street. And that other one just *crawled*. By God, do you know what this might tie in with?'

We were silent for a moment. Then Gonzales said, 'Of course!' And Burton said, 'The *holes*!'

'Exactly,' said Allenby. 'Maybe whatever made – or makes – the holes comes right down the centre of the street here. Maybe that's why they built the village this way – to make room for—'

'For what?' Randolph asked unhappily, shifting his feet.

'I don't know,' Allenby said. He looked thoughtfully at the chief. 'That circular motion he made – could he have been describing something that went around and around the planet? Something like – oh, no!' Allenby eyes glazed. 'I wouldn't believe it in a million years.'

His gaze went to the far end of the street, to the high sand dune that rose there. The chief seemed to be waiting for something to happen.

'I'm going to crawl,' Randolph stated. He got to his hands and knees and began to creep across the centre of the avenue.

The chief let him go.

The sand dune at the end of the street suddenly erupted. A forty-foot spout of dust shot straight out from the sloping side, as if a bullet had emerged. Powdered sand hazed the air, yellowed it almost the full length of the avenue. Grains of sand stung the skin and rattled minutely on the houses.

WhoooSSSHHHHHH!

Randolph dropped flat on his belly. He didn't have to continue his trip. He had made other arrangements.

That night in the ship, while we all sat around, still shaking our heads every once in a while, Allenby talked with Earth. He sat there, wearing the headphones, trying to make himself understood above the godawful static.

'. . . an exceedingly small body,' he repeated wearily to his unbelieving audience, 'about four inches in diameter. It travels at a mean distance of four feet above the surface of the planet, at a velocity yet to be calculated. Its unique nature results in many hitherto unobserved – I might say even unimagined – phenomena.' He stared blankly in front of him for a moment, then delivered the understatement of his life. 'The discovery may necessitate a re-examination of many of our basic postulates in the physical sciences.'

The headphones squawked.

Patiently, Allenby assured Earth that he was entirely serious, and reiterated the results of his observations. I suppose that he, an astronomer, was twice as flabbergasted as the rest of us. On the other hand, perhaps he was better equipped to adjust to the evidence.

'Evidently,' he said, 'when the body was formed, it travelled at such fantastic velocity as to enable it to' – his voice was almost a whisper – 'to punch holes in things.'

The headphones squawked.

'In rocks,' Allenby said, 'in mountains, in anything that got in its way. And now the holes form a large portion of its fixed orbit.'

Squawk.

'Its mass must be in the order of—'

Squawk.

'—process of making the holes slowed it, so that now it travels just fast enough—'

Squawk.

'—maintain its orbit and penetrate occasional objects such as—'

Squawk.

'—and sand dunes—'

Squawk.

'My God, I *know* it's a mathematical monstrosity,' Allenby snarled. '*I* didn't put it there!'

Squawk.

Allenby was silent for a moment. Then he said slowly, 'A name?'

Squawk.

'H'm,' said Allenby. 'Well, well.' He appeared to brighten just a little. 'So it's up to ɪne, as leader of the expedition, to name it?'

Squawk.

'Well, well,' he said.

That chop-licking tone was in his voice. We'd heard it all too often before. We shuddered, waiting.

'Inasmuch as Mars' outermost moon is called Deimos, and the next Phobos,' he said, 'I think I shall name the third moon of Mars – *Bottomos*.'

Arthur C. Clarke
The star

It is 3000 light-years to the Vatican. Once I believed that space could have no power over Faith. Just as I believed that the heavens declared the glory of God's handiwork. Now I have seen that handiwork, and my faith is sorely troubled.

I stare at the crucifix that hangs on the cabin wall above the Mark VI computer, and for the first time in my life I wonder if it is no more than an empty symbol.

I have told no one yet, but the truth cannot be concealed. The data are there for anyone to read, recorded on the countless miles of magnetic tape and the thousands of photographs we are carrying back to Earth. Other scientists can interpret them as easily as I can – more easily, in all probability. I am not one who would condone that tampering with the Truth which often gave my Order a bad name in the olden days.

The crew is already sufficiently depressed; I wonder how they will take this ultimate irony. Few of them have any religious faith, yet they will not relish using this final weapon in their campaign against me – that private, good-natured but fundamentally serious war which lasted all the way from Earth. It amused them to have a Jesuit as chief astrophysicist: Dr Chandler, for instance, could never get over it (why are medical men such notorious atheists?). Sometimes he would meet me on the observation deck, where the lights are always low so that the stars shine with undiminished glory. He would come up to me in the gloom and stand staring out of the great oval port, while the heavens crawled slowly round us as the ship turned end over end with the residual spin we had never bothered to correct.

'Well, Father,' he would say at last. 'It goes on for ever and for ever, and perhaps *Something* made it. But how you can believe that Something has a special interest in us and our miserable little world – that just beats me.' Then the argument would start, while the stars and nebulae would swing around us in silent, endless arcs beyond the flawlessly clear plastic of the observation port.

It was, I think, the apparent incongruity of my position which . . . yes, *amused* . . . the crew. In vain I would point to my three papers in the *Astrophysical Journal*, my five in the *Monthly Notices of the Royal Astronomical Society*. I would remind them that our Order has long been famous for its scientific works. We may be few now, but ever since the eighteenth century we have made contributions to astronomy and geophysics out of all proportion to our numbers.

Will my report on the Phoenix Nebula end our thousand years of history? It will end, I fear, much more than that.

I do not know who gave the Nebula its name, which seems to me a very bad one. If it contains a prophecy, it is one which cannot be verified for several thousand million years. Even the word 'nebula' is misleading: this is a far smaller object than those stupendous clouds of mist – the stuff of unborn stars – which are scattered throughout the length of the Milky Way. On the cosmic scale, indeed, the Phoenix Nebula is a tiny thing – a tenuous shell of gas surrounding a single star.

Or what is left of a star. . . .

The Rubens engraving of Loyola seems to mock me as it hangs there above the spectrophotometer tracings. What would *you*, Father, have made of this knowledge that has come into my keeping, so far from the little world that was all the universe you knew? Would your faith have risen to the challenge, as mine has failed to do?

You gaze into the distance, Father, but I have travelled a distance beyond any that you could have imagined when you founded our Order a thousand years ago. No other survey ship has been so far from Earth: we are at the very frontiers of the explored universe. We set out to reach the Phoenix Nebula, we succeeded, and we are homeward bound with our burden of knowledge. I wish I could lift that burden from my shoulders, but I call to you in vain across the centuries and the light-years that lie between us.

On the book you are holding the words are plain to read. AD

MAIOREM DEI GLORIAM the message runs, but it is a message I can no longer believe. Would you still believe it, if you could see what we have found?

We knew, of course, what the Phoenix Nebula was. Every year, in *our* galaxy alone, more than a hundred stars explode, blazing for a few hours or days with thousands of times their normal brilliance before they sink back into death and obscurity. Such are the ordinary novae – the commonplace disasters of the universe. I have recorded the spectrograms and light-curves of dozens, since I started working at the lunar observatory.

But three or four times in every thousand years occurs something beside which even a nova pales into total insignificance.

When a star becomes a *supernova*, it may for a little while outshine all the massed suns of the galaxy. The Chinese astronomers watched this happen in A.D. 1054, not knowing what it was they saw. Five centuries later, in 1572, a supernova blazed in Cassiopeia so brilliantly that it was visible in the daylight sky. There have been three more in the thousand years that have passed since then.

Our mission was to visit the remnants of such a catastrophe, to reconstruct the events that led up to it and, if possible, to learn its cause. We came slowly in through the concentric shells of gas that had been blasted out six thousand years before, yet were expanding still. They were immensely hot, radiating still with a fierce violet light, but far too tenuous to do us any damage. When the star had exploded, its outer layers had been driven upwards with such speed that they had escaped completely from its gravitational field. Now they formed a hollow shell large enough to engulf a thousand solar systems, and at its centre burned the tiny, fantastic object which the star had now become – a white dwarf, smaller than the Earth yet weighing a million times as much.

The glowing gas shells were all around us, banishing the normal night of interstellar space. We were flying into the centre of a cosmic bomb that had detonated millennia ago and whose incandescent fragments were still hurtling apart. The immense scale of the explosion, and the fact that the debris already covered a volume of space many billions of miles across, robbed the scene of any visible movement. It would take decades before the unaided eye could detect any motion in these tortured wisps and eddies of gas, yet the sense of turbulent expansion was over-whelming.

We had checked our primary drive hours before, and were drifting slowly towards the fierce little star ahead. Once it had been a sun like our own, but it had squandered in a few hours the energy that should have kept it shining for a million years. Now it was a shrunken miser, hoarding its resources as if trying to make amends for its prodigal youth.

No one seriously expected to find planets. If there had been any before the explosion, they would have been boiled into puffs of vapour, and their substance lost in the greater wreckage of the star itself. But we made the automatic search, as always when approaching an unknown sun, and presently we found a single small world circling the star at an immense distance. It must have been the Pluto of this vanished solar system, orbiting on the frontiers of the night. Too far from the central sun ever to have known life, its remoteness had saved it from the fate of all its lost companions.

The passing fires had seared its rocks and burnt away the mantle of frozen gas that must have covered it in the days before the disaster. We landed, and we found the Vault.

Its builders had made sure that we should. The monolithic marker that stood above the entrance was now a fused stump, but even the first long-range photographs told us that here was the work of intelligence. A little later we detected the continent-wide pattern of radioactivity that had been buried in the rock. Even if the pylon above the Vault had been destroyed, this would have remained, an immovable and all but eternal beacon calling to the stars. Our ship fell towards this gigantic bull's-eye like an arrow into its target.

The pylon must have been a mile high when it was built, but now it looked like a candle that had melted down into a puddle of wax. It took us a week to drill through the fused rock, since we did not have the proper tools for a task like this. We were astronomers, not archaeologists, but we could improvise. Our original programme was forgotten: this lonely monument, reared at such labour at the greatest possible distance from the doomed sun, could have only one meaning. A civilization which knew it was about to die had made its last bid for immortality.

It will take us generations to examine all the treasures that were placed in the Vault. *They* had plenty of time to prepare, for their sun must have given its first warnings many years before the final detonation. Everything that they wished to preserve, all the fruits of their genius, they brought here to this distant world in the days before the end, hoping that some other race would find them and that they would not be utterly forgotten.

If only they had had a little more time! They could travel freely enough between the planets of their own sun, but they had not yet learned to cross the interstellar gulfs, and the nearest solar system was a hundred light-years away.

Even if they had not been so disturbingly human as their sculpture shows, we could not have helped admiring them and grieving for their fate. They left thousands of visual records and the machines for projecting them, together with elaborate pictorial instructions from which it will not be difficult to learn their written language. We have examined many of these records, and brought to life for the first time in 6000 years the warmth and beauty of a civilization which in many ways must have been superior to our own. Perhaps they only showed us the best, and one can hardly blame them. But their worlds were very lovely, and their cities were built with a grace that matches anything of ours. We have watched them at work and play, and listened to their musical speech sounding across the centuries. One scene is still before my eyes – a group of children on a beach of strange blue sand, playing in the waves as children play on Earth.

And sinking into the sea, still warm and friendly and life-giving, is the sun that will soon turn traitor and obliterate all this innocent happiness.

Perhaps if we had not been so far from home and so vulnerable to loneliness we should not have been so deeply moved. Many of us had seen the ruins of ancient civilizations on other worlds, but they had never affected us so profoundly.

This tragedy was unique. It was one thing for a race to fail and die, as nations and cultures have done on Earth. But to be destroyed

so completely in the full flower of its achievement, leaving no sur-
vivors – how could that be reconciled with the mercy of God?

My colleagues have asked me that, and I have given what
answers I can. Perhaps you could have done better, Father Loyola,
but I have found nothing in the *Exercitia Spiritualia* that helps me
here. They were not an evil people: I do not know what gods they
worshipped, if indeed they worshipped any. But I have looked
back at them across the centuries, and have watched while the
loveliness they used their last strength to preserve was brought
forth again into the light of their shrunken sun.

I know the answers that my colleagues will give when they get
back to Earth. They will say that the universe has no purpose and
no plan; that, since a hundred suns explode every year in our
galaxy, at this very moment some race is dying in the depths of
space. Whether that race has done good or evil during its lifetime
will make no difference in the end: there is no divine justice, *for
there is no God.*

Yet, of course, what we have seen proves nothing of the sort.
Anyone who argues thus is being swayed by emotion, not logic.
God has no need to justify His actions to man. He who built the
universe can destroy it when He chooses. It is arrogance – it is
perilously near blasphemy – for us to say what He may or may
not do.

This I could have accepted, hard though it is to look upon
whole worlds and peoples thrown into the furnace. But there
comes a point when even the deepest faith must falter, and now,
as I look at my calculations, I know I have reached that point at
last.

We could not tell, before we reached the nebula, how long ago
the explosion took place. Now, from the astronomical evidence
and the record in the rocks of that one surviving planet, I have
been able to date it very exactly. I know in what year the light of
this colossal conflagration reached Earth. I know how brilliantly
the supernova whose corpse now dwindles behind our speeding
ship once shone in terrestrial skies. I know how it must have
blazed low in the East before sunrise, like a beacon in that
Oriental dawn.

There can be no reasonable doubt: the ancient mystery is solved at last. Yet – O God, there were so many stars you *could* have used.

What was the need to give these people to the fire, that the symbol of their passing might shine above Bethlehem?

Henry Kuttner
Two-handed engine

Ever since the days of Orestes there have been men with Furies following them. It wasn't until the twenty-second century that mankind made itself a set of real Furies, out of steel. Mankind had reached a crisis by then. They had a good reason for building man-shaped Furies that would dog the footsteps of all men who kill men. Nobody else. There was by then no other crime of any importance.

It worked very simply. Without warning, a man who thought himself safe would suddenly hear the steady footfalls behind him. He would turn and see the two-handed engine walking towards him, shaped like a man of steel, and more incorruptible than any man not made of steel could be. Only then would the murderer know he had been tried and condemned by the omniscient electronic minds that knew society as no human mind could ever know it.

For the rest of his days, the man would hear those footsteps behind him. A moving jail with invisible bars that shut him off from the world. Never in life would he be alone again. And one day – he never knew when – the jailer would turn executioner.

Danner leaned back comfortably in his contoured restaurant-chair and rolled expensive wine across his tongue, closing his eyes to enjoy the taste of it better. He felt perfectly safe. Oh, perfectly protected. For nearly an hour now he had been sitting here, ordering the most expensive food, enjoying the music breathing softly through the air, the murmurous, well-bred hush of his fellow diners. It was a good place to be. It was very good, having so much money – now.

True, he had had to kill to get the money. But no guilt troubled him. There was no guilt if you aren't found out, and Danner had

protection. Protection straight from the source, which was something new in the world. Danner knew the consequences of killing.
If Hartz hadn't satisfied him that he was perfectly safe, Danner
would never have pulled the trigger. . . .

The memory of an archaic word flickered through his mind
briefly. *Sin.* It evoked nothing. Once it had something to do with
guilt, in an incomprehensible way. Not any more. Mankind had
been through too much. Sin was meaningless now.

He dismissed the thought and tried the heart-of-palms salad.
He found he didn't like it. Oh well, you had to expect things like
that. Nothing was perfect. He sipped the wine again, liking the
way the glass seemed to vibrate like something faintly alive in his
hand. It was good wine. He thought of ordering more, but then
he thought no, save it, next time. There was so much before him,
waiting to be enjoyed. Any risk was worth it. And, of course, in
this there had been no risk.

Danner was a man born at the wrong time. He was old enough
to remember the last days of utopia, young enough to be trapped
in the new scarcity economy the machines had clamped down on
their makers. In his early youth he'd had access to free luxuries,
like everybody else. He could remember the old days when he was
an adolescent and the last of the Escape Machines were still
operating, the glamorous, bright, impossible, vicarious visions
that didn't really exist and never could have. But then the scarcity
economy swallowed up pleasure. Now you got necessities but no
more. Now you had to work. Danner hated every minute of it.

When the swift change came, he'd been too young and unskilled
to compete in the scramble. The rich men today were the men
who had built fortunes on cornering the few luxuries the machines
still produced. All Danner had left were bright memories and a
dull, resentful feeling of having been cheated. All he wanted were
the bright days back, and he didn't care how he got them.

Well, now he had them. He touched the rim of the wine glass
with his finger, feeling it sing silently against the touch. Blown
glass? he wondered. He was too ignorant of luxury items to
understand. But he'd learn. He had the rest of his life to learn in,
and be happy.

He looked up across the restaurant and saw through the transparent dome of the roof the melting towers of the city. They made a stone forest as far as he could see. And this was only one city. When he was tired of it, there were more. Across the country, across the planet the network lay that linked city with city in a webwork like a vast, intricate, half-alive monster. Call it society.

He felt it tremble a little beneath him.

He reached for the wine and drank quickly. The faint uneasiness that seemed to shiver the foundations of the city was something new. It was because – yes, certainly it was because of a new fear.

It was because he had not been found out.

That made no sense. Of course the city was complex. Of course it operated on a basis of incorruptible machines. They, and only they, kept man from becoming very quickly another extinct animal. And of these the analogue computers, the electronic calculators, were the gyroscope of all living. They made and enforced the laws that were necessary now to keep mankind alive. Danner didn't understand much of the vast changes that had swept over society in his lifetime, but this much even he knew.

So perhaps it made sense that he felt society shiver because he sat here luxurious on foam-rubber, sipping wine, hearing soft music, and no Fury standing behind his chair to prove that the calculators were still guardians for mankind. . . .

If not even the Furies are incorruptible, what can a man believe in?

It was at that exact moment that the Fury arrived.

Danner heard every sound suddenly die out around him. His fork was halfway to his lips, but he paused, frozen, and looked up across the table and the restaurant towards the door.

The Fury was taller than a man. It stood there for a moment, the afternoon sun striking a blinding spot of brightness from its shoulder. It had no face, but it seemed to scan the restaurant leisurely, table by table. Then it stepped in under the door-frame and the sun-spot slid away and it was like a tall man encased in steel, walking slowly between the tables.

Danner said to himself, laying down his untasted food, 'Not for me. Everyone else here is wondering. I *know*.'

And like a memory in a drowning man's mind, clear, sharp and condensed into a moment, yet every detail clear, he remembered what Hartz had told him. As a drop of water can pull into its reflection a wide panorama condensed into a tiny focus, so time seemed to focus down to a pinpoint the half-hour Danner and Hartz had spent together, in Hartz's office with the walls that could go transparent at the push of a button.

He saw Hartz again, plump and blond, with the sad eyebrows. A man who looked relaxed until he began to talk, and then you felt the burning quality about him, the air of driven tension that made even the air around him to be restlessly trembling. Danner stood before Hartz's desk again in memory, feeling the floor hum faintly against his soles with the heartbeat of the computers. You could see them through the glass, smooth, shiny things with winking lights in banks like candles burning in coloured glass cups. You could hear their faraway chattering as they ingested facts, mediated them, and then spoke in numbers like cryptic oracles. It took men like Hartz to understand what the oracles meant.

'I have a job for you,' Hartz said. 'I want a man killed.'

'Oh, no,' Danner said. 'What kind of a fool do you think I am?'

'Now, wait a minute. You can use money, can't you?'

'What for?' Danner asked bitterly. 'A fancy funeral?'

'A life of luxury. I know you're not a fool. I know damned well you wouldn't do what I ask unless you got money *and* protection. That's what I can offer. Protection.'

Danner looked through the transparent wall at the computers. 'Sure,' he said.

'No, I mean it. I—' Hartz hesitated, glancing around the room a little uneasily, as if he hardly trusted his own precautions for making sure of privacy. 'This is something new,' he said. 'I can re-direct any Fury I want to.'

'Oh, sure,' Danner said again.

'It's true. I'll show you. I can pull a Fury off any victim I choose.'

'How?'

'That's my secret. Naturally. In effect, though, I've found a way to feed in false data, so the machines come out with the wrong verdict before conviction, or the wrong orders after conviction.'

'But that's – dangerous, isn't it?'

'Dangerous?' Hartz looked at Danner under his sad eyebrows.

'Well, yes. I think so. That's why I don't do it often. I've done it only once, as a matter of fact. Theoretically, I'd worked out the method. I tested it, just once. It worked. I'll do it again, to prove to you I'm telling the truth. After that I'll do it once again, to protect you. And that will be it. I don't want to upset the calculators any more than I have to. Once your job's done, I won't have to.'

'Who do you want killed?'

Involuntarily Hartz glanced upward, towards the heights of the building where the top-rank executive officers were. 'O'Reilly,' he said.

Danner glanced upward too, as if he could see through the floor and observe the exalted shoe-soles of O'Reilly, Controller of the Calculators, pacing an expensive carpet overhead.

'It's very simple,' Hartz said. 'I want his job.'

'Why not do your own killing, then, if you're so sure you can stop the Furies?'

'Because that would give the whole thing away,' Hartz said impatiently. 'Use your head. I've got an obvious motive. It wouldn't take a calculator to figure out who profits most if O'Reilly dies. If I saved myself from a Fury, people would start wondering how I did it. But you've got no motive for killing O'Reilly. Nobody but the calculators would know, and I'll take care of them.'

'How do I know you can do it?'

'Simple. Watch.'

Hartz got up and walked quickly across the resilient carpet that gave his steps a falsely youthful bounce. There was a waist-high counter on the far side of the room, with a slanting glass screen on it. Nervously Hartz punched a button, and a map of a section ⋅ of the city sprang out in bold lines on its surface.

'I've got to find a sector where a Fury's in operation now,' he explained. The map flickered and he pressed the button again. The unstable outlines of the city streets wavered and brightened and then went out as he scanned the sections fast and nervously. Then a map flashed on which had three wavering streaks of coloured light criss-crossing it, intersecting at one point near the centre. The point moved very slowly across the map, at just about the speed of a walking man reduced to miniature in scale with the street he walked on. Around him the coloured lines wheeled slowly, keeping their focus always steady on the single point.

'There,' Hartz said, leaning forward to read the printed name of the street. A drop of sweat fell from his forehead on to the glass, and he wiped it uneasily away with his fingertip. 'There's a man with a Fury assigned to him. All right, now. I'll show you. Look here.'

Above the desk was a news-screen. Hartz clicked it on and watched impatiently while a street scene swam into focus. Crowds, traffic noises, people hurrying, people loitering. And in the middle of the crowd a little oasis of isolation, an island in the sea of humanity. Upon that moving island two occupants dwelt, like a Crusoe and a Friday, alone. One of the two was a haggard man who watched the ground as he walked. The other islander in this deserted spot was a tall, shining man-formed shape that followed at his heels.

As if invisible walls surrounded them, pressing back the crowds they walked through, the two moved in an empty space that closed in behind them, opened up before them. Some of the passers-by stared, some looked away in embarrassment or uneasiness. Some watched with a frank anticipation, wondering perhaps at just what moment the Friday would lift his steel arm and strike the Crusoe dead.

'Watch, now,' Hartz said nervously. 'Just a minute. I'm going to pull the Fury off this man. Wait.' He crossed to his desk, opened a drawer, bent secretively over it. Danner heard a series of clicks from inside, and then the brief chatter of tapped keys. 'Now,' Hartz said, closing the drawer. He moved the back of his hand across his forehead. 'Warm in here, isn't it? Let's get a closer look. You'll see something happen in a minute.'

Back to the news-screen. He flicked the focus switch and the street scene expanded, the man and his pacing jailer swooped upward into close focus. The man's face seemed to partake subtly of the impassive quality of the robot's. You would have thought they had lived a long time together, and perhaps they had. Time is a flexible element, infinitely long sometimes in a very short space.

'Wait until they get out of the crowd,' Hartz said. 'This mustn't be conspicuous. There, he's turning now.' The man, seeming to move at random, wheeled at an alley corner and went down the narrow, dark passage away from the thoroughfare. The eye of the news-screen followed him as closely as the robot.

'So you do have cameras that can do that,' Danner said with interest. 'I always thought so. How's it done? Are they spotted at every corner, or is a beam trans—'

'Never mind,' Hartz said. 'Trade secret. Just watch. We'll have to wait until— No, no! Look, he's going to try it now!'

The man glanced furtively behind him. The robot was just turning the corner in his wake. Hartz darted back to his desk and pulled the drawer open. His hand poised over it, his eyes watched the screen anxiously. It was curious how the man in the alley, though he could have no inkling that other eyes watched, looked up and scanned the sky, gazing directly for a moment into the attentive, hidden camera and the eyes of Hartz and Danner. They saw him take a sudden, deep breath, and break into a run.

From Hartz's drawer sounded a metallic click. The robot, which had moved smoothly into a run the moment the man did, checked itself awkwardly and seemed to totter on its steel for an instant. It slowed. It stopped like an engine grinding to a halt. It stood motionless.

At the edge of the camera's range you could see the man's face, looking backward, mouth open with shock as he saw the impossible happen. The robot stood there in the alley, making indecisive motions as if the new orders Hartz pumped into its mechanisms were grating against inbuilt orders in whatever receptor it had. Then it turned its steel back upon the man in the alley and went smoothly, almost sedately, away down the street, walking as precisely as if it were obeying valid orders, not stripping the very gears of society in its aberrant behaviour.

You got one last glimpse of the man's face, looking strangely stricken, as if his last friend in the world had left him.

Hartz switched off the screen. He wiped his forehead again. He went to the glass wall and looked out and down as if he were half afraid the calculators might know what he had done. Looking very small against the background of the metal giants, he said over his shoulder, 'Well, Danner?'

Was it well? There had been more talk, of course, more persuasion, a raising of the bribe. But Danner knew his mind had been made up from that moment. A calculated risk, and worth it. Well worth it. Except—

In the deathly silence of the restaurant all motion had stopped. The Fury walked calmly between the tables, threading its shining way, touching no one. Every face blanched, turned towards it. Every mind thought, 'Can it be for me?' Even the entirely innocent thought, 'This is the first mistake they've ever made, and it's come for me. The first mistake, but there's no appeal and I could never prove a thing.' For, while guilt had no meaning in this world, punishment did have meaning, and punishment could be blind, striking like the lightning.

Danner between set teeth told himself over and over, 'Not for me. I'm safe. I'm protected. It hasn't come for me.' And yet he thought how strange it was – what a coincidence, wasn't it – that there should be two murderers here under this expensive glass roof today? Himself, and the one the Fury had come for.

He released his fork and heard it clink on the plate. He looked down at it and the food, and suddenly his mind rejected everything around him and went diving off on a fugitive tangent like an ostrich into sand. He thought about food. How did asparagus grow? What did raw food look like? He had never seen any. Food came ready-cooked out of restaurant kitchens or automatic slots. Potatoes, now. What did they look like? A moist white mash? No, for sometimes they were oval slices, so the thing itself must be oval. But not round. Sometimes you got them in long strips, squared off at the ends. Something quite long and oval, then chopped into even lengths. And white, of course. And they grew underground, he was almost sure. Long, thin roots twining white arms among the pipes and conduits he had seen laid bare when the streets were under repair. How strange that he should be eating something like thin, ineffectual human arms that embraced the sewers of the city and writhed pallidly where the worms had their being. And where he himself, when the Fury found him, might. . . .

He pushed the plate away.

An indescribable rustling and murmuring in the room lifted his eyes for him as if he were an automaton. The Fury was halfway across the room now, and it was almost funny to see the relief of those whom it had passed by. Two or three of the women had buried their faces in their hands, and one man had slipped quietly from his chair in a dead faint as the Fury's passing released their private dreads back into their hidden wells.

The thing was quite close now. It looked to be about seven feet tall, and its motion was very smooth, which was unexpected when you thought about it. Smoother than human motions. Its feet fell with a heavy, measured tread upon the carpet. Thud, thud, thud. Danner tried impersonally to calculate what it weighed. You always heard that they made no sound except for that terrible tread, but this one creaked very slightly somewhere. It had no features, but the human mind couldn't help sketching in lightly a sort of airy face upon that blank steel surface, with eyes that seemed to search the room.

It was coming closer. Now all eyes were converging towards Danner. And the Fury came straight on. It almost looked as if—

'No!' Danner said to himself. 'Oh, no, this can't be!' He felt like a man in a nightmare, on the verge of waking. 'Let me wake soon,' he thought. 'Let me wake *now*, before it gets here!'

But he did not wake. And now the thing stood over him, and the thudding footsteps stopped. There was the faintest possible creaking as it towered over his table, motionless, waiting, its featureless face turned towards his.

Danner felt an intolerable tide of heat surge up into his face – rage, shame, disbelief. His heart pounded so hard the room swam and a sudden pain like jagged lightning shot through his head from temple to temple.

He was on his feet, shouting.

'No, no!' he yelled at the impassive steel. 'You're wrong! You've made a mistake! Go away, you damned fool! You're wrong, you're wrong!' He groped on the table without looking down, found his plate and hurled it straight at the armoured chest before him. China shattered. Spilled food smeared a white and green and brown stain over the steel. Danner floundered out of his chair, around the table, past the tall metal figure towards the door.

All he could think of now was Hartz.

Seas of faces swam by him on both sides as he stumbled out of the restaurant. Some watched with avid curiosity, their eyes seeking him. Some did not look at all, but gazed at their plates rigidly or covered their faces with their hands. Behind him the measured tread came on, and the rhythmic faint creak from somewhere inside the armour.

The faces fell away on both sides and he went through a door without any awareness of opening it. He was in the street. Sweat bathed him and the air struck icy, though it was not a cold day. He looked blindly left and right, and then plunged for a bank of phone booths half a block away, the image of Hartz swimming before his eyes so clearly he blundered into people without seeing them. Dimly he heard indignant voices begin to speak and then die into awestruck silence. The way cleared magically before him. He walked in the newly created island of his isolation up to the nearest booth.

After he had closed the glass door the thunder of his own blood in his ears made the little sound-proofed booth reverberate. Through the door he saw the robot stand passionlessly waiting, the smear of spilled food still streaking its chest like some robotic ribbon of honour across a steel shirt-front.

Danner tried to dial a number. His fingers were like rubber. He breathed deep and hard, trying to pull himself together. An irrelevant thought floated across the surface of his mind: I forgot to pay for my dinner. And then: A lot of good the money will do me now. Oh, damn Hartz, damn him, damn him!

He got the number.

A girl's face flashed into sharp, clear colours on the screen before him. Good, expensive screens in the public booths in this part of town, his mind noted impersonally.

'This is Controller Hartz's office. May I help you?'

Danner tried twice before he could give his name. He wondered if the girl could see him, and behind him, dimly through the glass, the tall waiting figure. He couldn't tell, because she dropped her eyes immediately to what must have been a list on the unseen table before her.

'I'm sorry. Mr Hartz is out. He won't be back today.'

The screen drained of light and colour.

Danner folded back the door and stood up. His knees were unsteady. The robot stood just far enough back to clear the hinge of the door. For a moment they faced each other. Danner heard himself suddenly in the midst of an uncontrollable giggling which even he realized verged on hysteria. The robot with the smear of food like a ribbon of honour looked so ridiculous. Danner to his dim surprise found that all this while he had been clutching the restaurant napkin in his left hand.

'Stand back,' he said to the robot. 'Let me out. Oh, you fool, don't you know this is a mistake?' His voice quavered. The robot creaked faintly and stepped back.

'It's bad enough to have you follow me,' Danner said. 'At least you might be clean. A dirty robot is too much – too much—' The thought was idiotically unbearable, and he heard tears in his voice. Half-laughing, half-weeping, he wiped the steel chest clean and threw the napkin to the floor.

And it was at that very instant, with the feel of the hard chest still vivid in his memory, that realization finally broke through the protective screen of hysteria, and he remembered the truth. He would never in life be alone again. Never while he drew breath. And when he died it would be at these steel hands, perhaps upon this steel chest, with the passionless face bent to his, the last thing in life he would ever see. No human companion, but the black steel skull of the Fury.

It took him nearly a week to reach Hartz. During the week, he changed his mind about how long it might take a man followed by a Fury to go mad. The last thing he saw at night was the street light shining through the curtains of his expensive hotel suite upon the metal shoulder of his jailer. All night long, waking from uneasy slumber, he could hear the faint creaking of some inward mechanism functioning under the armour. And each time he woke it was to wonder whether he would ever wake again. Would the blow fall while he slept? And what kind of blow? How did the Furies execute? It was always a faint relief to see the bleak light of early morning shine upon the watcher by his bed. At least he had lived through the night. But was this living? And was it worth the burden?

He kept his hotel suite. Perhaps the management would have liked him to go, but nothing was said. Possibly they didn't dare. Life took on a strange, transparent quality, like something seen through an invisible wall. Outside of trying to reach Hartz, there was nothing Danner wanted to do. The old desires for luxuries, entertainment, travel had melted away. He wouldn't have travelled alone.

He did spend hours in the public library, reading all that was available about the Furies. It was here that he first encountered the two haunting and frightening lines Milton wrote when the world was small and simple – mystifying lines that made no certain sense to anybody until man created a Fury out of steel, in his own image.

But that two-handed engine at the door
Stands ready to smite once, and smite no more. . . .

Danner glanced up at his own two-handed engine, motionless at his shoulder, and thought of Milton and the long-ago times when life was simple and easy. He tried to picture the past. The twentieth century, when all civilizations together crashed over the brink in one majestic downfall to chaos. And the time before that, when people were . . . different, somehow. But how? It was too far and too strange. He could not imagine the time before the machines.

But he learned for the first time what had really happened, back there in his early years, when the bright world finally blinked out entirely and grey drudgery began. And the Furies were first forged in the likeness of man.

Before the really big wars began, technology advanced to the point where machines bred upon machines like living things, and there might have been an Eden on earth, with everybody's wants fully supplied, except that the social sciences fell too far behind the physical sciences. When the decimating wars came on, machines and people fought side by side, steel against steel and man against man, but man was the more perishable. The wars ended when there were no longer two societies left to fight against each other. Societies splintered apart into smaller and smaller groups until a state very close to anarchy set in.

The machines licked their metal wounds meanwhile and healed

each other as they had been built to do. They had no need for the social sciences. They went on calmly reproducing themselves and handing out to mankind the luxuries which the age of Eden had designed them to hand out. Imperfectly, of course. Incompletely, because some of their species were wiped out entirely and left no machines to breed and reproduce their kind. But most of them mined their raw materials, refined them, poured and cast the needed parts, made their own fuel, repaired their own injuries and maintained their breed upon the face of the earth with an efficiency man never even approached.

Meanwhile mankind splintered and splintered away. There were no longer any real groups, not even families. Men didn't need each other much. Emotional attachments dwindled. Men had been conditioned to accept vicarious surrogates and escapism was fatally easy. Men reoriented their emotions to the Escape Machines that fed them joyous, impossible adventure and made the waking world seem too dull to bother with. And the birth rate fell and fell. It was a very strange period. Luxury and chaos went hand in hand, anarchy and inertia were the same thing. And still the birth rate dropped. . . .

Eventually a few people recognized what was happening. Man as a species was on the way out. And man was helpless to do anything about it. But he had a powerful servant. So the time came when some unsung genius saw what would have to be done. Someone saw the situation clearly and set a new pattern in the biggest of the surviving electronic calculators. This was the goal he set: 'Mankind must be made self-responsible again. You will make this your only goal until you achieve the end.'

It was simple, but the changes it produced were worldwide and all human life on the planet altered drastically because of it. The machines were an integrated society, if man was not. And now they had a single set of orders which all of them reorganized to obey.

So the days of the free luxuries ended. The Escape Machines shut up shop. Men were forced back into groups for the sake of survival. They had to undertake now the work the machines withheld, and slowly, slowly, common needs and common interests began to spawn the almost lost feeling of human unity again.

But it was so slow. And no machine could put back into man what he had lost – the internalized conscience. Individualism had reached its ultimate stage and there had been no deterrent to crime for a long while. Without family or clan relations, not even feud retaliation occurred. Conscience failed, since no man identified with any other.

The real job of the machines now was to rebuild in man a realistic superego to save him from extinction. A self-responsible society would be a genuinely interdependent one, the leader identifying with the group, and a realistically internalized conscience which would forbid and punish 'sin' – the sin of injuring the group with which you identify.

And here the Furies came in.

The machines defined murder, under any circumstances, as the only human crime. This was accurate enough, since it is the only act which can irreplaceably destroy a unit of society.

The Furies couldn't prevent crime. Punishment never cures the criminal. But it can prevent others from committing crime through simple fear, when they see punishment administered to others. The Furies were the symbol of punishment. They overtly stalked the streets on the heels of their condemned victims, the outward and visible sign that murder is always punished, and punished most publicly and terribly. They were very efficient. They were never wrong. Or, at least, in theory they were never wrong, and considering the enormous quantities of information stored by now in the analogue computers it seemed likely that the justice of the machines was far more efficient than that of humans could be.

Some day man would rediscover sin. Without it he had come near to perishing entirely. With it, he might resume his authority over himself and the race of mechanized servants who were helping him to restore his species. But until that day the Furies would have to stalk the streets, man's conscience in metal guise, imposed by the machines man created a long time ago.

What Danner did during this time he scarcely knew. He thought a great deal of the old days when the Escape Machines still worked, before the machines rationed luxuries. He thought of this sullenly and with resentment, for he could see no point at all in the experiment mankind was embarked on. He had liked it better in the old days. And there were no Furies then, either.

He drank a good deal. Once he emptied his pockets into the hat of a legless beggar, because the man like himself was set apart from society by something new and terrible. For Danner it was the Fury. For the beggar it was life itself. Thirty years ago he would have lived or died unheeded, tended only by machines. That a beggar could survive at all, by begging, must be a sign that society was beginning to feel twinges of awakened fellow feeling with its members, but to Danner that meant nothing. He wouldn't be around long enough to know how the story came out.

He wanted to talk to the beggar, though the man tried to wheel himself away on his little platform.

'Listen,' Danner said urgently, following, searching his pockets. 'I want to tell you. It doesn't feel the way you think it would. It feels—'

He was quite drunk that night, and he followed the beggar until the man threw the money back at him and thrust himself away rapidly on his wheeled platform, while Danner leaned against a building and tried to believe in its solidity. But only the shadow of the Fury, falling across him from the street lamp, was real.

Later that night, somewhere in the dark, he attacked the Fury. He seemed to remember finding a length of pipe somewhere, and he struck showers of sparks from the great, impervious shoulders above him. Then he ran, doubling and twisting up alleys, and in the end he hid in a dark doorway, waiting, until the steady footsteps resounded through the night.

He fell asleep, exhausted.

It was the next day that he finally reached Hartz.

'What went wrong?' Danner asked. In the past week he had changed a good deal. His face was taking on, in its impassivity, an odd resemblance to the metal mask of the robot.

Hartz struck the desk edge a nervous blow, grimacing when he hurt his hand. The room seemed to be vibrating not with the pulse of the machines below but with his now tense energy.

'*Something* went wrong,' he said. 'I don't know yet. I—'

'You don't know!' Danner lost part of his impassivity.

'Now, wait.' Hartz made soothing motions with his hands.

'Just hang on a little longer. It'll be all right. You can—'

'How much longer have I got?' Danner asked. He looked over his shoulder at the tall Fury standing behind him, as if he were really asking the question of it, not Hartz. There was a feeling, somehow, about the way he said it that made you think he must have asked that question many times, looking up into the blank steel face, and would go on asking hopelessly until the answer came at last. But not in words. . . .

'I can't even find that out,' Hartz said. 'Damn it, Danner, this was a risk. You knew that.'

'You said you could control the computer. I saw you do it. I want to know why you didn't do what you promised.'

'Something went wrong, I tell you. It should have worked. The minute this – business – came up I fed in the data that should have protected you.'

'But what happened?'

Hartz got up and began to pace the resilient flooring. 'I just don't know. We don't understand the potentiality of the machines, that's all. I thought I could do it. But—'

'You *thought*!'

'I know I can do it. I'm still trying. I'm trying everything. After all, this is important to me, too. I'm working as fast as I can. That's why I couldn't see you before. I'm certain I can do it, if I can work this out my way. Damn it, Danner, it's complex. And it's not like juggling a comptometer. Look at those things out there.'

Danner didn't bother to look.

'You'd better do it,' he said. 'That's all.'

Hartz said furiously. 'Don't threaten me! Let me alone and I'll work it out. But don't threaten me.'

'You're in this too,' Danner said.

'How?' he asked.

'O'Reilly's dead. You paid me to kill him.'

Hartz shrugged. 'The Fury knows that,' he said. 'The computers know it. And it doesn't matter a damn bit. Your hand pulled the trigger, not mine.'

'We're both guilty. If I suffer for it, you—'

'Now, wait a minute. Get this straight. I thought you knew it.

It's a basis of law enforcement, and always has been. Nobody's punished for intention. Only for actions. I'm no more responsible for O'Reilly's death than the gun you used on him.'

'But you lied to me! You tricked me! I'll—'

Hartz went back to his desk and sat down on the edge of it.

'You'll do as I say, if you want to save yourself. I didn't trick you, I just made a mistake. Give me time and I'll retrieve it.'

'*How long?*'

This time both men looked at the Fury. It stood impassive.

'I don't know how long,' Danner answered his own question. 'You say you don't. Nobody even knows how he'll kill me, when the time comes. I've been reading everything that's available to the public about this. Is it true that the method varies, just to keep people like me on tenterhooks? And the time allowed – doesn't that vary too?'

'Yes, it's true. But there's a minimum time – I'm almost sure. You must still be within it. Believe me, Danner, I can still call off the Fury. You saw me do it. You know it worked once. All I've got to find out is what went wrong this time. But the more you bother me the more I'll be delayed. I'll get in touch with you. Don't try to see me again.'

Danner was on his feet. He took a few quick steps towards Hartz, fury and frustration breaking up the impassive mask which despair had been forming over his face. But the solemn footsteps of the Fury sounded behind him. He stopped.

The two men looked at each other.

'Give me time,' Hartz said. 'Trust me, Danner.'

In a way it was worse, having hope. There must until now have been a kind of numbness of despair that had kept him from feeling too much. But now there was a chance that after all he might escape into the bright and new life he had risked so much for – if Hartz could save him in time.

Now, for a period, he began to savour experience again. He bought new clothes. He travelled, though never, of course, alone. He even sought human companionship again and found it – after a fashion. But the kind of people willing to associate with a man under this sort of death sentence was not a very appealing type.

He found, for instance, that some women felt strongly attracted to him, not because of himself or his money, but for the sake of his companion. They seemed enthralled by the opportunity for a close, safe brush with the very instrument of destiny. Over his very shoulder, sometimes, he would realize they watched the Fury in an ecstasy of fascinated anticipation. In a strange reaction of jealousy, he dropped such people as soon as he recognized the first coldly flirtatious glance one of them cast at the robot behind him.

He tried farther travel. He took the rocket to Africa, and came back by way of the rain-forests of South America, but neither the nightclubs nor the exotic newness of strange places seemed to touch him in any way that mattered. The sunlight looked much the same, reflecting from the curved steel surfaces of his follower, whether it shone over lion-coloured savannahs or filtered through the hanging gardens of the jungles. All novelty grew dull quickly because of the dreadful familiar thing that stood for ever at his shoulder. He could enjoy nothing at all.

And the rhythmic beat of footfalls behind him began to grow unendurable. He used earplugs, but the heavy vibration throbbed through his skull in a constant measure like an eternal headache. Even when the Fury stood still, he could hear in his head the imaginary beating of its steps.

He bought weapons and tried to destroy the robot. Of course he failed. And even if he succeeded he knew another would be assigned to him. Liquor and drugs were no good. Suicide came more and more often into his mind, but he postponed that thought, because Hartz had said there was still hope.

In the end, he came back to the city to be near Hartz – and hope. Again he found himself spending most of his time in the library, walking no more than he had to because of the footsteps that thudded behind him. And it was here, one morning, that he found the answer. . . .

He had gone through all available factual material about the Furies. He had gone through all the literary references collated under the heading, astonished to find how many there were and how apt some of them had become – like Milton's two-handed engine – after the lapse of all these centuries. *Those strong feet*

that followed, followed after, he read, . . . *with unhurrying chase,
And unperturbed pace, Deliberate speed, majestic instancy*. . . . He
turned the page and saw himself and his plight more literally than
any allegory:

*I shook the pillaring hours
And pulled my life upon me; grimed with smears,
I stand amid the dust of the mounded years –
My mangled youth lies dead beneath the heap.*

He let several tears of self-pity fall upon the page that pictured
him so clearly.

But then he passed on from literary references to the library's
store of filmed plays, because some of them were cross-indexed
under the heading he sought. He watched Orestes hounded in
modern dress from Argos to Athens with a single seven-foot robot
Fury at his heels instead of the three snake-haired Erinyes of
legend. There had been an outburst of plays on the theme when
the Furies first came into usage. Sunk in a half-dream of his own
boyhood memories when the Escape Machines still operated,
Danner lost himself in the action of the films.

He lost himself so completely that when the familiar scene first
flashed by him in the viewing booth he hardly questioned it. The
whole experience was part of a familiar boyhood pattern and he
was not at first surprised to find one scene more vividly familiar
than the rest. But then memory rang a bell in his mind and he sat
up sharply and brought his fist down with a bang on the stop-
action button. He spun the film back and ran the scene over again.

It showed a man walking with his Fury through city traffic, the
two of them moving in a little desert island of their own making,
like a Crusoe with a Friday at his heels. . . . It showed the man turn
into an alley, glance up at the camera anxiously, take a deep breath
and break into a sudden run. It showed the Fury hesitate, make
indecisive motions and then turn and walk quietly and calmly
away in the other direction, its feet ringing on the pavement
hollowly. . . .

Danner spun the film back again and ran the scene once more,
just to make doubly sure. He was shaking so hard he could scarcely
manipulate the viewer.

'How do you like that?' he muttered to the Fury behind him in the dim booth. He had by now formed a habit of talking to the Fury a good deal, in a rapid, mumbling undertone, not really aware he did it. 'What do you make of that, you? Seen it before, haven't you? Familiar, isn't it? Isn't it! *Isn't it!* Answer me, you damned dumb hulk!' And, reaching backward, he struck the robot across the chest as he would have struck Hartz if he could. The blow made a hollow sound in the booth, but the robot made no other response, though when Danner looked back inquiringly at it he saw the reflection of the over-familiar scene, running a third time on the screen, running in tiny reflection across the robot's chest and faceless head, as if it too remembered.

So now he knew the answer. And Hartz had never possessed the power he claimed. Or, if he did, had no intention of using it to help Danner. Why should he? His risk was over now. No wonder Hartz had been so nervous, running that film-strip off on a news-screen in his office. But the anxiety sprang not from the dangerous thing he was tampering with, but from sheer strain in matching his activities to the action in the play. How he must have rehearsed it, timing every move! And how he must have laughed afterwards.

'How long have I got?' Danner demanded fiercely, striking a hollow reverberation from the robot's chest. 'How long? Answer me! Long enough?'

Release from hope was an ecstasy now. He need not wait any longer. He need not try any more. All he had to do was get to Hartz and get there fast, before his own time ran out. He thought with revulsion of all the days he had wasted already, in travel and time-killing, when for all he knew his own last minutes might be draining away now. Before Hartz's did.

'Come along,' he said needlessly to the Fury. 'Hurry!'

It came, matching its speed to his, the enigmatic timer inside it ticking the moments away towards that instant when the two-handed engine would smite once, and smite no more.

Hartz sat in the Controller's office behind a brand-new desk, looking down from the very top of the pyramid now over the banks of computers that kept society running and cracked the whip over mankind. He sighed with deep content.

The only thing was he found himself thinking a good deal about

Danner. Dreaming of him, even. Not with guilt, because guilt implies conscience, and the long schooling in anarchic individualism was still deep in the roots of every man's mind. But with uneasiness, perhaps.

Thinking of Danner, he leaned back and unlocked a small drawer which he had transferred from his old desk to the new. He slid his hand in and let his fingers touch the controls lightly, idly. Quite idly.

Two movements, and he could save Danner's life. For, of course, he had lied to Danner straight through. He could control the Furies very easily. He could save Danner, but he had never intended to. There was no need. And the thing was dangerous. You tamper once with a mechanism as complex as that which controlled society, and there would be no telling where the maladjustment might end. Chain-reaction, maybe, throwing the whole organization out of kilter. No.

He might some day have to use the device in the drawer. He hoped not. He pushed the drawer shut quickly, and heard the soft click of the lock.

He was Controller now. Guardian, in a sense, of the machines which were faithful in a way no man could ever be. *Quis custodiet*, Hartz thought. The old problem. And the answer was: Nobody. Nobody, today. He himself had no superiors and his power was absolute. Because of this little mechanism in the drawer, nobody controlled the Controller. Not an internal conscience, and not an external one. Nothing could touch him. . . .

Hearing the footsteps on the stairs, he thought for a moment he must be dreaming. He had sometimes dreamed that he was Danner, with those relentless footfalls thudding after him. But he was awake now.

It was strange that he caught the almost subsonic beat of the approaching metal feet before he heard the storming steps of Danner rushing up his private stairs. The whole thing happened so fast that time seemed to have no connection with it. First he heard the heavy, subsonic beat, then the sudden tumult of shouts and banging doors downstairs, and then last of all the thump, thump of Danner charging up the stairs, his steps so perfectly matched by the heavier thud of the robot's that the metal trampling drowned out the tramp of flesh and bone and leather.

Then Danner flung the door open with a crash, and the shouts and tramplings from below funnelled upward into the quiet office like a cyclone rushing towards the hearer. But a cyclone in a nightmare, because it would never get any nearer. Time had stopped.

Time had stopped with Danner in the doorway, his face convulsed, both hands holding the revolver because he shook so badly he could not brace it with one.

Hartz acted without any more thought than a robot. He had dreamed of this moment too often, in one form or another. If he could have tampered with the Fury to the extent of hurrying Danner's death, he would have done it. But he didn't know how. He could only wait it out, as anxiously as Danner himself, hoping against hope that the blow would fall and the executioner strike before Danner guessed the truth. Or gave up hope.

So Hartz was ready when trouble came. He found his own gun in his hand without the least recollection of having opened the drawer. The trouble was that time had stopped. He knew, in the back of his mind, that the Fury must stop Danner from injuring anybody. But Danner stood in the doorway alone, the revolver in both shaking hands. And farther back, behind the knowledge of the Fury's duty, Hartz's mind held the knowledge that the machines could be stopped. The Furies could fail. He dared not trust his life to their incorruptibility, because he himself was the source of a corruption that could stop them in their tracks.

The gun was in his hand without his knowledge. The trigger pressed his finger and the revolver kicked back against his palm, and the spurt of the explosion made the air hiss between him and Danner.

He heard his bullet clang on metal.

Time started again, running double-pace to catch up. The Fury had been no more than a single pace behind Danner after all, because its steel arm encircled him and its steel hand was deflecting Danner's gun. Danner had fired, yes, but not soon enough. Not before the Fury reached him. Hartz's bullet struck first.

It struck Danner in the chest, exploding through him, and rang upon the steel chest of the Fury behind him. Danner's face smoothed out into a blankness as complete as the blankness of the mask above his head. He slumped backwards, not falling because of the robot's embrace, but slowly slipping to the floor between the Fury's arm and its impervious metal body. His revolver thumped softly to the carpet. Blood welled from his chest and back.

The robot stood there impassive, a streak of Danner's blood slanting across its metal chest like a robotic ribbon of honour.

The Fury and the Controller of the Furies stood staring at each other. And the Fury could not, of course, speak, but in Hartz's mind it seemed to.

'Self-defence is no excuse,' the Fury seemed to be saying. 'We never punish intent, but we always punish action. Any act of murder. Any act of murder.'

Hartz barely had time to drop his revolver in his desk drawer before the first of the clamorous crowd from downstairs came bursting through the door. He barely had the presence of mind to do it, either. He had not really thought the thing through this far.

It was, on the surface, a clear case of suicide. In a slightly unsteady voice he heard himself explaining. Everybody had seen the madman rushing through the office, his Fury at his heels. This wouldn't be the first time a killer and his Fury had tried to get at the Controller, begging him to call off the jailer and forestall the executioner. What had happened, Hartz told his underlings calmly enough, was that the Fury had naturally stopped the man from shooting Hartz. And the victim had then turned his gun upon himself. Powder-burns on his clothing showed it. (The desk was very near the door.) Back-blast in the skin of Danner's hands would show he had really fired a gun.

Suicide. It would satisfy any human. But it would not satisfy the computers.

They carried the dead man out. They left Hartz and the Fury alone, still facing each other across the desk. If anyone thought this was strange, nobody showed it.

Hartz himself didn't know if it was strange or not. Nothing like this had ever happened before. Nobody had ever been fool enough to commit murder in the very presence of a Fury. Even the Controller did not know exactly how the computers assessed evidence and fixed guilt. Should this Fury have been recalled, normally?

If Danner's death were really suicide, would Hartz stand here alone now?

He knew the machines were already processing the evidence of what had really happened here. What he couldn't be sure of was whether this Fury had already received its orders and would follow him wherever he went from now on until the hour of his death. Or whether it simply stood motionless, waiting recall.

Well, it didn't matter. This Fury or another was already, in the present moment, in the process of receiving instructions about him. There was only one thing to do. Thank God there was something he *could* do.

So Hartz unlocked the desk drawer and slid it open, touched the clicking keys he had never expected to use. Very carefully he fed the coded information, digit by digit, into the computers. As he did, he looked out through the glass wall and imagined he could see down there in the hidden tapes the units of data fading into blankness and the new, false information flashing into existence.

He looked up at the robot. He smiled a little.

'Now you'll forget,' he said. 'You and the computers. You can go now. I won't be seeing you again.'

Either the computers worked incredibly fast – as, of course, they did – or pure coincidence took over, because in only a moment or two the Fury moved as if in response to Hartz's dismissal. It had stood quite motionless since Danner slid through its arms. Now new orders animated it, and briefly its motion was almost jerky as it changed from one set of instructions to another. It almost seemed to bow, a stiff little bending motion that brought its head down to a level with Hartz's.

He saw his own face reflected in the blank face of the Fury. You could very nearly read an ironic note in that stiff bow, with the diplomat's ribbon of honour across the chest of the creature, symbol of duty discharged honourably. But there was nothing honourable about this withdrawal. The incorruptible metal was putting on corruption and looking back at Hartz with the reflection of his own face.

He watched it stalk towards the door. He heard it go thudding evenly down the stairs. He could feel the thuds vibrate in the floor, and there was a sudden sick dizziness in him when he thought the whole fabric of society was shaking under his feet.

The machines were corruptible.

Mankind's survival still depended on the computers, and the computers could not be trusted. Hartz looked down and saw that his hands were shaking. He shut the drawer and heard the lock click softly. He gazed at his hands. He felt their shaking echoed in an inner shaking, a' terrifying sense of the instability of the world.

A sudden, appalling loneliness swept over him like a cold wind. He had never felt before so urgent a need for the companionship of his own kind. No one person, but people. Just people. The sense of human beings all around him, a very primitive need.

He got his hat and coat and went downstairs rapidly, hands deep in his pockets because of some inner chill no coat could guard against. Halfway down the stairs he stopped dead still.

There were footsteps behind him.

He dared not look back at first. He knew those footsteps. But he had two fears and he didn't know which was worse. The fear that a Fury was after him – and the fear that it was not. There would be a sort of insane relief if it really was, because then he could trust the machines after all, and this terrible loneliness might pass over him and go.

He took another downward step, not looking back. He heard the ominous footfall behind him, echoing his own. He sighed one deep sigh and looked back.

There was nothing on the stairs.

He went on down after a timeless pause, watching over his shoulder. He could hear the relentless feet thudding behind him, but no visible Fury followed. No visible Fury.

The Erinyes had struck inward again, and an invisible Fury of the mind followed Hartz down the stairs.

It was as if sin had come anew into the world, and the first man felt again the first inward guilt. So the computers had not failed, after all.

Hartz went slowly down the steps and out into the street, still hearing as he would always hear the relentless, incorruptible footsteps behind him that no longer rang like metal.

Howard Fast
The large ant

There have been all kinds of notions and guesses as to how it would end. One held that sooner or later there would be too many people; another that we would do each other in, and the atom bomb made that a very good likelihood. All sorts of notions, except the simple fact that we were what we were. We could find a way to feed any number of people and perhaps even a way to avoid wiping each other out with the bomb; those things we are very good at, but we have never been any good at changing ourselves or the way we behave.

I know. I am not a bad man or a cruel man; quite to the contrary, I am an ordinary, humane person, and I love my wife and my children and I get along with my neighbours. I am like a great many other men, and I do the things they would do and just as thoughtlessly. There it is in a nutshell.

I am also a writer, and I told Lieberman, the curator, and Fitzgerald, the government man, that I would like to write down the story. They shrugged their shoulders. 'Go ahead,' they said, 'because it won't make one bit of difference.'

'You don't think it would alarm people?'

'How can it alarm anyone when nobody will believe it?'

'If I could have a photograph or two.'

'Oh, no,' they said then. 'No photographs.'

'What kind of sense does that make?' I asked them. 'You are willing to let me write the story – why not the photographs so that people could believe me?'

'They still won't believe you. They will just say you faked the photographs, but no one will believe you. It will make for more confusion; and, if we have a chance of getting out of this, confusion won't help.'

'What will help?'

They weren't ready to say that, because they didn't know. So here is what happened to me, in a very straightforward and ordinary manner.

Every summer, sometime in August, four good friends of mine and I go for a week's fishing on the St Regis chain of lakes in the Adirondacks. We rent the same shack each summer; we drift around in canoes, and sometimes we catch a few bass. The fishing isn't very good, but we play cards well together, and we cook out and generally relax. This summer past, I had some things to do that couldn't be put off. I arrived three days late, and the weather was so warm and even and beguiling that I decided to stay on by myself for a day or two after the others left. There was a small flat lawn in front of the shack, and I made up my mind to spend at least three or four hours at short putts. That was how I happened to have the putting iron next to my bed.

The first day I was alone, I opened a can of beans and a can of beer for my supper. Then I lay down in my bed with *Life on the Mississippi*, a pack of cigarettes, and an eight-ounce chocolate-bar. There was nothing I had to do, no telephone, no demands and no newspapers. At that moment, I was about as contented as any man can be in these nervous times.

It was still light outside, and enough light came in through the window above my head for me to read by. I was just reaching for a fresh cigarette, when I looked up and saw it on the foot of my bed. The edge of my hand was touching the golf club, and with a single motion I swept the club over and down, struck it a savage and accurate blow, and killed it. That was what I referred to before. Whatever kind of a man I am, I react as a man does. I think that any man, black, white or yellow, in China, Africa or Russia, would have done the same thing.

First I found that I was sweating all over, and then I knew I was going to be sick. I went outside to vomit, recalling that this hadn't happened to me since 1943, on my way to Europe on a tub of a liberty ship. Then I felt better and was able to go back into the shack and look at it. It was quite dead, but I had already made up my mind that I was not going to sleep alone in this shack.

I couldn't bear to touch it with my bare hands. With a piece of brown paper, I picked it up and dropped it into my fishing creel. That I put into the trunk case of my car, along with what luggage

I carried. Then I closed the door of the shack, got into my car and drove back to New York. I stopped once along the road, just before I reached the Thruway, to nap in the car for a little over an hour. It was almost dawn when I reached the city, and I had shaved, had a hot bath and changed my clothes before my wife awoke.

During breakfast, I explained that I was never much of a hand at the solitary business, and since she knew that, and since driving alone all night was by no means an extraordinary procedure for me, she didn't press me with any questions. I had two eggs, coffee and a cigarette. Then I went into my study, lit another cigarette and contemplated my fishing creel, which sat upon my desk.

My wife looked in, saw the creel, remarked that it had too ripe a smell and asked me to remove it to the basement.

'I'm going to dress,' she said. The kids were still at camp. 'I have a date with Ann for lunch – I had no idea you were coming back. Shall I break it?'

'No, please don't. I can find things to do that have to be done.'

Then I sat and smoked some more, and finally I called the museum, and asked who the curator of insects was. They told me his name was Bertram Lieberman, and I asked to talk to him. He had a pleasant voice. I told him that my name was Morgan, and that I was a writer, and he politely indicated that he had seen my name and read something that I had written. That is formal procedure when a writer introduces himself to a thoughtful person.

I asked Lieberman if I could see him, and he said that he had a busy morning ahead of him. Could it be tomorrow?

'I am afraid it has to be now,' I said firmly.

'Oh? Some information you require.'

'No. I have a specimen for you.'

'Oh?' The 'oh' was a cultivated, neutral interval. It asked and answered and said nothing. You have to develop that particular 'oh'.

'Yes. I think you will be interested.'

'An insect?' he asked mildly.

'I think so.'

'Oh? Large?'

'Quite large,' I told him.

'Eleven o'clock? Can you be here then? On the main floor, to the right, as you enter.'

'I'll be there,' I said.

'One thing – dead?'

'Yes, it's dead.'

'Oh?' again. 'I'll be happy to see you at eleven o'clock, Mr Morgan.'

My wife was dressed now. She opened the door to my study and said firmly, 'Do get rid of that fishing creel. It smells.'

'Yes, darling. I'll get rid of it.'

'I should think you'd want to take a nap after driving all night.'

'Funny, but I'm not sleepy,' I said. 'I think I'll drop around to the museum.'

My wife said that was what she liked about me, that I never tired of places like museums, police courts and third-rate nightclubs.

Anyway, aside from a racetrack, a museum is the most interesting and unexpected place in the world. It was unexpected to have two other men waiting for me, along with Mr Lieberman, in his office. Lieberman was a skinny, sharp-faced man of about sixty. The government man, Fitzgerald, was small, dark-eyed, and wore gold-rimmed glasses. He was very alert, but he never told me what part of the Government he represented. He just said 'we', and it meant the Government. Hopper, the third man, was comfortable-looking, pudgy, and genial. He was a United States senator with an interest in entomology, although before this morning I would have taken better than even money that such a thing not only wasn't, but could not be.

The room was large and square and plainly furnished, with shelves and cupboards on all walls.

We shook hands, and then Lieberman asked me, nodding at the creel, 'Is that it?'

'That's it.'

'May I?'

'Go ahead,' I told him. 'It's nothing that I want to stuff for the parlour. I'm making you a gift of it.'

'Thank you, Mr Morgan,' he said, and then he opened the creel and looked inside. Then he straightened up, and the other two men looked at him inquiringly.

He nodded. 'Yes.'

The senator closed his eyes for a long moment. Fitzgerald took off his glasses and wiped them industriously. Lieberman spread a piece of plastic on his desk, and then lifted the thing out of my creel and laid it on the plastic. The two men didn't move. They just sat where they were and looked at it.

'What do you think it is, Mr Morgan?' Lieberman asked me.

'I thought that was your department.'

'Yes, of course. I only wanted your impression.'

'An ant. That's my impression. It's the first time I saw an ant fourteen, fifteen inches long. I hope it's the last.'

'An understandable wish,' Lieberman nodded.

Fitzgerald said to me, 'May I ask how you killed it, Mr Morgan?'

'With an iron. A golf club, I mean. I was doing a little fishing with some friends up at St Regis in the Adirondacks, and I brought the iron for my short shots. They're the worst part of my game, and when my friends left I intended to stay on at our shack and do four or five hours of short putts. You see—'

'There's no need to explain,' Hopper smiled, a trace of sadness on his face. 'Some of our very best golfers have the same trouble.'

'I was lying in bed, reading, and I saw it at the foot of my bed. I had the club—'

'I understand,' Fitzgerald nodded.

'You avoid looking at it,' Hopper said.

'It turns my stomach.'

'Yes – yes, I suppose so.'

Lieberman said, 'Would you mind telling us why you killed it, Mr Morgan?'

'Why?'

'Yes – why?'

'I don't understand you,' I said. 'I don't know what you're driving at.'

'Sit down, please, Mr Morgan,' Hopper nodded. 'Try to relax. I'm sure this has been very trying.'

'I still haven't slept. I want a chance to dream before I say how trying.'

'We are not trying to upset you, Mr Morgan,' Lieberman said. 'We do feel, however, that certain aspects of this are very important. That is why I am asking you why you killed it. You must have had a reason. Did it seem about to attack you?'

'No.'

'Or make any sudden motion towards you?'

'No. It was just there.'

'Then, why?'

'This is to no purpose,' Fitzgerald put in. 'We know why he killed it.'

'Do you?'

'The answer is very simple, Mr Morgan. You killed it because you are a human being.'

'Oh?'

'Yes. Do you understand?'

'No, I don't.'

'Then why did you kill it?' Hopper put in.

'I was scared to death. I still am, to tell the truth.'

Lieberman said, 'You are an intelligent man, Mr Morgan. Let me show you something.' He then opened the doors of one of the wall cupboards, and there eight jars of formaldehyde and in each jar a specimen like mine – and in each case mutilated by the violence of its death. I said nothing. I just stared.

Lieberman closed the cupboard doors. 'All in five days,' he shrugged.

'A new race of ants,' I whispered stupidly.

'No. They're not ants. Come here!' He motioned me to the desk and the other two joined me. Lieberman took a set of dissecting instruments out of his drawer, used one to turn the thing over and then pointed to the underpart of what would be the thorax in an insect.

'That looks like part of him, doesn't it, Mr Morgan?'

'Yes, it does.'

Using two of the tools, he found a fissure and pried the bottom apart. It came open like the belly of a bomber; it was a pocket, a pounch, a receptacle that the thing wore, and in it were four beautiful little tools or instruments or weapons, each about an inch and a half long. They were beautiful the way any object of functional purpose and loving creation is beautiful – the way the creature itself would have been beautiful, had it not been an insect and myself a man. Using tweezers, Lieberman took each instrument off the brackets that held it, offering each to me. And I took each one, felt it, examined it, and then put it down.

I had to look at the ant now, and I realized that I had not truly looked at it before. We don't look carefully at a thing that is horrible or repugnant to us. You can't look at anything through a screen of hatred. But now the hatred and the fear was diluted and, as I looked, I realized it was not an ant although like an ant. It was nothing that I had ever seen or dreamed of.

All three men were watching me, and suddenly I was on the defensive. 'I didn't know! What do you expect when you see an insect that size?'

Lieberman nodded.

'What in the name of God is it?'

From his desk, Lieberman produced a bottle and four small glasses. He poured and we drank it neat. I would not have expected him to keep good Scotch in his desk.

'We don't know,' Hopper said. 'We don't know what it is.'

Lieberman pointed to the broken skull from which a white substance oozed. 'Brain material – a great deal of it.'

'It could be a very intelligent creature,' Hopper nodded.

Lieberman said, 'It is an insect in developmental structure. We know very little about intelligence in our insects. It's not the same as what we call intelligence. It's a collective phenomenon – as if you were to think of the component parts of our bodies. Each part is alive, but the intelligence is a result of the whole. If that same pattern were to extend to creatures like this one—'

I broke the silence. They were content to stand there and stare at it.

'Suppose it were?'

'What?'

'The kind of collective intelligence you were talking about.'

'Oh? Well, I couldn't say. It would be something beyond our wildest dreams. To us – well, what we are to an ordinary ant.'

'I don't believe that,' I said shortly, and Fitzgerald, the government man, told me quietly, 'Neither do we. We guess.'

'If it's that intelligent, why didn't it use one of those weapons on me?'

'Would that be a mark of intelligence?' Hopper asked mildly.

'Perhaps none of these are weapons,' Lieberman said.

'Don't you know? Didn't the others carry instruments?'

'They did,' Fitzgerald said shortly.

'Why? What were they?'

'We don't know,' Lieberman said.

'But you can find out. We have scientists, engineers— Good God, this is an age of fantastic instruments. Have them taken apart!'

'We have.'

'Then what have you found out?'

Nothing.'

'Do you mean to tell me', I said, 'that you can find out nothing about these instruments – what they are, how they work, what their purpose is?'

'Exactly,' Hopper nodded. 'Nothing, Mr Morgan. They are meaningless to the finest engineers and technicians in the United States. You know the old story – suppose you gave a radio to Aristotle? What would he do with it? Where would he find power? And what would he receive with no one to send? It is not that these instruments are complex. They are actually very simple. We simply have no idea of what they can or should do.'

'But they must be a weapon of some kind.'

'Why?' Lieberman demanded. 'Look at yourself, Mr Morgan – a cultured and intelligent man, yet you cannot conceive of a mentality that does not include weapons as a prime necessity. Yet a weapon is an unusual thing, Mr Morgan. An instrument of murder. We don't think that way, because the weapon has become the symbol of the world we inhabit. Is that civilized, Mr Morgan? Or is the weapon and civilization in the ultimate sense incompatible? Can you imagine a mentality to which the concept of murder is impossible – or let me say absent. We see everything through our own subjectivity. Why shouldn't some other – this creature, for example – see the process of mentation out of his subjectivity? So he approaches a creature of our world – and he is slain. Why? What explanation? Tell me, Mr Morgan, what conceivable explanation could we offer a wholly rational creature for this—' pointing to the thing on his desk. 'I am asking you the question most seriously. What explanation?'

'An accident?' I muttered.

'And the eight jars in my cupboard? Eight accidents?'

'I think, Dr Lieberman,' Fitzgerald said, 'that you can go a little too far in that direction.'

'Yes, you would think so. It's a part of your own background. Mine is as a scientist. As a scientist, I try to be rational when I can. The creation of a structure of good and evil, or what we call morality and ethics, is a function of intelligence – and unquestionably the ultimate evil may be the destruction of conscious intelligence. That is why, so long ago, we at least recognized the injunction, "Thou shalt not kill!" even if we never gave more than lip-service to it. But to a collective intelligence, such as this might be a part of, the concept of murder would be monstrous beyond the power of thought.'

I sat down and lit a cigarette. My hands were trembling. Hopper apologized. 'We have been rather rough with you, Mr Morgan. But over the past days eight other people have done just what you did. We are caught in the trap of being what we are.'

'But tell me – where do these things come from?'

'It almost doesn't matter where they come from,' Hopper said hopelessly. 'Perhaps from another planet – perhaps from inside this one – or the moon or Mars. That doesn't matter. Fitzgerald thinks they come from a smaller planet, because their movements are apparently slow on earth. But Dr Lieberman thinks that they move slowly because they have not discovered the need to move quickly. Meanwhile, they have the problem of murder and what to do with it. Heaven knows how many of them have died in other places – Africa, Asia, Europe.'

'Then why don't you publicize this? Put a stop to it before it's too late!'

'We've thought of that,' Fitzgerald nodded. 'What then – panic, hysteria, charges that this is the result of the atom bomb? We can't change. We are what we are.'

'They may go away,' I said.

'Yes, they may,' Lieberman nodded. 'But, if they are without the curse of murder, they may also be without the curse of fear. They may be social in the highest sense. What does society do with a murderer?'

'There are societies that put him to death – and there are other societies that recognize his sickness and lock him away, where he can kill no more,' Hopper said. 'Of course, when a whole world is on trial, that's another matter. We have atom bombs now and other things, and we are reaching out to the stars—'

'I'm inclined to think that they'll run,' Fitzgerald put in. 'They may just have that curse of fear, Doctor.'

'They may,' Lieberman admitted. 'I hope so.'

But the more I think of it the more it seems to me that fear and hatred are the two sides of the same coin. I keep trying to think back, to re-create the moment when I saw it standing at the foot of my bed in the fishing shack. I keep trying to drag out of my memory a clear picture of what it looked like, whether behind that chitinous face and the two gently waving antennae there was any evidence of fear and anger. But, the clearer the memory becomes, the more I seem to recall a certain wonderful dignity and repose. Not fear and not anger.

And more and more, as I go about my work, I get the feeling of what Hopper called 'a world on trial'. I have no sense of anger myself. Like a criminal who can no longer live with himself, I am content to be judged.

Robert Sheckley
Early model

The landing was almost a catastrophe. Bentley knew his co-ordination was impaired by the bulky weight on his back; he didn't realize how much until, at a crucial moment, he stabbed the wrong button. The ship began to drop like a stone. At the last moment, he overcompensated, scorching a black hole into the plain below him. His ship touched, teetered for a moment, then sickeningly came to rest.

Bentley had effected mankind's first landing on Tels IV.

His immediate reaction was to pour himself a sizeable drink of strictly medicinal scotch.

When that was out of the way, he turned on his radio. The receiver was imbedded in his ear, where it itched, and the microphone was a surgically implanted lump in his throat. The portable sub-space set was self-tuning, which was all to the good, since Bentley knew nothing about narrowcasting on so tight a beam over so great a distance.

'All's well,' he told Professor Sliggert over the radio. 'It's an Earth-type planet, just as the survey reports said. The ship is intact. And I'm happy to report that I did not break my neck in landing.'

'Of course not,' Sliggert said, his voice thin and emotionless through the tiny receiver. 'What about the Protec? How does it feel? Have you become used to it yet?'

Bentley said, 'Nope. It still feels like a monkey on my back.'

'Well, you'll adjust,' Sliggert assured him. 'The Institute sends it congratulations and I believe the Government is awarding you a medal of some sort. Remember, the thing now is to fraternize with the aborigines, and if possible to establish a trade agreement of some sort, any sort. As a precedent. We need this planet, Bentley.'

'I know.'

'Good luck. Report whenever you have a chance.'

'I'll do that,' Bentley promised and signed off.

He tried to stand up, but didn't make it on the first attempt. Then, using the handholds that had been conveniently spaced above the control board, he managed to stagger erect. Now he appreciated the toll that no-weight extracts from a man's muscles. He wished he had done his exercises more faithfully on the long trip out from Earth.

Bentley was a big, jaunty young man, over six feet tall, widely and solidly constructed. On Earth, he had weighed 200 pounds and had moved with an athlete's grace. But, ever since leaving Earth, he'd had the added encumbrance of seventy-three pounds strapped irrevocably and immovably to his back. Under the circumstances, his movements resembled those of a very old elephant wearing tight shoes.

He moved his shoulders under the wide plastic straps, grimaced, and walked to a starboard porthole. In the distance, perhaps half a mile away, he could see a village, low and brown on the horizon. There were dots on the plain moving toward him. The villagers apparently had decided to discover what strange object had fallen from the skies breathing fire and making an uncanny noise.

'Good show,' Bentley said to himself. Contact would have been difficult if these aliens had shown no curiosity. This eventuality had been considered by the Earth Interstellar Exploration Institute, but no solution had been found. Therefore it had been struck from the list of possibilities.

The villagers were drawing closer. Bentley decided it was time to get ready. He opened a locker and took out his linguascene, which, with some difficulty, he strapped to his chest. On one hip, he fastened a large canteen of water. On the other hip went a package of concentrated food. Across his stomach, he put a package of assorted tools. Strapped to one leg was the radio. Strapped to the other was a medicine kit.

Thus equipped, Bentley was carrying a total of 148 pounds, every ounce of it declared essential for an extraterrestrial explorer.

The fact that he lurched rather than walked was considered unimportant.

The natives had reached the ship now and were gathering around it, commenting disparagingly. They were bipeds. They had short thick tails and their features were human, but nightmare human. Their colouring was a vivid orange.

Bentley also noticed that they were armed. He could see knives, spears, lances, stone hammers and flint axes. At the sight of this armament, a satisfied smile broke over his face. Here was the justification for his discomfort, the reason for the unwieldy seventy-three pounds which had remained on his back ever since leaving Earth.

It didn't matter what weapons these aboriginals had, right up to the nuclear level. They couldn't hurt him.

That's what Professor Sliggert, head of the Institute, inventor of the Protec, had told him.

Bentley opened the port. A cry of astonishment came from the Telians. His linguascene, after a few seconds' initial hesitation, translated the cries as, 'Oh! Ah! How strange! Unbelievable! Ridiculous! Shockingly improper!'

Bentley descended the ladder on the ship's side, carefully balancing his 148 pounds of excess weight. The natives formed a semicircle around him, their weapons ready.

He advanced on them. They shrank back. Smiling pleasantly, he said, 'I come as a friend.' The linguascene barked out the harsh consonants of the Telian language.

They didn't seem to believe him. Spears were poised and one Telian, larger than the others and wearing a colourful headdress, held a hatchet in readiness.

Bentley felt the slightest tremor run through him. He was invulnerable, of course. There was nothing they could do to him as long as he wore the Protec. Nothing! Professor Sliggert had been certain of it.

Before takeoff, Professor Sliggert had strapped the Protec to Bentley's back, adjusted the straps and stepped back to admire his brainchild.

'Perfect,' he had announced with quiet pride.

Bentley had shrugged his shoulders under the weight. 'Kind of heavy, isn't it?'

'But what can we do?' Sliggert asked him. 'This is the first of its kind, the prototype. I have used every weight-saving device possible – transistors, light alloys, printed circuits, pencil power packs and all the rest. Unfortunately, early models of any invention are invariably bulky.'

'Seems as though you could have streamlined it a bit,' Bentley objected, peering over his shoulder.

'Streamlining comes much later. First must be concentration, then compaction, then group-function, and finally styling. It's always been that way and it will always be. Take the typewriter. Now it is simply a keyboard almost as flat as a briefcase. But the prototype typewriter worked with foot pedals and required the combined strength of several men to lift. Take the hearing aid, which actually shrank pounds through the various stages of its development. Take the linguascene, which began as a very massive, complicated electronic calculator weighing several tons—'

'Okay,' Bentley broke in. 'If this is the best you could make it, good enough. How do I get out of it?'

Professor Sliggert smiled.

Bentley reached around. He couldn't find a buckle. He pulled ineffectually at the shoulder straps, but could find no way of undoing them. Nor could he squirm out. It was like being in a new and fiendishly efficient straitjacket.

'Come on, Professor, how do I get it off?'

'I'm not going to tell you.'

'Huh?'

'The Protec is uncomfortable, is it not?' Sliggert asked. 'You would rather not wear it?'

'You're damned right.'

'Of course. Did you know that in wartime, on the battlefield, soldiers have a habit of discarding essential equipment because it is bulky or uncomfortable? But we can't take chances on you. You are going to an alien planet, Mr Bentley. You will be exposed to wholly unknown dangers. It is necessary that you be protected at all times.'

'I know that,' Bentley said. 'I've got enough sense to figure out when to wear this thing.'

'But do you? We selected you for attributes such as resource-fulness, stamina, physical strength – and, of course, a certain amount of intelligence. But—'

'Thanks!'

'But those qualities do not make you prone to caution. Suppose you found the natives seemingly friendly and decided to discard the heavy, uncomfortable Protec? What would happen if you had misjudged their attitude? This is very easy to do on Earth; think how much easier it will be on an alien planet!'

'I can take care of myself,' Bentley said.

Sliggert nodded grimly. 'That is what Atwood said when he left for Durabella II and we have never heard from him again. Nor have we heard from Blake, or Smythe, or Korishell. Can you turn a knife-thrust from the rear? Have you eyes in the back of your head? No, Mr Bentley, you haven't – *but the Protec has!*'

'Look,' Bentley had said, 'believe it or not, I'm a responsible adult. I will wear the Protec at all times when on the surface of an alien planet. Now tell me how to get it off.'

'You don't seem to realize something, Bentley. If only your life were at stake, we would let you take what risks seemed reasonable to you. But we are also risking several billion dollars' worth of spaceship and equipment. Moreover, this is the Protec's field test. The only way to be sure of the results is to have you wear it all the time. The only way to ensure *that* is by not telling you how to remove it. We want results. You are going to stay alive whether you like it or not.'

Bentley had thought it over and agreed grudgingly. 'I guess I might be tempted to take it off, if the natives were really friendly.'

'You will be spared that temptation. Now, do you understand how it works?'

'Sure,' Bentley said. 'But will it really do all you say?'

'It passed the lab test perfectly.'

'I'd hate to have some little thing go wrong. Suppose it pops a fuse or blows a wire?'

'That is one of the reasons for its bulk,' Sliggert explained patiently. 'Triple everything. We are taking no chance of mechanical failure.

'And the power supply?'

'Good for a century or better at full load. The Protec is perfect, Bentley! After this field test, I have no doubt it will become standard equipment for all extraterrestrial explorers.' Professor Sliggert permitted himself a faint smile of pride.

'All right,' Bentley had said, moving his shoulders under the wide plastic straps. 'I'll get used to it.'

But he hadn't. A man just doesn't get used to a seventy-three-pound monkey on his back.

The Telians didn't know what to make of Bentley. They argued for several minutes, while the explorer kept a strained smile on his face. Then one Telian stepped forward. He was taller than the others and wore a distinctive headdress made of glass, bones and bits of rather garishly painted wood.

'My friends,' the Telian said, 'there is an evil here which I, Rinek, can sense.'

Another Telian wearing a similar headdress stepped forward and said, 'It is not well for a ghost doctor to speak of such things.'

'Of course not,' Rinek admitted. 'It is not well to speak of evil in the presence of evil, for evil then grows strong. But a ghost doctor's work is the detection and avoidance of evil. In this work, we must persevere, no matter what the risk.'

Several other men in the distinctive headdress, the ghost doctors, had come forward now. Bentley decided that they were the Telian equivalent of priests and probably wielded considerable political power as well.

'I don't think he's evil,' a young and cheerful-looking ghost doctor named Huascl said.

'Of course he is. Just look at him.'

'Appearances prove nothing, as we know from the time the good spirit Ahut M'Kandi appeared in the form of a—'

'No lectures, Huascl. All of us know the parables of Lalland. The point is, can we take a chance?'

Huascl turned to Bentley. 'Are you evil?' the Telian asked earnestly.

'No,' Bentley said. He had been puzzled at first by the Telians' intense preoccupation with his spiritual status. They hadn't even asked him where he'd come from, or how, or why. But, then, it was not so strange. If an alien had landed on Earth during certain periods of religious zeal, the first question asked might have been, 'Are you a creature of God or of Satan?'

'He says he's not evil,' Huascl said.

'How would he know?'

'If he doesn't, who does!'

'Once the great spirit G'tal presented a wise man with three kdal and said to him—'

And on it went. Bentley found his legs beginning to bend under the weight of all his equipment. The linguascene was no longer able to keep pace with the shrill theological discussion that raged around him. His status seemed to depend upon two or three disputed points, none of which the ghost doctors wanted to talk about, since to talk about evil was in itself dangerous.

To make matters more complicated, there was a schism over the concept of the penetrability of evil, the younger ghost doctors holding to one side, the older to the other. The factions accused each other of rankest heresy, but Bentley couldn't figure out who believed what or which interpretation aided him.

When the sun drooped low over the grassy plain, the battle still raged. Then, suddenly, the ghost doctors reached an agreement, although Bentley couldn't decide why or on what basis.

Huascl stepped forward as spokesman for the younger ghost doctors.

'Stranger,' he declared, 'we have decided not to kill you.'

Bentley suppressed a smile. That was just like a primitive people, granting life to an invulnerable being!

'Not yet, anyhow,' Huascl amended quickly, catching a frown upon Rinek and the older ghost doctors. 'It depends entirely upon you. We will go to the village and purify ourselves and we will feast. Then we will initiate you into the society of ghost doctors. No evil thing can become a ghost doctor; it is expressly forbidden. In this manner, we will detect your true nature.'

'I am deeply grateful,' Bentley said.

'But, if you *are* evil, we are pledged to destroy evil. And, if we must, we can!'

The assembled Telians cheered his speech and began at once the mile trek to the village. Now that a status had been assigned

Bentley, even tentatively, the natives were completely friendly. They chatted amiably with him about crops, droughts and famines.

Bentley staggered along under his equipment, tired, but inwardly elated. This was really a *coup*! As an initiate, a priest, he would have an unsurpassed opportunity to gather anthropological data, to establish trade, to pave the way for the future development of Tels IV.

All he had to do was pass the initiation tests. And not get killed, of course, he reminded himself, smiling.

It was funny how positive the ghost doctors had been that they could kill him.

The village consisted of two dozen huts arranged in a rough circle. Beside each mud-and-thatch hut was a small vegetable garden, and sometimes a pen for the Telian version of cattle. There were small green-furred animals roaming between the huts, which the Telians treated as pets. The grassy central area was common ground. Here was the community well and here were the shrines to various gods and devils. In this area, lighted by a great bonfire, a feast had been laid out by the village women.

Bentley arrived at the feast in a state of near-exhaustion, stooped beneath his essential equipment. Gratefully, he sank to the ground with the villagers and the celebration began.

First the village women danced a welcoming for him. They made a pretty sight, their orange skin glinting in the firelight, their tails swinging gracefully in unison. Then a village dignitary named Occip came over to him, bearing a full bowl.

'Stranger,' Occip said, 'you are from a distant land and your ways are not our ways. Yet let us be brothers! Partake, therefore, of this food to seal the bond between us, and in the name of all sanctity!'

Bowing low, he offered the bowl.

It was an important moment, one of those pivotal occasions that can seal forever the friendship between races or make them eternal enemies. But Bentley was not able to take advantage of it. As tactfully as he could, he refused the symbolic food.

'But it is purified!' Occip said.

Bentley explained that, because of a tribal taboo, he could eat only his own food. Occip could not understand that different species have different dietary requirements. For example, Bentley pointed out, the staff of life on Tels IV might well be some strychnine compound. But he did not add that, even if he wanted to take the chance, his Protec would never allow it.

Nonetheless, his refusal alarmed the village. There were hurried conferences among the ghost doctors. Then Rinek came over and sat beside him.

'Tell me,' Rinek inquired after a while, 'what do you think of evil?'

'Evil is not good,' Bentley said solemnly.

'Ah!' The ghost doctor pondered that, his tail flicking nervously over the grass. A small green-furred pet, a mog, began to play with his tail. Rinek pushed him away and said, 'So you do not like evil.'

'No.'

'And you would permit no evil influence around you?'

'Certainly not,' Bentley said, stifling a yawn. He was growing bored with the ghost doctor's tortuous examining.

'In that case, you would have no objection to receiving the sacred and very holy spear that Kran K'leu brought down from the abode of the Small Gods, the brandishing of which confers good upon a man.'

'I would be pleased to receive it,' said Bentley, heavy-eyed, hoping this would be the last ceremony of the evening.

Rinek grunted his approval and moved away. The women's dances came to an end. The ghost doctors began to chant in deep, impressive voices. The bonfire flared high.

Huascl came forward. His face was now painted in thin black and white stripes. He carried an ancient spear of black wood, its head of shaped volcanic glass, its length intricately although primitively carved.

Holding the spear aloft, Huascl said: 'O Stranger from the Skies, accept from us this spear of sanctity! Kran K'leu gave this lance to Trin, our first father, and bestowed upon it a magical nature and caused it to be a vessel of the spirits of the good. Evil cannot abide the presence of this spear! Take, then, our blessings with it.'

Bentley heaved himself to his feet. He understood the value of a ceremony like this. His acceptance of the spear should end, once and for all, any doubts as to his spiritual status. Reverently he inclined his head.

Huascl came forward, held out the spear and—

The Protec snapped into action.

Its operation was simple, in common with many great inventions. When its calculator-component received a danger cue, the Protec threw a force field around its operator. This field rendered him invulnerable, for it was completely and absolutely impenetrable. But there were certain unavoidable disadvantages.

If Bentley had had a weak heart, the Protec might have killed him there and then, for its action was electronically sudden, completely unexpected and physically wrenching. One moment, he was standing in front of the great bonfire, his hand held out for the sacred spear. In the next moment, he was plunged into darkness.

As usual, he felt as though he had been catapulted into a musty, lightless closet, with rubbery walls pressing close on all sides. He cursed the machine's super-efficiency. The spear had not been a threat; it was part of an important ceremony. But the Protec, with its literal senses, had interpreted it as a possible danger.

Now, in the darkness, Bentley fumbled for the controls that would release the field. As usual, the force field interfered with his positional sense, a condition that seemed to grow worse with each subsequent use. Carefully he felt his way along his chest, where the button should have been, and located it at last under his right armpit, where it had twisted around to. He released the field.

The feast had ended abruptly. The natives were standing close together for protection, weapons ready, tails stretched stiffly out. Huascl, caught in the force field's range, had been flung twenty feet and was slowly picking himself up.

The ghost doctors began to chant a purification dirge, for protection against evil spirits. Bentley couldn't blame them.

When a Protec force field goes on, it appears as an opaque black sphere, some ten feet in diameter. If it is struck, it repels with a force equal to the impact. White lines appear in the sphere's surface, swirl, coalesce, vanish. And, as the sphere spins, it screams in a thin, high-pitched wail.

All in all, it was a sight hardly calculated to win the confidence of a primitive and superstitious people.

'Sorry,' Bentley said, with a weak smile. There hardly seemed anything else to say.

Huascl limped back, but kept his distance. 'You cannot accept the sacred spear,' he stated.

'Well, it's not exactly that,' said Bentley. 'It's just – well, I've got this protective device, kind of like a shield, you know, it doesn't like spears. Couldn't you offer me a sacred gourd?'

'Don't be ridiculous,' Huascl said. 'Who ever heard of a sacred gourd?'

'No, I guess not. But please take my word for it – I'm not evil. Really I'm not. I've just got a taboo about spears.'

The ghost doctors talked among themselves too rapidly for the linguascene to interpret it. It caught only the words 'evil', 'destroy', and 'purification'. Bentley decided his forecast didn't look too favourable.

After the conference, Huascl came over to him and said, 'Some of the others feel that you should be killed at once, before you bring some great unhappiness upon the village. I told them, however, that you cannot be blamed for the many taboos that restrict you. We will pray for you through the night. And perhaps, in the morning, the initiation will be possible.'

Bentley thanked him. He was shown to a hut and then the Telians left him as quickly as possible. There was an ominous hush over the village; from his doorway, Bentley could see little groups of natives talking earnestly and glancing covertly in his direction.

It was a poor beginning for co-operation between two races.

He immediately contacted Professor Sliggert and told him what had happened.

'Unfortunate,' the Professor said. 'But primitive people are notoriously treacherous. They might have meant to kill you with the spear instead of actually handing it to you. Let you have it, that is, in the most literal sense.'

'I'm positive there was no such intention,' Bentley said. 'After all, you have to start trusting people sometime.'

'Not with a billion dollars' worth of equipment in your charge.'

'But I'm not going to be able to *do* anything!' Bentley shouted. 'Don't you understand? They're suspicious of me already. I wasn't able to accept their sacred spear. That means I'm very possibly evil. Now, what if I can't pass the initiation ceremony tomorrow? Suppose some idiot starts to pick his teeth with a knife and the Protec saves me? All the favourable first impression I built up will be lost.'

'Goodwill can be regained,' Professor Sliggert said sententiously. 'But a billion dollars' worth of equipment—'

'—can be salvaged by the next expedition. Look, Professor, give me a break. Isn't there some way I can control this thing manually?'

'No way at all,' Sliggert replied. 'That would defeat the entire purpose of the machine. You might just as well not be wearing it if you're allowed to rely on your own reflexes rather than electronic impulses.'

'Then tell me how to take it off.'

'The same argument holds true – you wouldn't be protected at all times.'

'Look,' Bentley protested, 'you chose me as a competent explorer. I'm the guy on the spot. I know what the conditions are here. Tell me how to get it off.'

'No! The Protec must have a full field test. And we want you to come back alive.'

'That's another thing,' Bentley said. 'These people seem kind of sure they can kill me.'

'Primitive peoples always overestimate the potency of their strength, weapons and magic.'

'I know, I know. But you're certain there's no way they can get through the field? Poison, maybe?'

'Nothing can get through the field,' Sliggert said patiently. 'Not even light rays can penetrate. Not even gamma radiation. You are wearing an impregnable fortress, Mr Bentley. Why can't you manage to have a little faith in it?'

'Early models of inventions sometimes need a lot of ironing out,' Bentley grumbled. 'But have it your way. Won't you tell me how to take it off, though, just in case something goes wrong?'

'I wish you would stop asking me that, Mr Bentley. You were chosen to give Protec a *full* field test. That's just what you are going to do.'

When Bentley signed off, it was deep twilight outside and the villagers had returned to their huts. Campfires burned low and he could hear the call of night creatures.

At that moment, Bentley felt very alien and exceedingly homesick.

He was tired almost to the point of unconsciousness, but he forced himself to eat some concentrated food and drink a little water. Then he unstrapped the tool kit, the radio and the canteen, tugged defeatedly at the Protec and lay down to sleep.

Just as he dozed off, the Protec went violently into action, nearly snapping his neck out of joint.

Wearily he fumbled for the controls, located them near his stomach and turned off the field.

The hut looked exactly the same. He could find no source of attack.

Was the Protec losing its grip on reality, he wondered, or had a Telian tried to spear him through the window?

Then Bentley saw a tiny mog puppy scuttling away frantically, its legs churning up clouds of dust.

The little beast probably just wanted to get warm, Bentley thought. But of course it was alien. Its potential for danger could not be overlooked by the ever-wary Protec.

He fell asleep again and immediately began to dream that he was locked in a prison of bright red sponge rubber. He could push the walls out and out and out, but they never yielded, and at last he would have to let go and be gently shoved back to the centre of the prison. Over and over, this happened, until suddenly he felt his back wrenched and awoke within the Protec's lightless field.

This time he had real difficulty finding the controls. He hunted desperately by feel until the bad air made him gasp in panic. He located the controls at last under his chin, released the field, and began to search groggily for the source of the new attack.

He found it. A twig had fallen from the thatch roof and had tried to land on him. The Protec, of course, had not allowed it.

'Aw, come on now,' Bentley groaned aloud. 'Let's use a little judgement!'

But he was really too tired to care. Fortunately, there were no more assaults that night.

Huascl came to Bentley's hut in the morning, looking very solemn and considerably disturbed.

'There were great sounds from your hut during the night,' the ghost doctor said. 'Sounds of torment, as though you were wrestling with a devil.'

'I'm just a restless sleeper,' Bentley explained.

Huascl smiled to show that he appreciated the joke. 'My friend, did you pray for purification last night and for release from evil?'

'I certainly did.'

'And was your prayer granted?'

'It was,' Bentley said hopefully. 'There's no evil around me. Not a bit.'

Huascl looked dubious. 'But can you be sure? Perhaps you should depart from us in peace. If you cannot be initiated, we shall have to destroy you—'

'Don't worry about it,' Bentley told him. 'Let's get started.'

'Very well,' Huascl said, and together they left the hut.

The initiation was to be held in front of the great bonfire in the village square. Messengers had been sent out during the night and ghost doctors from many villages were there. Some had come as far as twenty miles to take part in the rites and to see the alien with their own eyes. The ceremonial drum had been taken from its secret hiding-place and was now booming solemnly. The villagers watched, chattered together, laughed. But Bentley could detect an undercurrent of nervousness and strain.

There was a long series of dances. Bentley twitched worriedly when the last figure started, for the leading dancer was swinging a glass-studded club around his head. Nearer and nearer the dancer whirled, now only a few feet away from him, his club a dazzling streak.

The villagers watched, fascinated. Bentley shut his eyes, expecting to be plunged momentarily into the darkness of the force field.

But the dancer moved away at last and the dance ended with a roar of approval from the villagers.

Huascl began to speak. Bentley realized with a thrill of relief that this was the end of the ceremony.

'O brothers,' Huascl said, 'this alien has come across the great emptiness to be our brother. Many of his ways are strange and around him there seems to hang a strange hint of evil. And yet who can doubt that he means well? Who can doubt that he is, in essence, a good and honourable person? With this initiation, we purge him of evil and make him one of us.'

There was dead silence as Huascl walked up to Bentley.

'Now,' Huascl said, 'you are a ghost doctor and indeed one of us.' He held out his hand.

Bentley felt his heart leap within him. He had won! He had been accepted! He reached out and clasped Huascl's hand.

Or tried to. He didn't quite make it, for the Protec, ever alert, saved him from the possibly dangerous contact.

'You damned idiotic gadget!' Bentley bellowed, quickly finding the control and releasing the field.

He saw at once that the fat was in the fire.

'Evil!' shrieked the Telians, frenziedly waving their weapons.

'Evil!' screamed the ghost doctors.

Bentley turned despairingly to Huascl.

'Yes,' the young ghost doctor said sadly, 'it is true. We had hoped to cure the evil by our ancient ceremonial. But it could not be. This evil must be destroyed! *Kill the devil!*'

A shower of spears came at Bentley. The Protec responded instantly.

Soon it was apparent that an impasse had been reached. Bentley would remain for a few minutes in the field, then override the controls. The Telians, seeing him still unharmed would renew their barrage and the Protec would instantly go back into action.

Bentley tried to walk back to his ship. But the Protec went on again each time he shut it off. It would take him a month or two to cover a mile at that rate, so he stopped trying. He would simply wait the attackers out. After a while, they would find out they couldn't hurt him and the two races would finally get down to business.

He tried to relax within the field, but found it impossible. He was hungry and extremely thirsty. And his air was starting to grow stale.

Then Bentley remembered, with a sense of shock that air had not gone through the surrounding field the night before. Naturally – nothing could get through. If he wasn't careful, he could be asphyxiated.

Even an impregnable fortress could fall, he knew, if the defenders were starved or suffocated out.

He began to think furiously. How long could the Telians keep up the attack? They would have to grow tired sooner or later, wouldn't they?

Or would they?

He waited as long as he could, until the air was all but unbreathable, then overrode the controls. The Telians were sitting on the ground around him. Fires had been lighted and food was cooking. Rinek lazily threw a spear at him and the field went on.

So, Bentley thought, they had learned. They were going to starve him out.

He tried to think, but the walls of his dark closet seemed to be pressing against him. He was growing claustrophobic and already his air was stale again.

He thought for a moment, then overrode the controls. The Telians looked at him coolly. One of them reached for a spear.

'Wait!' Bentley shouted. At the same moment, he turned on his radio.

'What do you want?' Rinek asked.

'Listen to me! It isn't fair to trap me in the Protec like this!'

'Eh? What's going on?' Professor Sliggert asked, through the ear receiver.

'You Telians know –' Bentley said hoarsely, 'you know that you can destroy me by continually activating the Protec. I can't turn it off! I can't get out of it!'

'Ah!' said Professor Sliggert. 'I see the difficulty. Yes.'

'We are sorry,' Huascl apologized. 'But evil must be destroyed.'

'Of course it must,' Bentley said desperately. 'But not me. Give me a chance, *Professor*!'

'This is indeed a flaw,' Professor Sliggert mused, 'and a serious one. Strange but things like this, of course, can't show up in the lab, only in a full-scale field test. The fault will be rectified in the new models.'

'Great! But I'm here now! How do I get this thing off?'

'I am sorry,' Sliggert said. 'I honestly never thought the need would arise. To tell the truth, I designed the harness so that you could not get out of it under any circumstances.'

'Why, you lousy—'

'Please!' Sliggert said sternly. 'Let's keep our heads. If you can hold out for a few months, we might be able—'

'I can't! The air! Water!'

'Fire!' cried Rinek, his face contorted. 'By fire, we will chain the demon!'

And the Protec snapped on.

Bentley tried to think things out carefully in the darkness. He would have to get out of the Protec. But how? There was a knife in his tool kit. Could he cut through the tough plastic straps? He would have to!

But what then? Even if he emerged from his fortress, the ship was a mile away. Without the Protec, they could kill him with a single spear thrust. And they were pledged to, for he had been declared irrevocably evil.

But, if he ran, he at least had a chance. And it was better to die of a spear thrust than to strangle slowly in absolute darkness.

Bentley turned off the field. The Telians were surrounding him with campfires, closing off his retreat with a wall of flame.

He hacked frantically at the plastic web. The knife slithered and slipped along the strap. And he was back in Protec.

When he came out again, the circle of fire was complete. The Telians were cautiously pushing the fires toward him, lessening the circumference of his circle.

Bentley felt his heart sink. Once the fires were close enough, the Protec would go on and stay on. He would not be able to override a continuous danger signal. He would be trapped within the field for as long as they fed the flames.

And, considering how primitive people felt about devils, it was just possible that they would keep the fire going for a century or two.

He dropped the knife, used side-cutters on the plastic strap and succeeded in ripping it halfway through.

He was in Protec again.

Bentley was dizzy, half-fainting from fatigue, gasping great mouthfuls of foul air. With an effort, he pulled himself together. He couldn't drop now. That would be the end.

He found the controls, overrode them. The fires were very near him now. He could feel their warmth against his face. He snipped viciously at the strap and felt it give.

He slipped out of the Protec just as the field activated again. The force of it threw him into the fire. But he fell feet-first and jumped out of the flames without getting burned.

The villagers roared. Bentley sprinted away; as he ran, he dumped the linguascene, the tool kit, the radio, the concentrated food and the canteen. He glanced back once and saw that the Telians were after him.

But he was holding his own. His tortured heart seemed to be pounding his chest apart and his lungs threatened to collapse at any moment. But now the spaceship was before him, looming great and friendly on the flat plain.

He was going to just make it. Another twenty yards. . . .

Something green flashed in front of him. It was a small, green-furred mog puppy. The clumsy beast was trying to get out of his way.

He swerved to avoid crushing it and realized too late that he should never have broken stride. A rock turned under his foot and he sprawled forward.

He heard the pounding feet of the Telians coming toward him and managed to climb on one knee.

Then somebody threw a club and it landed neatly on his forehead.

'Ar gwy dril?' a voice asked incomprehensibly from far off.

Bentley opened his eyes and saw Huascl bending over him. He was in a hut, back in the village. Several armed ghost doctors were at the doorway, watching.

'Ar dril?' Huascl asked again.

Bentley rolled over and saw, piled neatly beside him, his canteen, concentrated food, tools, radio and linguascene. He took a deep drink of water, then turned on the linguascene.

'I asked if you felt all right,' Huascl said.

'Sure, fine,' Bentley grunted, feeling his head. 'Let's get it over with.'

'Over with?'

'You're going to kill me, aren't you? Well, let's not make a production out of it.'

'But we didn't want to destroy *you*,' Huascl said. 'We knew you for a good man. It was the devil we wanted!'

'Eh?' asked Bentley in a blank, uncomprehending voice.

'Come, look.'

The ghost doctors helped Bentley to his feet and brought him outside. There, surrounded by lapping flames, was the glowing great black sphere of the Protec.

'You didn't know, of course,' Huascl said, 'but there was a devil riding upon your back.'

'Huh!' gasped Bentley.

'Yes, it is true. We tried to dispossess him by purification, but he was too strong. We had to force you, brother, to face that evil and throw it aside. We knew you would come through, and you did!'

'I see,' Bentley said. 'A devil on my back. Yes, I guess so.'

That was exactly what the Protec would have to be, to them. A heavy, misshapen weight on his shoulders, hurling out a black sphere whenever they tried to purify it. What else could a religious people do but try to free him from its grasp?

He saw several women of the village bring up baskets of food and throw them into the fire in front of the sphere. He looked inquiringly at Huascl.

'We are propitiating it,' Huascl said, 'for it is a very strong devil, undoubtedly a miracle-working one. Our village is proud to have such a devil in bondage.'

A ghost doctor from a neighbouring village stepped up. 'Are there more such devils in your homeland? Could you bring *us* one to worship?'

Several other ghost doctors pressed eagerly forward. Bentley nodded. 'It can be arranged,' he said.

He knew that the Earth–Tels trade was now begun. And at last a suitable use had been found for Professor Sliggert's Protec.

Philip Jose Farmer
Sail on! Sail on!

Friar Sparks sat wedged between the wall and the realizer. He was motionless except for his forefinger and his eyes. From time to time his finger tapped rapidly on the key upon the desk, and now and then his irises, grey-blue as his native Irish sky, swivelled to look through the open door of the *toldilla* in which he crouched, the little shanty on the poop deck. Visibility was low.

Outside was dusk and a lantern by the railing. Two sailors leaned on it. Beyond them bobbed the bright lights and dark shapes of the *Niña* and the *Pinta*. And beyond them was the smooth horizon-brow of the Atlantic, edged in black and blood by the red dome of the rising moon.

The single carbon-filament bulb above the monk's tonsure showed a face lost in fat – and in concentration.

The luminiferous ether crackled and hissed tonight, but the phones clamped over his ears carried, along with them, the steady dots and dashes sent by the operator at the Las Palmas station on the Grand Canary.

'*Zzisss!* So you are out of sherry already.... *Pop!* ... Too bad ... *crackle* ... you hardened old winebutt.... *Zzz.*... May God have mercy on your sins....

'Lots of gossip, news, et cetera.... *Hisses!* ... Bend your ear instead of your neck, impious one. ... The Turks are said to be gathering ... *crackle* ... an army to march on Austria. It is rumoured that the flying sausages, said by so many to have been seen over the capitals of the Christian world, are of Turkish origin. The rumour goes they have been invented by a renegade Rogerian who was converted to the Muslim religion. ... I say ... *zziss* ... to that. No one of us would do that. It is a falsity spread by our enemies in the Church to discredit us. But many people believe that....

'How close does the Admiral calculate he is to Cipangu now?

'Flash! Savonarola today denounced the Pope, the wealthy of Florence, Greek art and literature, and the experiments of the disciples of Saint Roger Bacon. . . . *Zzz!* . . . The man is sincere but misguided and dangerous. . . . I predict he'll end up on the stake he's always prescribing for us. . . .

'*Pop!* . . . This will kill you. . . . Two Irish mercenaries by the name of Pat and Mike were walking down the street of Granada when a beautiful Saracen lady leaned out of a balcony and emptied a pot of . . . *hiss!* . . . and Pat looked up and. . . . *Crackle.* . . . Good, hah? Brother Juan told that last night. . . .

'P.V. . . . P.V. . . . Are you coming in? . . . P.V. . . . P.V. . . . Yes, I know it's dangerous to bandy such jests about, but nobody is monitoring us tonight. . . . *Zzz.* . . . I think they're not, anyway. . . .'

And so the ether bent and warped with their messages. And presently Friar Sparks tapped out the P.V. that ended their talk – the *Pax vobiscum.* Then he pulled the plug out that connected his earphones to the set and, lifting them from his ears, clamped them down forward over his temples in the regulation manner.

After sidling bent-kneed from the *toldilla*, punishing his belly against the desk's hard edge as he did so, he walked over to the railing. De Salcedo and de Torres were leaning there and talking in low tones. The big bulb above gleamed on the page's red-gold hair and on the interpreter's full black beard. It also bounced pinkishly off the priest's smooth-shaven jowls and the light scarlet robe of the Rogerian order. His cowl, thrown back, served as a bag for scratch paper, pens, an ink bottle, tiny wrenches and screwdrivers, a book on cryptography, a slide rule, and a manual of angelic principles.

'Well, old rind,' said young de Salcedo familiarly, 'what do you hear from Las Palmas?'

'Nothing now. Too much interference from that.' He pointed to the moon riding the horizon ahead of them. 'What an orb!' bellowed the priest. 'It's as big and red as my revered nose!'

The two sailors laughed, and de Salcedo said, 'But it will get smaller and paler as the night grows, Father. And your proboscis will, on the contrary, become larger and more sparkling in inverse proportion according to the square of the ascent—'

He stopped and grinned, for the monk had suddenly dipped his nose, like a porpoise diving into the sea, raised it again, like the same animal jumping from a wave, and then once more plunged it into the heavy currents of their breath. Nose to nose, he faced them, his twinkling little eyes seeming to emit sparks like the realizer in his *toldilla*.

Again, porpoise-like, he sniffed and snuffed several times, quite loudly. Then, satisfied with what he had gleaned from their breaths, he winked at them. He did not, however, mention his findings at once, preferring to sidle towards the subject.

He said, 'This Father Sparks on the Grand Canary is so entertaining. He stimulates me with all sorts of philosophical notions, both valid and fantastic. For instance, tonight, just before we were cut off by that' – he gestured at the huge bloodshot eye in the sky – 'he was discussing what he called worlds of parallel time-tracks, an idea originated by Dysphagius of Gotham. It's his idea there may be other worlds in coincident but not contacting universes, that God, being infinite and of unlimited creative talent and ability, the Master Alchemist, in other words, has possibly – perhaps necessarily – created a plurality of continua in which every probable event has happened.'

'Huh?' grunted de Salcedo.

'Exactly. Thus, Columbus was turned down by Queen Isabella, so this attempt to reach the Indies across the Atlantic was never made. So we would not now be standing here plunging ever deeper into Oceanus in our three cockleshells, there would be no booster buoys strung out between us and the Canaries, and Father Sparks at Las Palmas and I on the *Santa María* would not be carrying on our fascinating conversations across the ether.

'Or, say, Roger Bacon was persecuted by the Church, instead of being encouraged and giving rise to the order whose inventions have done so much to ensure the monopoly of the church on alchemy and its divinely inspired guidance of that formerly pagan and hellish practice.'

De Torres opened his mouth, but the priest silenced him with a magnificent and imperious gesture and continued.

'Or, even more ridiculous, but thought-provoking, he speculated just this evening on universes with different physical laws. One, in particular, I thought very droll. As you probably don't know, Angelo Angelei has proved, by dropping objects from the Leaning Tower of Pisa, that different weights fall at different speeds. My delightful colleague on the Grand Canary is writing a satire which takes place in a universe where Aristotle is made out to be a liar, where all things drop with equal velocities, no matter what their size. Silly stuff, but it helps to pass the time. We keep the ether busy with our little angels.'

De Salcedo said, 'Uh, I don't want to seem too curious about the secrets of your holy and cryptic order, Friar Sparks. But these little angels your machine realizes intrigue me. Is it a sin to presume to ask about them?'

The monk's bull roar slid to a dove cooing. 'Whether it's a sin or not depends. Let me illustrate, young fellows. If you were concealing a bottle of, say, very scarce sherry on you, and you did not offer to share it with a very thirsty old gentleman, that would be a sin. A sin of omission. But if you were to give that desert-dry, that pilgrim-weary, that devout, humble and decrepit old soul a long, soothing, refreshing, and stimulating draught of life-giving fluid, daughter of the vine, I would find it in my heart to pray for you for that deed of loving-kindness, of encompassing charity. And it would please me so much I might tell you a little of our realizer. Not enough to hurt you, just enough so you might gain more respect for the intelligence and glory of my order.'

De Salcedo grinned conspiratorially and passed the monk the bottle he'd hidden under his jacket. As the friar tilted it, and the chug-chug-chug of vanishing sherry became louder, the two sailors glanced meaningfully at each other. No wonder the priest, reputed to be so brilliant in his branch of the alchemical mysteries, had yet been sent off on this half-baked voyage to devil-knew-where. The Church had calculated that, if he survived, well and good. If he didn't, then he would sin no more.

The monk wiped his lips on his sleeve, belched loudly as a horse, and said, '*Gracias*, boys. From my heart, so deeply buried in this fat, I thank you. An old Irishman, dry as a camel's hoof, choking to death with the dust of abstinence, thanks you. You have saved my life.'

'Thank rather that magic nose of yours,' replied de Salcedo. 'Now, old rind, now that you're well greased again, would you mind explaining as much as you are allowed about that machine of yours?'

Friar Sparks took fifteen minutes. At the end of that time, his listeners asked a few permitted questions.

'. . . and you say you broadcast on a frequency of eighteen hundred k.c.?' the page asked. 'What does "k.c." mean?'

'*K* stands for the French *kilo*, from a Greek word meaning thousand. And *c* stands for the Hebrew *cherubim*, the "little angels". Angel comes from the Greek *angelos*, meaning messenger. It is our concept that the ether is crammed with these cherubim, these little messengers. Thus, when we Friar Sparkses depress the key of our machine, we are able to realize some of the infinity of "messengers" waiting for just such a demand for service.

'So, eighteen hundred k.c. means that in a given unit of time one million, eight hundred thousand cherubim line up and hurl themselves across the ether, the nose of one being brushed by the feathertips of the cherub's wings ahead. The height of the wing crests of each little creature is even, so that, if you were to draw an outline of the whole train, there would be nothing to distinguish one cherub from the next, the whole column forming that grade of little angels known as C.W.'

'C.W.?'

'Continuous wing-height. My machine is a C.W. realizer.'

Young de Salcedo said, 'My mind reels. Such a concept! Such a revelation! It almost passes comprehension. Imagine, the aerial of your realizer is cut just so long, so that the evil cherubim surging back and forth on it demand a predetermined and equal number of good angels to combat them. And this seduction coil on the realizer crowds "bad" angels into the left-hand, the sinister, side. And, when the bad little cherubim are crowded so closely and numerously that they can't bear each other's evil company, they jump the spark gap and speed around the wire to the "good" plate. And in this racing back and forth they call themselves to the attention of the "little messengers", the yea-saying cherubim. And you, Friar Sparks, by manipulating your machine thus and so, and by lifting and lowering your key, you bring these invisible and friendly lines of carriers, your etheric and winged postmen, into reality. And you are able, thus, to communicate at great distances with your brothers of the order.'

'Great God!' said de Torres.

It was not a vain oath but a pious exclamation of wonder. His eyes bulged; it was evident that he suddenly saw that man was not alone, that on every side, piled on top of each other, flanked on every angle, stood a host. Black and white, they presented a solid chessboard of the seemingly empty cosmos, black for the nay-sayers, white for the yea-sayers, maintained by a Hand in delicate balance and subject as the fowls of the air and the fish of the sea to exploitation by man.

Yet de Torres, having seen such a vision as has made a saint of many a man, could only ask, 'Perhaps you could tell me how many angels may stand on the point of a pin?'

Obviously, de Torres would never wear a halo. He was destined, if he lived, to cover his bony head with the mortar-board of a university teacher.

De Salcedo snorted. 'I'll tell you. Philosophically speaking, you may put as many angels on a pinhead as you want to. Actually speaking, you may put only as many as there is room for. Enough of that. I'm interested in facts, not fancies. Tell me, how could the moon's rising interrupt your reception of the cherubim sent by the Sparks at Las Palmas?'

'Great Caesar, how would I know? Am I a repository of universal knowledge? No, not I! A humble and ignorant friar, I! All I can tell you is that last night it rose like a bloody tumour on the horizon, and that when it was up I had to quit marshalling my little messengers in their short and long columns. The Canary station was quite overpowered, so that both of us gave up. And the same thing happened tonight.'

'The moon sends messages?' asked de Torres.

'Not in a code I can decipher. But it sends, yes.'

'Santa María!'

'Perhaps,' suggested de Salcedo, 'there are people on that moon, and they are sending.'

Friar Sparks blew derision through his nose. Enormous as were his nostrils, his derision was not small-bore. Artillery of contempt laid down a barrage that would have silenced any but the strongest of souls.

'Maybe' – de Torres spoke in a low tone – 'maybe, if the stars are windows in heaven, as I've heard said, the angels of the higher hierarchy, the big ones, are realizing – uh – the smaller? And they only do it when the moon is up so we may know it is a celestial phenomenon?'

He crossed himself and looked around the vessel.

'You need not fear,' said the monk gently. 'There is no Inquisitor leaning over your shoulder. Remember, I am the only priest on this expedition. Moreover, your conjecture has nothing to do with dogma. However, that's unimportant. Here's what I don't understand: How can a heavenly body broadcast? Why does it have the same frequency as the one I'm restricted to? Why—'

'I could explain,' interrupted de Salcedo with all the brashness and impatience of youth. 'I could say that the Admiral and the Rogerians are wrong about the earth's shape. I could say the earth is not round but is flat. I could say the horizon exists, not because we live upon a globe, but because the earth is curved only a little way, like a greatly flattened-out hemisphere. I could also say that the cherubim are coming, not from Luna, but from a ship such as ours, a vessel which is hanging in the void off the edge of the earth.'

'What?' gasped the other two.

'Haven't you heard', said de Salcedo, 'that the King of Portugal secretly sent out a ship after he turned down Columbus' proposal? How do we know he did not, that the messages are from our predecessor, that he sailed off the world's rim and is now suspended in the air and becomes exposed at night because it follows the moon around Terra – is, in fact, a much smaller and unseen satellite?'

The monk's laughter woke many men on the ship. 'I'll have to tell the Las Palmas operator your tale. He can put it in that novel of his. Next you'll be telling me those messages are from one of those fire-shooting sausages so many credulous laymen have been seeing flying around. No, my dear de Salcedo, let's not be ridiculous. Even the ancient Greeks knew the earth was round. Every university in Europe teaches that. And we Rogerians have measured the circumference. We know for sure that the Indies lie just across the Atlantic. Just as we know for sure, through mathematics, that heavier-than-air machines are impossible. Our Friar Ripskulls, our mind doctors, have assured us these flying creaticns are mass hallucinations or else the tricks of heretics or Turks who want to panic the populace.

'That moon radio is no delusion, I'll grant you. What it is, I don't know. But it's not a Spanish or Portuguese ship. What about its different code? Even if it came from Lisbon, that ship would still have a Rogerian opeɪator. And he would, according to our policy, be of a different nationality from the crew so he might the easier stay out of political embroilments. He wouldn't break our laws by using a different code in order to communicate with Lisbon. We disciples of Saint Roger do not stoop to petty boundary intrigues. Moreover, that realizer would not be powerful enough to reach Europe, and must, therefore, be directed at us.'

'How can you be sure?' said de Salcedo. 'Distressing though the thought may be to you, a priest could be subverted. Or a layman could learn your secrets and invent a code. I think that a Portuguese ship is sending to another, a ship perhaps not too distant from us.'

De Torres shivered and crossed himself again. 'Perhaps the angels are warning us of approaching death? Perhaps?'

'Perhaps? Then why don't they use our code? Angels would know it as well as I. No, there is no perhaps. The order does not permit perhaps. It experiments and finds out; nor does it pass judgement until it knows.'

'I doubt we'll ever know,' said de Salcedo gloomily. 'Columbus has promised the crew that if we come across no sign of land by evening tomorrow, we shall turn back. Otherwise' – he drew a finger across his throat – '*kkk!* Another day, and we'll be pointed east and getting away from that evil bloody-looking moon and its incomprehensible messages.'

'It would be a great loss to the order and to the Church,' sighed the friar. 'But I leave such things in the hands of God and inspect only what He hands me to look at.'

With which pious statement Friar Sparks lifted the bottle to ascertain the liquid level. Having determined in a scientific manner its existence, he next measured its quantity and tested its quality by putting all of it in that best of all chemistry tubes, his enormous belly.

Afterwards, smacking his lips and ignoring the pained and disappointed looks on the faces of the sailors, he went on to speak enthusiastically of the water screw and the engine which turned it, both of which had been built recently at the St Jonas College at Genoa. If Isabella's three ships had been equipped with those, he declared, they would not have to depend upon the wind. However, so far, the fathers had forbidden its extended use because it was feared the engine's fumes might poison the air and the terrible speeds it made possible might be fatal to the human body. After which he plunged into a tedious description of the life of his patron saint, the inventor of the first cherubim realizer and receiver, Jonas of Carcassonne, who had been martyred when he grabbed a wire he thought was insulated.

The two sailors found excuses to walk off. The monk was a good fellow, but hagiography bored them. Besides, they wanted to talk of women. . . .

If Columbus had not succeeded in persuading his crews to sail one more day, events would have been different.

At dawn the sailors were very much cheered by the sight of several large birds circling their ships. Land could not be far off; perhaps these winged creatures came from the coast of fabled Cipangu itself, the country whose houses were roofed with gold.

The birds swooped down. Closer, they were enormous and very strange. Their bodies were flattish and almost saucer-shaped and small in proportion to the wings, which had a spread of at least thirty feet. Nor did they have legs. Only a few sailors saw the significance of that fact. These birds dwelt in the air and never rested upon land or sea.

While they were meditating upon that, they heard a slight sound as of a man clearing his throat. So gentle and far off was the noise that nobody paid any attention to it, for each thought his neighbour had made it.

A few minutes later, the sound had become louder and deeper, like a lute string being twanged.

Everybody looked up. Heads were turned west.

Even yet they did not understand that the noise like a finger plucking a wire came from the line that held the earth together, and that the line was stretched to its utmost, and that the violent finger of the sea was what had plucked the line.

It was some time before they understood. They had run out of horizon.

When they saw that, they were too late.

The dawn had not only come up *like* thunder, it *was* thunder. And, though the three ships heeled over at once and tried to sail close-hauled on the port tack, they suddenly speeded up and relentless current made beating hopeless.

Then it was the Rogerian wished for the Genoese screw and the wood-burning engine that would have made them able to resist the terrible muscles of the charging and bull-like sea. Then it was that some men prayed, some raved, some tried to attack the Admiral, some jumped overboard, and some sank into a stupor.

Only the fearless Columbus and the courageous Friar Sparks stuck to their duties. All that day the fat monk crouched wedged in his little shanty, dot-dashing to his fellow on the Grand Canary. He ceased only when the moon rose like a huge red bubble from the throat of a dying giant. Then he listened intently all night and worked desperately, scribbling and swearing impiously and checking cipher books.

When the dawn came up again in a roar and a rush, he ran from the *toldilla*, a piece of paper clutched in his hand. His eyes were wild, and his lips were moving fast, but nobody could understand that he had cracked the code. They could not hear him shouting, 'It is the Portuguese! It is the Portuguese!'

Their ears were too overwhelmed to hear a mere human voice. The throat clearing and the twanging of the string had been the noises preliminary to the concert itself. Now came the mighty overture; as compelling as the blast of Gabriel's horn was the topple of Oceanus into space.